commencing our descent
suzannah**dunn**

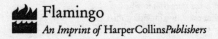

Flamingo
An Imprint of HarperCollins*Publishers*

Flamingo
An Imprint of HarperCollins*Publishers*
77–85 Fulham Palace Road,
Hammersmith, London W6 8JB

Flamingo is a registered trade mark of
HarperCollins Publishers Limited

www.fireandwater.com

Published by Flamingo 2000
9 8 7 6 5 4 3 2 1

First published in Great Britain by
Flamingo 1999

Author photograph by © Claire McNamee

ISBN 0 00 655088 6

Set in Sabon by
Rowland Phototypesetting Ltd, Bury St Edmunds, Suffolk

Printed and bound in Great Britain by
Clays Ltd, St Ives plc

ACKNOWLEDGEMENTS

I am grateful to South East Arts for a Writers' Bursary in 1997.

Many thanks to: Charlotte Windsor, Jon Butler, Mandy Kirkby, and Philip Gwyn Jones at Flamingo; Harriet Guggenheim, and Deborah Rogers of Rogers, Coleridge and White Ltd.;

Peter Hunter, for detective stories;

and David Kendall, for reading the manuscript with such good grace.

Flying too high
With some guy
In the sky
Is my idea
Of nothing to do.

Yet I get a kick
Out of you.

'I Get a Kick Out of You'
Cole Porter

CONTENTS

Things which are not	1
A weep from a wound	24
Treaclier	37
Quick, slow	53
Dead give-aways	75
Tripwire tense	102
Ruinous blue	130
Waylaid	160
Wish	181
Make no bones	213
Good as gold	232

THINGS WHICH ARE NOT

'Decisions? Don't look at me.'

But this is exactly what he does: he stops sawing through the thin copper pipe as I reach the top stair, he turns around and looks. And when he has looked for several seconds, he says, 'You're so pale, you know, Sadie.'

Jason's own hair and eyes are the colour of charcoal, perhaps a touch warmer, closer to burned wood, scorches on wood.

'Yes, thanks, I do know.'

My pallor is more than compensated for by hair the colour of pomegranate pulp. I am a lucky redhead, if that is not a contradiction in terms: none of the legendary temper, no incendiary freckles, and my skin lacks that blue tint of exposed bone. Philip says that my skin is the colour of Chardonnay; but he is kind, he is my husband. He says that I caramelise to muscat whenever I catch the sun.

Jason says, 'But because you're pale, you'll always look young. Younger than me, anyway.'

'I *am* younger than you.'

He is thirty-five, I am thirty-one. Earlier in our lives, when we had had fewer years, four of them would have made the difference of a generation: he would have been playing rugby on Saturday mornings when I was playing with my dolls; he would have been into punk when I was impressed by Genesis; smoking dope when I was sipping Pernod-and-black. Nowadays, four years is no time at all, but our lives are incomparable for other reasons. He is a father of four, the eldest of whom is fifteen.

'Decision number one: I want to know where you'd prefer

me to run this pipe. You have two options: beneath these floorboards here, or . . .' he swivels, to point, 'along this wall, which is less pretty but less work for me, less of a bill for you.'

I sit down on the top stair. 'Give me a moment.'

He resumes his sawing: a sound effect for a music hall magician. 'Enjoy your walk?'

Hal's walk. Before Hal came, four months ago, I rarely walked as far as the local shops. When I agreed to take him on, I read in a book that a Labrador should have an hour each day off the lead. And I do everything by the book. He lives for his trips to the park, which seems very little to ask. So I take him twice each day. Between these excursions, he dozes on his bed, slumped or curled but somehow tuned in for the sound of my arm slithering into a sleeve or for the change in tempo of my movements that implies that I am going to leave the house. Sometimes he knows before I do that I am thinking of leaving. I have had to become careful, self-conscious of my signals, because I hate to turn him down, to have to watch the droop of his ears, those blond velvet triangles. Whenever I do leave the house without him, his stare – sideways, heavily-lidded – seems to accuse me of going alone to the park.

During our walk this morning, the clear sky was punctured by a knuckle of half-moon. Leaf-laden trees made a foreshortened horizon of green thunderclouds. The hedgerows were scattered with convolvulus flowers like washed but un-ironed hankerchiefs. Hal and I encountered other regulars. Firstly, the childminders: a bespectacled, tattooed man and a hennaed woman with their two battalions. Childminders, surely, because the children are too numerous, too similarly-aged and dissimilarly dressed to be their own. Four toddlers were strapped into two double buggies. Others were on foot, on small and unsteady feet, taking small and sometimes reluctant, even petulant, steps.

Further on, I exchanged nods and smiles with the polite

middle-aged couple as he, with her support, was venturing from his wheelchair; he managed a little more than last week. Then we passed the elderly, hobbling man and woman, both of them as arthritic as their dogs, her Alsatian and his dachshund. We were passed in turn by the cheerful, late-thirties mum who strides behind her baby's plush pushchair and kicks a tennis ball ahead for her puppy to chase. We avoided the wrinkled but elaborately made-up woman who throws a small plastic naked doll for her miniature dog to fetch. Today, there were irregulars too: one of the benches was occupied by a canoodling couple of kids with masses of matted hair and layers of army surplus clothing. They were sharing a bottle of vodka for their elevenses. As Hal neared, they bellowed to their dog to 'Play nicely'.

None of them will be there when we go back this afternoon: by four o'clock the day will have drained from the park. Even the groundsmen will have stopped work and gone home. Hal and I, too, fail to take the afternoons as seriously as the mornings: in our half-hour we will manage a lap rather than a lap and a half. A mere break, a breath of fresh air. Hal will be contemplative, his nose close to the ground, his concentration as thorough as that of an avid reader.

'Anyway, this pipe. Oh, don't pull that face, Sadie. And don't tell me that I'll have to wait for the man of the house to come home before I can have a decision.'

'You could build an Eiffel Tower from these pipes before he comes home.'

'Still working hard?'

'Still working hard.'

'Still at the hostel?'

'Manager now.'

'And how is he?'

'The same. Fine. Thriving. Busy.'

'Good. Let's give the Eiffel Tower a miss and hurry up with this.' He brandishes the sawn-off pipe.

'I'm a Libran.'

'So?'

'So, I can't make decisions.'

'You believe in all that?'

'No. Just happens to be true, in my case.'

Hal is coming up behind me. He is only ever inelegant when on the stairs, his four legs encountering something designed for two. Determinedly digging his way up the steps, plucky but gawky, he looks like a puppy.

'Hal's a Taurus.'

'Hal's a *dog*.'

'He's a typical Taurus.'

'He's a typical *dog*, Sadie.'

While I rub Hal's head, his ears, he is butting my hands. I am perversely proud of his prettiness. Would I love him quite so much if he were plain? I did adopt him unseen. His previous owners, friends of friends, were going to live abroad for several years. Having been persuaded to take him, I drove the two hundred miles to fetch him. I had been told that he was a Labrador cross: the look of a Labrador, but smaller. I had not been told that he had the slender face of a deer, that he was all cheekbones.

'You spoil that mutt.'

'So? Isn't life hard enough without a bit of spoiling? And he's four. Didn't people spoil you when you were four?'

'I was a person.'

'When you were four? You sure, Jason?'

Hal, with his impeccable manners, his love of home and liking for everything to be just so, seems human. He is more domesticated than I am.

Jason's mobile phone screams from the tool box. During all the years that he has been coming here, he has carried this particular prop: a workhorse of a mobile phone, antiquated and bulky.

He tells me, 'I'm not answering.'

'Mobiles are for answering; that's what they're for.'

Despairing of me, he snatches the phone from the box, stops the noise, listens intently.

'Yep. Okay. Six-ish. In a while, crocodile.'

He slots down the aerial, and I think of the shop on the way to the park: *For all your satellite and aerial needs*. Needs that I do not know that I have. Every day, I resist the urge to go in there and ask, *All my satellite and aerial needs?*

Jason says, 'My eldest: could I pick her up from rehearsal on my way home.'

I am awed by his daughters' social schedules, by their mother's fixing of old-fashioned girlhoods for them: stage school, horse-riding, hockey club and music lessons. The household seems to run like a finishing school, but the finish is a tough one: from what Jason says, the activities do not revolve around an aim to become accomplished, to learn, but a desire to be equipped: with competitiveness and a sense of fair play, improved posture and strengthened bones.

As a child, I had no place in any world apart from that of my mother's. Unless I was in school, I went everywhere with her, which was nowhere: the park, the shops. The only advice that I remember from her was that there is nothing more important than a good marriage, but she never told me how to make one because she did not know. Odd to think of my parents now, in early retirement, relatively companionable, apparently having reached some kind of truce.

'Just one more year of school for my eldest.'

'And then?'

'Wants to work in a shoe shop. Says she loves shoes.' He frowns into the tool box. 'Does that mean that I love power showers and central heating systems? Suppose I do, though.' He looks up at me. 'Do you think you'll have kids, now?'

'I have to find a job first: that's the plan.' Instantly, I realise how ridiculous this must sound to him. I try to explain, 'I need a life, Jason.'

'You have a life, don't you?' He is genuinely puzzled.

* * *

I used to be a carer: that is the currently favoured term. *Caring* is the buzz word for what I did, here, at home, for eight years. So perhaps, now that it is all over, I should turn professional. There is nothing professional, though, about the jobs in nursing homes that are advertised every week in our local newspaper. Unsociable hours and low pay. If I had such a job, I would see even less of Philip. Hard work for very little money, he says, and we have no real need of the money, so why work simply for the sake of working? He says that I should do something that I want to do. But this is exactly my problem: what do I want to do? What *can* I do? I have a sense that I should train for something, learn something, but training is extensive, expensive, and I have no experience of anything, so no one would want me for their over-subscribed courses. And even if I did train, would there be a job for me? My problem is that I have been away from the world for too long. I cannot imagine how other people cope with the power struggles, timetables, deadlines, and expec-tations, not least the expectation that they will leave the house every day, for most of the day. No, I do not want to do anything. But I know that I cannot stay as I am.

'You're looking for a job?'

I wrinkle my nose: ambivalent confirmation. This morn-ing's cursory look through the newspaper ended prematurely in a perusal of adverts, one of which was entitled, *Impotence problems?*

Impotence *problems?* Problems over and above the impotence?

There were other adverts: *Hair loss?*, *Flabby belly?*, *Panic attacks?*

And I thought that I had problems.

'Coffee?'

'Wonderful.'

As soon as I move, Hal whips from his prone position. He is due his lunch. What would he have done if I had forgotten?

I love to watch him with his food. Fast but fastidious, he laps up the gravy before beginning on the biscuits. His tail, usually wagging, will droop: serious happiness.

I am a couple of stairs down when Jason calls, 'You love piano music, don't you. What's playing, now, downstairs? Scott Joplin?'

'No, but you're close. It's a . . .' I flinch from using the word *pastiche*, '. . . fake, a modern fake.'

Will he ask why a fake, when we can have the real Scott Joplin? Could I explain that but for the work of this particular, later composer, William Bolcom, there would have been no Scott Joplin? No Scott Joplin as we know him. He would have been unknown; dead and unknown.

'Would you rather hear something else?' Philip says that my listening to piano music is pathological. He reels from Czerny, Nancarrow. 'Because I can play you . . . oh, I don't know' . . . – what was I playing earlier? – 'The Au Pairs?'

He laughs. 'Seriously? The Au Pairs?'

'An *old* tape.'

'A *very* old tape, I imagine. No, this is nice. What's it called?'

'*Graceful Ghost.*'

I am half-way down the stairs when I hear him say, 'Your theme tune.' He says it lightly, without irony or reservation.

Glancing upwards, I see that he is already busy again; absorbed.

I love the word *grace*, how it seems to elude definition. I would love to be graceful. Perhaps I would be, if not for the dead weight of my left foot.

Coming down into the hallway, I sense the house recovering from the presence of Annie, living poltergeist. She had said that she would *pop over*, but she never pops, she takes root. Arriving on Saturday afternoon, she stayed overnight and until mid-afternoon yesterday. A whole weekend. Just as she did on the weekend before last. The current problem is the break-up, a month or so ago, with her latest: someone called Pete, who, she told us, had been around for three or four months.

When she arrived, she laughed, 'No one as beautiful and talented as I am should have to stay home alone on a Saturday night.'

While she was upstairs, unpacking, Philip said, 'She's harmless.'

He could have said, *She's your friend*.

He says that we should have her to stay because she has a flat in London; we have a Victorian terraced house with a garden, close to the countryside, and she has a 'sixties studio on an estate in a backwater of Edmonton. Perhaps, to Philip, this counts as a kind of homelessness; perhaps I misheard, perhaps he said *homeless* rather than *harmless*.

When she had unpacked she came downstairs cooing to Hal, 'How's my favourite, then?'

I said, 'I'm fine, thanks.'

'Oh, *you*,' she derided.

She likes Hal, and Hal likes her. But Hal likes anyone who likes him.

As she passed me, I detected the usual pot-pourri of cosmetics: perfume and deodorant, soap and shampoo, lotions and fabric conditioner. As ever, her breath was scented with garlic, alcohol and chocolate. Perhaps she breathes harder than other people. Perhaps she stands closer.

With the slightest turn of her head, her long, sleek brown hair becomes a blade. On the rare occasions during her visits when she moves from my settee, the cushions are more crushed than anyone else would leave them. In her pillow, in the mornings, there is a hollow of awesome proportions and duration: eerily suggestive, somehow, of a catastrophe. And for days after she has gone home, I come across crockery in unnerving places: a cup in a soap dish, this morning.

All weekend I worried that she would stay and call in sick this morning. She takes lots of sick leave – a couple of days every couple of weeks – despite burgeoning health. In her manager's office is a folder labelled *The sick and late book*, in which she stars. She works in her local library, on general desk duties, but also with responsibility for activities, which is ironic in view of her own stupendous inertia. She organises occasional storytelling sessions for children, and a talk or two each month with a display of books on a subject chosen by the Chief Librarian. *Alpines* last month. She has had this job for a while now – six months or more? – so she is due for the usual dismissal or resignation. She has had so many jobs during the twelve years that I have known her. Once, for almost a year, she was a croupier, and this is the job which she cites whenever complaining of her current situation: *Look how I've come down in the world.*

When we met, fourteen years ago, we were working in a garden centre on Saturdays. Most of those Saturdays are boiled down in my memory to one never-ending queue of customers and an overloaded till drawer. There were days which were different, though, during the few months of the year when business was slack. We had two winters of Saturdays, when we were stationed alone together in the chillier of the two vast greenhouses, a crystalline enclave which smelled of old, cold water in potted soil. With our hands idle but ostensibly ready for work in fingerless gloves, we spent the empty days speculating on the excitement of the coming evening, the coming years. Whenever the screech of the sliding door signalled a customer, Annie would turn, slowly, stately, so that her face was visible only to me, and complain in a fervent whisper, 'Bastard, bastard, bastard . . .', an incantation which would continue until she turned back around with impeccable timing and a winning smile. She was as irresistible to me as to those hapless customers. I would never have stuck those winters of Saturdays without her.

Of all my friends, she is the only one who has always been utterly uninvolved in her work, having always purposefully chosen utterly uninvolving work. All that she ever takes home of her work is her name badge, which she tends to forget to remove: *Rhiannon Ritchie*. We both revelled in her disaffection when we were seventeen, but she has become too old for this. We both know that this lassitude is bad for her. But if and when I find a job, how will I be any different from her? How unlike Philip, who lives for work: in all the years that I have known him, he has never taken a day of sick leave. His stated reason is that someone else would have to cover for him. He is needed; nothing is more important to him.

This weekend, he and I were Annie's audience once again. We spent most of our time in the garden, Annie and I sitting in sunshine and shade respectively, while Philip was weeding, digging, planting, pruning. Annie's sunburn was slapped with strap marks and cropped by hem lines. Her skin swelled around the straps of her sandals, her watch strap, the shoulder straps which were in turn shadowed by black bra straps. On her thighs, a strip of pallor blazed beneath her hem whenever she slithered lower in her chair. She looked frighteningly robust; the chair, worryingly less so.

For a while, early on the Saturday evening, she talked about her latest ex-, concluding, 'He thinks with his cock.'

Philip was crouching on the far border of the lawn, snipping with a pair of shears, and the rhythm was faultless, crisp: either he did not hear, or he was lying low.

'And that's fine,' Annie boomed, 'when you're on the receiving end of his attention. The problem is that the attention span of that kind of bloke tends to be *short* . . .'

The regular chirp of the shears' blades sounded like a slow walk on stiletto heels.

'What *am* I saying? *All* men are like that. Slaves to testosterone, and they have the cheek to imply that we women are heavy on the hormones.' She added, 'Men are dogs.'

'Annie,' I countered, 'dogs are loyal.'

'You're thinking of Hal, and Hal's a eunuch.' She reached to stroke him. Even her hands provided no rest for the eye, demanded attention: her fingernails were scarlet. 'Ah, Hal,' she purred, 'life is simple, for you, eh?'

'But short,' I qualified.

'But *sweet*,' she enthused.

'And of course: with only twelve years or so to live, he should have nothing but pleasure.'

'Hal, you hear that? Don't you have a good deal.'

'Twelve years is a good deal?'

Suddenly, she said, 'You've had a bad couple of years.' And then, looking across the garden at Philip, 'You're so lucky, to have him.'

He was lunging into the long grass with each snap of the steel jaws as if he were trying to catch something.

'I know, I know.'

Closing my eyes, I detected the scent of the honeysuckle that Philip had planted for me. The white wisteria had finished flowering; Philip planted that for me as well. Opening my eyes, I saw the pastel Icelandic poppies that were mine too. And behind, indoors, at the south-facing sash window, my terracotta-potted banana tree: a present from Philip. I had wanted that plant not for bananas, of course, but for the leaves: the broad, thick, bottle-green leaves typical of a tropical plant, but with irregular marks that look so endearingly artificial they could have come from brushstrokes.

It was midsummer's eve, but suddenly I was thinking of its shadow, the winter solstice; some lines from a Donne poem:

He ruin'd mee, and I am re-begot
Of absence, darknesse, death; things which are not.

Philip rose, with more of a bounce than an unfolding. Rubbing his head, he probably smeared soil on to his bristly hair, dulling the grey. He had his back turned to us, and seemed to be puzzling over something in the flowerbed, but I knew that whatever his expression, his face would bear the impression of a smile: even his frowns are teased by smile lines. Earlier, he had told me that he was going to cook my favourite risotto for our evening meal: my compensation, he had whispered, for having to cope with Annie.

I knew, and he knew, that he was the one who would have to cope with her for hours while she scraped the remains from each bowl and confided in her captive audience. He tolerates her very well. He tolerates anyone and everyone: his tolerance is diligent, perhaps even enthusiastic, if that is not a contradiction in terms; certainly practised, because of his job. Watching him focusing on his flowers, I was struck that his relation to the social world is primarily one of tolerance: he deals with the world, and then he comes home.

Often he says to me, *At the end of the day, all that I want is you.*

And, always, I wonder why; why me?

Annie mused, 'He's good-looking . . . funny . . . kind . . .' This lacked envy: her kind of man is a rogue; she is that kind of woman. She decided, 'He's perfect.'

I laughed. 'If he's perfect, why is he married *to me*?'

'Oh, he loves you to death.'

Do I want to be loved to death?

'Annie, you said that all men are dogs.'

She prepared to concede, 'Well, of course, you know him better than I do . . .'

'No, he *is* perfect.'

'So: the exception that proves the rule. You're very lucky.'

'Yes.' Perfect husband, perfect marriage.

Whatever is wrong, is wrong with me.

The first time I ran away from Philip, I went to Venice: Venice, late last November. Venice, on the brink of winter. I told him that I was going away for the weekend with an old but rarely-seen friend, Lizzie, to her parents' cottage in Dorset: she had been low, lately, I said. The truth was that she was in Dublin with her new lover.

Ran away? I flew. I have been flying since before I can remember, and have seen so many changes: year by year, there is more of everything. Except propellers. And accidents. The only problem with flying, nowadays, is the boredom. Airports are purgatory. I hate that they have so little sky: so few windows, none of which open. The air sticks to my skin as a thin, burning layer. Too many smokers savour a last cigarette in the queues for check-in and passport control; again, as they sprawl in the departure lounge; again, as they pace before boarding.

Passing the time before my flight to Venice, I drank coffee and read the destinations on the screens: my favourite, Port au Prince, that tricky mix of foreign and familiar. I watched names of cities moving very slowly up the screens, approaching their evocative, flashing *last call*. I watched for pilots: stray pilots, on the ground, always in pairs, just as in the air; always a path clearing for them, just as in the air. Those creases in their trousers, those caps, cuffs, shoes: I have never seen a pilot with scuffed shoes. No wonder, if they so rarely touch the ground, and then only the tiled floors of terminals.

I delayed passing into Departures, into the queue of people who are tense for the alarm that they imagine they will cause even though they know that they have nothing to hide. One of the X-ray operators yelled at people to stop looking over his shoulder for the juddering geometry that was their own bared luggage.

My guidebook claims that Venice has an annual total of twenty million tourists. I was happy, for those few days, to disappear into that immense crowd. The book complains that native inhabitants are in a minority, but I like cities that belong to no one in particular, cities that people have to make their own. I arrived by a vaporetto which veered, slammed into and bounced off each platform of wooden planks, and swayed on oil-black water, the motor groaning like a fog horn. The route was busy, the subdued air of the cabin was sheared time and time again by the sliding door. I envied the passengers their impressive coats. Most were travelling singly, and briskly; busy with newspapers. Several of them made perfunctory calls on their mobile phones, and I presumed that I was overhearing the Italian equivalent of, *I'm on my way home, darling.*

Close to St Mark's, I found a one-star, family-run hotel: family photos on the wall amid the obligatory views of the Piazza under floodwater. A tabby prowled the reception desk while a cheerful, pregnant twentysomething recorded my details in her curly continental script. An inquisitive feline nose scanned the drying ink. The building was typically Venetian: tall and narrow, badly lit and poorly plumbed. On the way to my room, I made several turns of the shadowy wooden staircase to a soundtrack of distant cisterns. In my room there was a radiator which was cold, so that my scarce breath turned into translucent, billowing clouds. I went to bed to keep warm, and read for an hour or so before turning off the lamp and falling asleep.

I woke to voices, disembodied voices in the utter darkness of my room. Clear, jovial voices. I took a moment to realise that they were outside, below my window, three floors down in the alleyway. Two men, Italian. I turned to my alarm clock: twenty to one. From the rhythm of the conversation, I guessed that they were saying their goodbyes, patching the farewells with arrangements to meet again and then swapping suddenly-recalled, last-minute gossip: all the usual. What was unusual was that the voices were undiluted by any sounds of traffic; the silence around them, and beyond them, was stunning.

I was there for four days. I did very little traditional sight-seeing, avoiding the interiors of most of the famous buildings and all of the galleries. Instead, I walked: in this city of water, I walked myself into the ground. Frequently, I stopped for coffee in tiny bakeries and bars, where, despite my attempts to conduct the exchange in Italian, the staff would reply in English and smile as if my nationality were a joke between us. As I downed musky little coffees at chrome counters, I watched the proprietors wiping surfaces, washing crockery, conversing dolefully with customers, and wondered whether they had come from elsewhere to try to make their living in this flood-troubled city. Every day, I breakfasted, lunched and dined on bread, cheese and fruit from the Rialto market, and developed the predictable but passionate conviction that this was how I should spend the rest of my life. All day, every day, I wandered, going nowhere in particular but purposefully crisscrossing the many, narrow, smooth canals of jade water.

The first two days I was freezing; the next two days I was too warm because the fog which seeped from the sea into the lagoon had burned away into a clear continental sky. I walked after dark, too, but never late because the locals seemed to be home by ten and most of the tourists were daytrippers. I sensed that no one was afraid of anyone else, that there was no one to be afraid of; but I was afraid of losing my way. Even on the main routes, the lanterns were few and sepia.

So, in the evenings I would venture from the Piazza San Marco along the main, broad waterfront, with the crowds of disembarking, homeward-bound Italians. Passing the Doges' Palace, I heard the dozens of moored gondolas flapping on wavelets. Twenty minutes further down the esplanade was another world: no one but a few dog-walkers; and perhaps a young couple clinging to each other, theatrically threatening each other with the sheer drop into deeper water. Here, I would turn inland and take a detour down the Via Garibaldi – crowds, again, around market stalls, and in hardware shops – before returning to the open water and walking as far as the parkland that my map named as *Giardini Pubblici*. The greenery always came as a shock to me in the disused dock-land darkness, in the far corner of such a treeless city.

By my second day, sore from so much walking, I was desperate to loosen up with a swim. At the tourist information office I was told that I would have to travel to Mestre, on the mainland, to find an indoor pool.

Water, water everywhere, and not a drop to swim in.

The woman who was advising me, who was dressed and made up like an air stewardess, drew my attention to the map beneath the glass surface of the desk. She tapped three specific areas, announcing with an air of efficiency, 'One, two, three.'

'Times?' I asked, unnecessarily pidgin. 'Open?'

She shrugged elaborately, and her gaze switched to the person who was behind me. But one of her colleagues stepped towards me. 'Sports centre?' she checked.

I shook my head, specified, 'Swimming pool.'

The tip of a pink-painted fingernail landed on the glass and scratched circles of deliberation before skidding to the far south-west of the island of La Giudecca. 'Here,' she said, dubiously, then a little more decisively, 'yes, here.'

'There?' Perilously close to the island marked *inceneritore* was a small extension of the furthest inhabited island.

Smiling, she reached for a phone and a phone book in which she re-enacted the ritual of the fingernail for some time and with increasing ferocity before she was satisfied. Then, having dialled, she had a brief conversation which sounded like a blazing row before she turned back to me with a slip of paper on which she had scribbled some days and times. Bashing the paper with the busy nail, she explained, 'Open for the public.'

And so that was why, on my second day in Venice, I went out to Sacca Fisola, home to many of the workers. I travelled on a vaporetto away from the city into the wide Canale della Giudecca, the sludge-coloured water churned by a wind from the sea. When I reached the island and stepped from the wooden platform on to dry land, I bumped into a man who was running with a baby in a pushchair. Behind me, I heard the vaporetto perform a slow, aquatic equivalent of a skid, the ringing of the bollard by the rope lasso, the cheers of the crowd on deck in reply to his breathless thanks.

To cross the island, I took paths across patchy communal lawns and around blocks of flats which were concrete but comfortably low. In the shadows, children played ball, and above them, laundry flared on balconies. Every step of the way, I was scrutinised by cats; dozens of cats, marooned but content. I imagined a life for myself, there. On the far shore was a small, bridged swamp beyond which was a brick building. And that was how I came to spend half an hour swimming lengths in a brand new indoor glass-walled pool on the tip of an ancient, convoluted, and sinking city.

For four days, I never once looked at a painting and there was no one with me to know. Despite my aversion to sightseeing, though, I did read my guidebook from cover to cover, and, occasionally, I was enticed. I went to see the church which had a keel for a roof and loomed from Campo Francesco Morosini like a capsized ship; the work of ship-builders during a slack period. My only serious excursions were to the Basilica. Heeding the guidebook, I returned at various times of day to see the mosaic-encrusted ceilings and walls in differently-angled daylight. Mostly, they were lit by their own gold: that half a square mile of biblical scenes begun in the twelfth century and not completed until the nineteenth. I loved the thin but muscular angels, prophets, disciples and saints of the early scenes, with their cheekbone-sharpened scowls, ramrod spines and strappy sandals. By the fifteenth century, the Virgin Mary had developed jointed fingers and a slouch. The few nineteenth-century mosaics featured crowds of pastel-coloured characters who were swooning, reclining, or lunging with spears. As I paced the intricately patterned and unevenly worn floors, the only women who appeared in the scenes above me were the many Marys and a lone thirteenth-century Salome with a slinky, scarlet, fur-trimmed dress, a suggestion of high heels and a pronounced wiggle to her hips.

I was inside another church when I realised what had happened to me. I was trawling the distant, dilapidated Cannaregio, looking through a pane of glass at something tiny and white that my guidebook told me was St Catherine's foot.

That was when I realised: if anyone from home pushed through the door and glanced over, they would almost certainly fail to see me. They would see somebody, an anonymous body, but *not me*, because I was so unlikely to be there, on my own, peering at a relic in the chilly gloom of an unexceptional church in a work-a-day area of Venice. I was invisible, I had disappeared.

The only traces of my disappeared days are in some of the thousands or millions of photos taken by my fellow tourists. In those photos, there are pieces of me – perhaps a turning shoulder, the toe of a shoe, a swing of my hair – and they are all over the world, making a worldwide splintered mosaic of my disappearance. There was something else that I realised: Venice had become mine, mine alone rather than the place where Philip and I had had our honeymoon. Never once, for me, was Venice missing Philip; never once did I miss him.

Pondering, yesterday, that first disappearance of mine, reminded me of George, his old photo. 'I've found a photo,' he told me, last week, '1942 written on the back. A close-up of me, but my sister's beau is there: his arm, his shoulder, the side of his head. I was ten or eleven, and he used to take me fishing, bike-riding, exploring. I wonder, now, whether he did all that to impress her. He was the brother I never had; I worshipped him. I had two sisters, older, outgoing girls, marvellous. Then suddenly he never came to our house again. I don't know which of them had the cause for complaint, or why. For years, I was desperate to see him again, hoped I'd bump into him. Never did. When I came across that photo, the other day, I wondered what became of him, and there was no one to ask.'

With some trepidation, I asked, 'Your sisters?'

'One's dead – years ago – and the other, I'm afraid, can't remember her own name. I hope to God that I don't go the same way.'

I had first met George in the library, a couple of months ago, in the tiny photocopying room beyond the reference section. Taped to the back of the door was the handwritten puzzle, *Do you have your original?*, which made sense when I raised the lid and found a local history pamphlet. The cover illustration was an old photograph of what is now the town's General Infirmary, but the title was *The Workhouse*.

'Sorry.' Someone had come into the doorway, was reaching with a liver-spotted hand for the pamphlet.

I looked back at the illustration, squinted at the familiar but shadowed landmark.

'You didn't know, did you, that the hospital was once the workhouse.' This was a statement rather than a question, but surprised.

I smiled, amenable. 'I didn't, no.'

He was tweedy, tidy, balding, bespectacled; his accent was local, rural. 'Oh, Gawd, yes,' he winced, 'I hated going there.'

'Oh.' *Ah, a madman: the reference room's resident madman.*

'With my job, I mean.'

I calculated: if he was in his sixties, he would have begun work between forty and fifty years ago. Was there still a workhouse in this town during the 'forties or 'fifties?

'What *was* your job?'

'Policeman.'

'Oh.' Instinctively, I focused on the room beyond him, on escape.

'Well, detective.'

I had to admit, 'You must have seen some things,' and for a moment I was truly envious.

'Yes,' his tone echoed mine; but behind his square, gold-rimmed lenses, the pale eyes had a reflective glaze. 'I was never bored. Sounds odd, because I had some pretty awful jobs – I worked with a coroner for a while – but there was never a moment that I didn't enjoy. And not many people can say that of their work.' Folding his arms, he contemplated me. 'And I liked the people: the villains, I mean. They had some stories to tell; when I think of the statements that I took . . .' He shrugged.

'Must have been hard work.'

'Oh, no. my father – who was also a policeman, like his own father – said that the force was ideal for men who didn't want to work. My reason for joining was the house: in those days, we were given a house.'

'Oh.' *Not a bad reason.*

'But my father was right about the police force as the last refuge for mavericks.'

'Really?' I tried to hide my scepticism with a smile.

'Oh, yes.'

Carefully polite, I ventured, 'And you'd think the opposite was true.'

'Would you?' A widening of his eyes; eyes which, I suddenly realised, had been watching mine ever since he had appeared in the doorway. Was *he* humouring *me*? 'You don't watch those telly chaps?'

'You're telling me that real detectives are like Morse?'

'Well, to be honest with you, I don't see many of those serials; only in passing, because my wife watches. But, yes, detectives do everything their own way. Or did.'

'Not nowadays?'

'Well . . .' he shrugged, 'there have been changes.'

'I can imagine.' I even knew the word: *rationalisation*.

He stepped backwards through the doorway, apologising. 'I've been rambling, I've kept you from your photocopying.'

'Oh, no, no, not at all,' and I was surprised that this was true. I wanted him to tell me more.

He asked, 'Do you work? Or perhaps you're at home with children?'

'No children. I'm looking for work.'

'I don't envy you. One of my sons has been unemployed for a year, and he's bored brainless, poor sod. Me, I'm ten months into retirement and finding something to do every day. Somewhere to go or something to do, or to read, to look up.' He held the pamphlet aloft.

'Mustn't keep you.'

But a week or so later, we came across each other in the park, and he invited me to join him in the café.

'By the way, I'm harmless,' he reassured me, laughing. 'Too old to be otherwise.'

Yesterday, Annie left me unsettled, so I decided to drop in on George, hoping for a serene half hour with him in his garden. But when he came to the door, he said, 'I've a chap, here, from London, he's come for some stories from me.'

'Stories?'

'Of work. Of working in the police force. Oral history. He's taping me.'

I stepped back off the doorstep, but he insisted, 'No, we're finishing up, he has a train to catch. Two minutes, and then you and I can make some tea and take a tray into the garden.'

Hal and I followed him into his front room. The historian, in an armchair in the corner, was middle-aged and dressed in a dark suit. Looking up into sunshine, his small round lenses became medallions. He rose, tall amid the armchairs, and George began the obligatory chant, 'Dr Robinson, Sadie Summerfield; Sadie, Dr Robinson.'

The man's smile looked like a wince. I wished that he had stayed in his armchair, that George had not been provoked to compere this display; I could have slipped into the room. I dreaded looking down to see the fleece of Hal's blond fur on those black trousers. The man was holding one of his hands towards me. I hate to shake hands, I become all thumbs; I hate the judgements that people make from hand-shakes. He said his first name, which I missed because he spoke quietly and I was saying hello. His hand had come and gone from mine before I had noticed.

I sat down; he sat down; Hal went towards him and had his head stroked. The hand was unmarked, ivory; the nails, too. Hal returned to me and lay down, panting close to the microphone on the coffee table. George settled into his chair. The interviewer leaned forward and pressed a switch on the tape recorder.

'As I was saying,' George told him, 'this chap was well known to us.'

Watching the historian's black wool sleeve scrape over a white cuff, I wondered why anyone would wear a suit in such weather and then not even remove the jacket in a stiflingly double-glazed, net-curtained, upholstered room. His face, though, was untouched by heat. Even the pink of lips was missing because he seemed to have none, he had a mere line for his mouth. He was colourless in a room slapped with sunshine, splashed with chintz, dotted with vases. Looking downwards, head inclined in listening pose, he was eerily motionless in the company of animated monologue and con-vulsive canine panting. He could have been a black-and-white photograph of a person, he was no more than an arrangement of shadows, the smallest and darkest of which resembled the indentation of a fingertip in the inner corner of each eye. By contrast, his temples shone below a receding hairline.

'He used to go into the countryside and pick this moss which is important to florists, then he'd come into a town when the florist had shut up shop for the day, he'd go next door and ask if he could leave Mrs Bloggs' order of moss with them, and would they pay him the two quid or whatever? The following day, of course, Mrs Bloggs breaks the news to her neighbour that she's never heard of this man or his moss.'

A tightening of one corner of the interviewer's mouth, the screwing down of a smile, then he glanced at me and I saw how all his colour was in his eyes: china blue; very dark, for a blue.

'And he did the same with blackberries and greengrocers, in season. Hard for us to keep the evidence, in those cases. I suspect that many shopkeepers didn't complain, but some did. I was never particularly interested in bringing him in, I wasn't going to go and look for him, I knew that he was around, so when we'd had a lot of complaints, I'd contact the spike –'

'Spike?' the interviewer queried.

'Workhouse. And I'd ask them to let me know when he turned up. And he always turned up, for the winter. He knew that I'd come for him, and then he'd be sent down, which was what he wanted because then he had food and shelter for the winter.'

I shuddered to think of that hopeless trading of workhouse for prison.

'Mind you, in the end, a judge lost patience and sent him down for three years – *three years*, quite unnecessary – and I never came across him again.'

Suddenly the session seemed to have finished: the historian was packing away his paraphernalia, going for his train.

A WEEP FROM A WOUND

Yesterday, I was on a train, gazing through the window, with my headphones on and a CD spinning, when, from beyond the foam cushions of my earpieces, I heard, 'Sadie.' I looked up at a man in a suit as he reminded me, 'Edwin Robinson: we met on Sunday at George Reynolds' house.'

'Oh, yes.' I smiled, not knowing what else to say or do. I knocked the headphones down the length of my hair; the foam pads became pincers on the base of my throat. 'Yes, hello. Edwin.' His name was news to me.

'Hello.' He smiled, in return, without moving a facial muscle: somehow he gave an impression of smiling. 'Do you mind?'

Mind what? What had I done?

He indicated the vacant seat opposite me.

'Oh, no, no.'

But, of course, I did; I did mind. Already, I had been captivated by the view, a screening of endlessly familiar suburbs, as slick as an advert. I was giving myself up to solitude, indolence, music: that unique, magical combination, my compensation for having to endure the train. The horrors of train travel: sunshine baked inside double-glazed, dirt-glazed windows; the ferocious slams of doors; blocked toilets and waterless taps; depleted buffets; delays. And now someone with whom I would be hard-pressed to pass the time of day, but with whom I would have to spend forty minutes.

He looked exactly as he had looked at George's house: he could have been waiting at the station all week. I was dressed very differently from how I had been dressed on Sunday: I was in clothes for a trip to town rather than something that resembled a tennis dress. But even with a disc of black glass over each eye and a contraption over my head and ears, I had been recognisable: my hair, a beacon.

He was apologetic: 'Actually, there's nowhere else.'

As far as I could see, every vacant seat bore a white card. 'Reservations?'

He muttered, 'Reservations, I've had a few.' Then, 'Don't let me stop you.'

I had no idea what he meant.

He pointed to my CD player.

'Oh,' I smiled my thanks, 'no.'

'No, please: listen away. Do.'

'No, really.' My solitude, indolence and music in front of him? I would have taken more kindly to a proposal that he watch me have a bath.

'I'd hate to think that I could come between you and . . .' He looked away, to the window, before asking, 'something poppy?'

Momentary confusion, for me, so I explained, 'That's my nickname.'

An eyebrow kinked, questioning.

'Poppy.'

'Oh, I *am* sorry.'

Was this sympathy? and how dare he? or an apology? and if so, for what? for the inadvertent familiarity?

He continued, 'How nice. Because of your hair?'

I inclined my head, to give him what was intended as a long look: *Stupid question*. For a second, I pondered the symbolism of poppies: late-blooming? death-defying? full of opium?

'Who uses this nickname of yours?' But suddenly he back-tracked, 'I suppose that's rather a personal question.'

'Not at all.'

How quaint: a *personal question*.

I replied, 'Almost everyone.' This was the best that I could do; a more adequate account would have required my life story, friend by friend. I said, 'Friends, family.'

Old friends, I had been about to say, before realising that I had no other kind: *new friend* being, for me, I realised, a contradiction in terms. With the exception of George; if I could count George.

'So, the hair colour's natural?'

'You think anyone would try to sell this?'

He smiled. And this time, I saw how: a narrowing of the eyes; a tightening in one corner of the mouth. 'Perhaps they should.'

Then he nodded towards my CD player. 'So, something poppy? Something I'm too old to know?'

I was amused: 'How old do you think *I* am.' A rhetorical question.

But he replied. 'Mid-twenties.'

I shook my head, owned up, 'I'm the wrong side of thirty.'

'Mid-twenties *is* the wrong side of thirty.'

I wanted to say, *For a man, perhaps*. Instead, I told him what he wanted to know: 'I was listening to something called "NYC's no lark".'

'Well, however old you are,' he said to the window, to the swill of suburbs, 'I'm sure that you're not old enough to have come across that the first time around.'

So, either he knew his Bill Evans, or he had glanced over and read the CD case. Suddenly I saw how he was different from Sunday: no glasses; on Sunday he had been wearing glasses. Did he wear glasses for work? Even if that work consisted only of listening? He had shadows of tiredness, a purple petal dropped beneath each eye.

He said, 'Not the happiest of tracks.'

'Schubert said there's no happy music. Obviously, he hadn't heard Jelly Roll Morton.' Then I asked, 'Did George tell you, this morning, about his mother?'

'I'm a historian, not a psychoanalyst.'

'She used to cook for the prisoners in the cell in the station;

even though she loathed cooking, and couldn't cook, she had to provide those meals because she was the policeman's wife.'

He was paying attention, now.

'She'd been a flapper, George says; lots of tennis and parties. Then she married his father, late; in the days when late-twenties was late. Never took to small-town life, though.'

A wince of a smile, again: an unspoken, *Who does?*

I asked him, 'Do *you* have a nickname?'

'No.'

'Not one that you know, anyway.'

And he laughed, but barely: an admission, his head bowed. The reserved seats remained unoccupied throughout the journey: a mass missing of a train. Our unmaterialised travelling companions had a lucky escape. The train had been in a station for a few minutes when a disembodied, distorted voice informed us that we were *experiencing a delay due to an electrical fault which has caused a failure of the doors.*

Edwin worried, '*How* do doors fail? How do doors *fail?*'

'They fail to open.'

'Are you saying that we're stuck?' He stared at me, in disbelief. His irises were a visceral blue.

'Well, that's what *he's* saying.'

'Do you think that he's having us on?'

Inside my head was the refrain, *Jeepers, creepers, where d'you get those peepers?*

He slid a mobile phone from his pocket. 'Necessary,' he remarked, apologetically, indicating it, 'because I'm mobile, much of the time. Or, rather, because I'm *not.*' He pushed a single button, told someone, 'I'm stuck on a train, and I do mean stuck.' He would ring again, he said, when he reached London.

'Work?' I sympathised, when he had finished.

'Wife. Late lunch.'

It hardly needed saying, but I said it anyway: 'Even later, now.'

'Looks as if she'll be lucky to see me for breakfast

tomorrow.' Then he asked me where I was going, and what I would be doing.

I said that I was on my way into London to meet up with my friend Fern.

'*Fern*? Fern and Poppy? What *is* this? The flower fairies?'

'Fern's her *real* name,' I qualified, rather pointlessly.

She is nothing like a fern; she is silvery, and brisk.

I was going to see Fern because, last week, Philip had said, 'Why don't you take the day off, on Friday?'

All that I could say was, 'Off from what?'

Sagely, he had replied, 'From your routine.'

He would be covering a sleep-in for one of his staff, so would have a day in lieu at home with Hal.

'Hal and I'll be boys together,' he enthused. 'We'll kick a football around the park and then go to the pub.' London was his suggestion for me: he knows how I like to spend my time; he seems to know better than I do, nowadays.

Edwin offered me his phone: 'Can you reach her, to warn her that you'll be late?'

I did not tell him that I had my own phone, and merely declined his offer. I had time in hand: Fern was doing something else over lunchtime. She is always doing something. Free time, of which she has so little, seems to hold a terror for her: time, for her, is to be used. Having fitted me into her schedule with a coffee or two, she would then travel across town to the offices of a Sunday newspaper. She works two evenings each week as a subeditor. The job helps to fund her expensive training.

'Fern's training as an analyst,' I told Edwin, and clarified, 'psycho.'

'Freudian Fern.'

'Lacanian,' I admitted, 'sounds like a baby milk formula, to me.'

'Appropriately, somehow.'

Why had I thought of Fern when planning my day in London? Probably because I knew that she, the busiest of my friends, would make time to see me at such short notice. I knew, too, though, that she makes the time not because she is generous or keen, but because she is organised. She lives to a schedule, and so she rises to the challenge, allocates me a slot. Sitting there in that train carriage, my journey suspended, I became aware of how I was braced, dreading her. During the past couple of years, she has changed. Hers is that state of mind into which most of my friends disappeared for a while during their twenties. They had time on their side, and eventually eased up, stopped trying to prove themselves and distance themselves from the past. In time, they relaxed; they came round. For Fern, late developer, the new identity could be permanent.

Lately, I have been wondering why I like her. The same, perhaps, as wondering if I like her. The same as wondering why I ever liked her. Originally, when we were sixth-formers, I liked her because she was likeable. The words that come to mind – *funny* and *warm* – say no more than that: she was likeable; I liked her. In recent years, she seems to have gone through a sense of humour menopause. The world is simply something with which she deals, and there is no give in her. I make rare appearances in her diary, but otherwise there is no place for me in that dealt-with life, not even as a memory. Perhaps especially not as a memory. In latter years, she has made a series of advantageous moves to become who she is now: wife of a BBC producer; mother of a year-old son; homeowner in Crouch End; sub on a Sunday paper; and Tavistock-trainee. Having taken the steps as they became available to her, she has kicked over the traces. I am an unwelcome reminder of how far she has come.

The doors continued to fail, and the train was delayed for an hour. We weathered the heatwave in a block of conditioned, manufactured air. Outside, on the station platform, the kiosk's newspapers detailed disasters that had happened elsewhere on the tracks in a week of jinxed journeys: a nine-hour delay on one train, a fire and fatality on another, and the driver who had turned by mistake into the grounds of a nuclear power station.

When there had been no more from the disembodied voice for ten minutes, one of our fellow passengers stood up and announced to the carriage that he was going to find the guard.

'I'd hate to have that guard's job,' I said to Edwin.

He said, 'I'd hate to have any job other than mine,' and asked, 'what about you? What do you do?' Properly cautious, he revised: 'Or what *did* you do? or would you *like* to do?'

So, I told him about Jacqueline: for five years before her death from pneumonia a year and a half ago, she lived with me; we were best friends when students, and then, just after graduation, she was injured in a car accident.

'Head injuries,' I said.

Those who never knew us before the accident assumed that we were sisters and that was why she lived with me. In fact, I explained to Edwin, there was nowhere for her to go: her father was dead; her mother, ill for years with depression; her brother and sister-in-law busy with a toddler and new baby. The only solution, in Jacque's case, was a rehabilitation centre, nearly a hundred miles away, where she was the youngest resident by more than thirty years.

'The staff were nice, but they were staff, if you know what I mean.'

And there were so many of them. So many hands. Timetables, job titles, *Key Worker*.

'She needed a home. I couldn't leave her there. And I wasn't working, at the time; I wasn't doing anything else.' I shrugged – *no big deal* – but below these words, the whole truth slid like a fish, barely detectable and faintly repulsive.

'I had the help of Philip, my husband.'

Not that he was my husband, then. But we were living together, because I had taken him up on his offer: if I wanted to provide a home for Jacqueline, I should live with him. She is part of our past, was part of our start. Caring for Jacque was possible because we had compensation money, we had equipment, help, and because we had each other. I had muscles, too, in time.

'She was very small,' I reassured Edwin.

She had always been small, but was smaller when she came home from the residential centre, her muscles wasted from lack of use. Smaller still when she died: barely able to move a muscle, she had barely a muscle to move. She shrank, over the years, and I grew. I am small again now. We both wore clothes labelled *eight* or *ten*: in my case, size; in hers, years. Did she ever glimpse and comprehend her labels, those graphic illustrations of her diminution? It occurs to me, now: why did I never think to remove them?

More than a year ago, she was already dead; a year ago, she had been dead for months. During that whole first year, my grief was undiminished. Almost as shocking to me as her death was how that gaping loss remained unmitigated, month by month. Her absence was raw; her death, a fundamental and disabling severance. But the slow passage of that time had an odd effect: when I was still near to her death, I was very near; and then suddenly I was worlds away. And that is where I am, nowadays: worlds away, with no prospect of return; remembering surprisingly little, and vaguely resentful that even her loss has moved away from me.

How strange, on that train, with Edwin, to be saying and hearing Jacque's name. She rarely, if ever, surfaces in conversation, nowadays. Not even with Philip. Perhaps especially not with Philip. I remember how, a couple of days after her funeral, I mentioned beginning to look for work, because I felt that I should, because I was clueless as to what else I should do; and, gently, kindly, Philip admonished me with, 'After this, you'll need time to find your feet.' That was the moment when I wanted to scream, *And what about you?* Why didn't I? He has always been careful of me, but more so since Jacqueline died. I feel that I am forever protecting him from me.

I never doubted that Jacqueline understood me, on some level: that she caught the drift, detected the undercurrent. She was incapable of more than indicating the most basic of preferences – her speech badly affected, practically obliterated – but I am certain that what was happening inside her head was nothing like that which happens inside the head of a small child. She was nothing like a child; she was Jacqueline, changed, but not into a child. No one ever changes back into a child. Nothing so uncomplicated. I talked a lot to her, told her a lot. We were together almost all the time. We passed the days listening to music, to the radio, watching television, going shopping and to the Day Centre, and to her various medical and therapeutic appointments, of which there were many. Everyone seems so sure that I gave up on something for her. But what? What else – what more – would I have had? People think that I lost the world, that I was lost to the world. And, yes, that is what accidents do: they befall you and you keep on falling; they take you from the world, either for a while or forever. But what was the world, to me? Only now that I am having to return to the world, am I lost. I have never been as lost as I am now.

Glancing over, I saw that he was watching me; he was watching more than listening. Or listening to more than the words. And he was opened up for more. All of him was in that wide-open gaze, and I was on the brink, hushed, buoyed by my unspoken words. Then, a pulse of eyelashes before once again he was self-contained, self-conscious, that gaze folded away.

After my day in London, I travelled home quite late, the land dipped into shadow, the sky a blue like the white of an eye. Darkness hardened around the train; but above, delicate plane trails were splashed by the sinking sun and tinted peach-coloured. For a while, several of them ran parallel, as if in a race; a slow race, the speed shrunk within the expanse of sky. For the first time ever, I wondered how many more summers

I would see. Probably no more than could be counted on my fingers and toes, twice over. A finite number of summers.

This morning the sky is cloudless again, but looks breathed upon. Hal and I have come a little later than usual to the park because a man came to advise me on the polishing of the floorboards in the front room.

Yesterday, when he had heard the story of Jacqueline, Edwin had asked, tentatively, 'And now?'

'Oh, now. Well, for now, I'm doing the house.'

'Doing what to the house?'

'Everything. Everything needs doing, nothing was done for years.'

Nothing, during the years when I was busy with Jacqueline; and then nothing during my listless year of mourning. And then, gradually, a couple of months ago, I realised how much needed to be done, and how little else there was for me to do. All the usual maintenance is taking place alongside the necessary re-conversion: when Jacqueline came to live with us, the house was converted; now that she has gone, ramps and handrails are being removed, some flooring replaced, her elaborate bathroom dismantled, and the front room – which was her bedroom – redecorated, reinstated. I am re-converting the house so that we can live without her.

The floorboards man, who came to the house this morning, was a twin; he told me that he had never had a room of his own when he was a child, because he was a twin. I had always wanted a twin: no mere sib, but a twin. He told me that his two elder brothers were twins too, and two of his own three children, one of whom had twins of her own. I was enchanted by this fairytale family, twins within twins, a Siamese version of a Russian doll.

'I never realised that they ran so clearly in families.'

'Children?' he quipped.

But he had saved the biggest surprise until last: the kind of twinning that runs in families is the non-identical kind.

The twins in his extraordinary family are the ordinary kind.

What then, I wonder, is the chance of such a family having identical twins? The same chance, presumably, as that of any other family having identical twins. I like to turn the puzzle around: what is the chance of being born an identical twin to such a family, of all families; to a family which specialises in the non-identical kind? Surely a tiny chance, quite spectacular.

None of this matters to Hal: he was one puppy in a multiple birth, the others unknown to him and insignificant. All that matters to him is me. And a few minutes ago, here in the park, he lost me. He was trotting ahead when he saw a spaniel, the spaniel saw him, and they were compelled to bound towards each other with the usual reckless enthusiasm. Predictably, they stopped short and stood tall before embarking on the final few cautious, mannered paces. The noses touched for a second, then glided down the other's body. I wondered how dogs regard human handshakes. What is so civilised about the taking, holding, squeezing of a hand? Because who knows where a hand has been? Hands go everywhere; that is what hands do. How intimate, to reach for the hand of another person, to place one's own hand into that of another person.

As soon as Hal had fulfilled his social obligation to the spaniel he was ready to return to me. He looked up but somehow missed me. He stiffened, straining to peer into the distance, but panic blinded him to me.

I called, 'Hal!' but he failed to hear. His outline, usually slack with contentment, was crystal clear with desolation.

I hurried towards him, yelling, 'Hal! Hal! *Here*!' My final note hit home and he scampered, but in the opposite direction.

I bellowed again, 'HERE!' but by then he was further away than my voice could carry. I was losing him, he was galloping away from me towards the road. I stopped, as if this would stop him too and make him turn around.

'HALHALHAL!'

Suddenly his radar worked: he circled, skidding, to lock

on to this ululation of mine; suddenly he was running fiercely towards me, doubled-up, his body tightened for speed. Nearer, he slowed down, feigned nonchalance, trotted to a tree trunk. We have suffered these panics of his on previous occasions and each time I have been aghast that he could think that I would leave him: here one minute and quite simply gone the next? Why else does he think that I am here with him but to follow him, to watch for him and take him home with me again?

Now we are winding down, meandering towards the café. The man who is sometimes still asleep beneath blankets on a bench in the Scented Garden is awake and sitting on the low wall which borders the café's terrace. Beside him is a café cup, but no saucer: tea, no trimmings. The word for men like him, when I was a child, was *tramp*; a word not dissimilar in connotation to *grandpa*. Tramps knew their place, which was benches and ditches; they did not camp in shop doorways as homeless people do nowadays. And they were given food rather than money. George told me that the tramps of his own childhood were shell-shocked veterans of the First World War, of which his father was a fellow veteran; and that his father, not known for his benevolence, took care of them, bathed and fed them. 'They came to their own kind,' he said.

When I was a child, the term *homeless* was never used, and instead I remember talk of *the open road*. I was under no illusions, I knew that our local tramps were afflicted with madness of the mumbling, visionary variety; I knew that they were infested with fleas and lice; but I knew, too, that they inspired an awe that had something to do with those roads, to do with walking away from our comfortable world like saints. The awe had something to do with their return, too. I remember how people spoke of them: *Yesterday I saw Hop-along in the churchyard, I hadn't seen him for, ooh, a couple of years*; *Haven't seen old Jack since that terrible Christmas*. Our tramps were landmarks, even in their absence. Perhaps especially in their absence. We were touched that within their nomadism lived a homing instinct, like a weep from a wound.

This man, who has been living here for a couple of months, is a throwback, a storybook tramp: he has the bushy beard and hair, and sleeps on a bench. But the beard is dark rather than grandpa-grey, and well-kept. His clothes, too, look fairly new and clean; unstylish, but new-ish, clean-ish. Sometimes he wears a pair of sunglasses which are too small for him, the frame slightly splayed: children's sunglasses, perhaps; perhaps given to him, perhaps found. Today his eyes are bare, he is squinting in the sunshine. Sometimes he wears a pair of startlingly white trainers; other times, his feet are bare. Today he has his back to us, he is facing the sun, so I cannot see.

We often pass each other on these paths. He walks purposefully, trainers or no trainers. During the past couple of months I have passed him so many times that these days I am unsure whether to acknowledge him. There is no one else here whom I pass daily but do not acknowledge. What I am unsure of is whether he would want to be acknowledged. I wonder what he sees whenever he sees me approaching: me, in a crisp little summer dress; following my glossy, golden hound; stepping out to savour the sunshine, circling the park, and returning home. I wonder if he wonders why I am so often in tears.

TREACLIER

Yesterday I went to London again. There are friends who I should have planned to see; some of whom I have not seen for years. But arrangements would have required energy and forethought, neither of which I had. Philip is always encouraging me to do as I please; this time, I took him up on his suggestion. I went to London to see Edwin.

I had enjoyed the time spent with him on that train, last week, even though much of the conversation was far from fun, and the journey was hell. What I had enjoyed was his company. Time spent with friends these days, for me, is in anticipation of a return to my natural state of solitude.

I knew that the phone number that he had given me was his home number, he had told me that he was working from home for the months that he was on sabbatical.

Sabbatical: a lovely word. I would love to have a job whereby that word could apply to me.

I phoned him, said that I was going to be in London. 'I thought that it might be nice to have that coffee.'

'I can't imagine anything nicer: a coffee is what we shall have.'

We settled on a time, which was lunchtime, twelve-thirty, before turning to the question of where. He started with, 'Where would be convenient for you?'

'Oh, anywhere fairly central.'

'Well . . .' he was thinking aloud, '. . . I'll be in the library . . .'

'The British Library? Bloomsbury it is, then.'

We agreed to meet on the library steps.

'The only problem,' he said, 'is if there's a bomb scare. The last time that there was a bomb scare, they locked us in.'

'Out.'

'No, in.'

'Who did? The IRA?'

'No, the library staff.'

'The *staff* locked you *in*? they took the chance to see off Britain's entire intelligentsia in one go? to retire early *en masse* to Marbella?'

He explained, 'The bomb wasn't *in* the library; the bomb was somewhere nearby. I suppose that whoever makes these decisions believed that we were safer inside the library than outside roaming the streets.'

'Which is, of course, the *raison d'être* of libraries.'

There was a pause, during which I feared that I had offended him, but then came a sigh that was close to a laugh and he said, 'You're a cynic, Sadie.'

I had to tell him, 'It's been said before.'

So, yesterday, I went to the steps of the British Museum. I have only ever been into the building on school trips. When I was a child, I was fascinated by the ancient Egyptians. Why? Because of their appealing, pictorial literacy? their extensive, opulent monarchy? their literally earth-moving faith? My primary school years teemed with projects, drawings, stories and library loans on the subject of the pharoahs. I was confident that I was going to be an Egyptologist.

Egyptologist: even the word captivates me; that ringing stress on the third syllable, the kind of sound that usually compensates for a silent consonant, although in this case everything is spoken.

How odd, that the passing of my passion was so thorough and so unconscious: a passion of which I had no memory until yesterday when I walked into Coptic Street. As soon as I saw the building, I wondered why I had never achieved that ambition of mine, and decided that I must have lacked resolve.

But then I pondered the real, live curators in there: what had they wanted to be when they were eight, nine, ten years old? Train drivers, probably, or nurses, or ice skaters: the usual; something action-packed. What was puzzling was why, as a child, I had been drawn to a disappeared civilisation, to corpses that were buried bizarrely with their earthly essentials in the hope of some further, fantastical life.

To me, as a child, the British Museum meant ancient Egyptians. Yesterday, approaching the building, I had no clearer idea of its contents: it was still a misshapen pyramid in central London, a massive mausoleum for the wrapped husks of people who, over thousands of years, have been excavated, ripped open, broken up, and stripped of their treasures. The journey that they have endured is not the one that they had in mind when they chose to have their brains drained down their noses. For them, the vital organ was not the brain but the heart; the state of one's heart decided one's fate. On their version of judgement day, the heart was placed on some scales with a feather, and if the heart fell, then the owner was condemned. How would I have fared? During the past year or so, my brain could well have leaked away down my nose. But with a heart like mine, I am sure as hell not going to heaven.

From their chosen site on the banks of the Nile to captivity in the vicinity of Russell Square tube station: that building must be alive with ghosts.

Plunder: a faintly sickening word, with echoes, to my mind, of *asunder, lunge* and *pluck*, all words that have in common a sense of utter disregard.

What an irony: the more precautions, the more plunder. Massively, absurdly fortified, both materially and spiritually, they were unable to prevent their inevitable downfall. What goes up, must come down, and down they came, with so very far to fall. And then the final insult: the all-seeing, unstoppable assault from X-rays. In my library books, the mummies' remaining embedded charms were exposed in black-and-white, along with their frailties and fatalities. I was horrified to see that their jewels looked like stupidly-swallowed sixpences. To those who knew the code, who could read the X-rays, the pristinely-preserved bones displayed indelible patterns of fractures, erosions and misplacements. Those embalmed bodies, which had been biding their time, became mere bundles of dietary deficiencies, diseases, domestic accidents and treasons.

As I walked through the gateway, I saw Edwin in the distance. He was sitting on the steps, and had not seen me; he was reading, his attention locked down over a book. I did not recognise the clothes that he was wearing; jeans and a shirt. I stopped, struck that this was the first time that I had ever seen him from anywhere but up close. He was, of course, so much more than the person to whom I had chatted on a train. He had a whole life that was unknown to me; and there he was, in that life, back in that life, quite beyond me. I had everything to learn about him.

Standing there, I realised that he would look up and see me before I could reach him. I was going to have to walk towards him for whole seconds while he watched me. The crowds of tourists added to the problem: he would watch me blundering through those intangible tripwires between posers and photographers. And my dress was too short. My entire wardrobe flashed before me, every article of clothing tantalisingly more appropriate than the one that I had chosen. I had only two options: to rush towards him, or to try to creep up on him. That was when he saw me, and spared me: he smiled but then became busy, slotting his book into his bag and removing his glasses. Reaching him, I closed the remaining distance between us with a kiss on his cheek. As I came away, his hand stayed for a moment in the small of my back.

We headed back towards the road.

'How was your journey?' he asked.

'Fine, but I'm in need of refreshments, to use a good, old-fashioned word.'

'Rehydration, to be more prosaic.'

'And cake, to be blunt.' I indicated his bag. 'What were you reading?'

He fished for the book, showed me: a novel, not one that I had read.

'What's it about?'

'Oh, you know, the usual: life, love . . .' Having delved into his bag, he had found some sunglasses and was now staring blackly into the crowds.

'With jokes?'

He laughed, or almost laughed. 'They *are* the jokes, aren't they?'

'And you said that *I* was a cynic.'

'I didn't say that *I wasn't*.'

Listening to the jauntiness in his step, I thought, *No, but you're not, you know; not quite.*

He asked me, 'Are you reading anything?'

'Rereading,' I had to admit. I have been unable to settle to anything new for some time.

'Rereading Grace Paley.'

Airily, over my head, he said, 'I don't know her.'

'Well, you should.'

'Well of course, but there are so many books that I should read.'

I stopped, so that he had to stop. 'No, I mean *for your own sake*.' For me, returning to her stories had been like turning up treasure that I had forgotten I had hidden. I had experienced a sense of reprieve. 'The pleasures in life are so few and so brief that I don't think that you can afford to be without her.'

'I'll do my best, then.'

'You do that.'

We went into a coffee shop which, like all the others that we had passed, was crowded. We were lucky to have one of the few tables for two by the window. Our tiny tabletop barely accommodated two tall glasses, gaudy with ice cubes and lemon, and two bottles of mineral water; big, bulbous bottles of green glass, ostentatiously Italian. Edwin checked, 'Not tempted by the cakes?'

'No room.'

'You've already had lunch somewhere?'

'No, I mean, no room on this table. When I've had my water, I'll consider cake.' Then, to be polite, I asked him: 'You?'

'No room because I devoured a not-insignificantly-sized bar of chocolate while I was waiting for you.'

I was alarmed, 'Was I late?'

'No, I was greedy.'

I laughed. A man with a sweet tooth is a man that I can trust.

Despite the cramped conditions, I was thankful that we were in Bloomsbury, I could cope with Bloomsbury. The scene on the other side of the window was quite unlike anywhere else in central London in this undertow of a heatwave. Across the narrow street, people were loitering in the shade of the awnings of a bookshop, a gallery and a deli. I made a start on my designer water. Sharing our neighbouring and similarly stool-sized table were two men who clearly had nothing to do with each other. One was chopping his spoon into a slice of cream-dolloped Dutch apple pie, his back overlapping the slats of his chair, his shirt's lower buttonholes taut. Next to his plate was the *Telegraph*, firmly folded into the shape that is ideal for fly-swatting or worse. Opposite him, a bespectacled and bearded man in black jeans and T-shirt was hunched over a paperback entitled *From Plato to NATO, readings in political philosophy*, and nibbling a lettuce-sodden bap.

Edwin asked, 'So, anyway, what have you been doing to that house of yours, since I last saw you?'

Because, of course, that was what I was doing: the house; that was all I was doing.

Between sips of water, I told him about the man who had come to advise on the floorboards, the man who was a twin from a family of two sets of twins and who had twins of his own, one of whom had twins of *her* own. And I received appropriately appreciative responses as I worked through this particular box of tricks.

Then he asked, 'Do you want children?'

'A coffee will do for now.'

His smile was quick, small, uncertain.

'Do *you* have children?' I asked him. I had been wanting to ask, on that train journey; there had been no mention of any.

'No.'

I said, 'I don't know whether I want to stay married.'

There: *said*. Said concisely and calmly. Said as if I had been saying the words casually every day for years, for all the years that they had been unsaid. Close friends are too close to be told; this burden of mine would simply become theirs too. So the truth was said to a man who I barely know. But if he is to know me, then this is what he has to know; this is who I am.

And, anyway, he asked.

Sort of.

He was silent for a moment, presumably giving me a chance to say more, before he responded with a careful, 'Ah.'

This *ah* somehow served to lessen the impact for me: *Ah, that little brain-teaser*. Suddenly I was so grateful, hopeful: *that* little brain-teaser, the one that other people have; the one to which there is a solution. I reached for my glass, craving a salutary, celebratory mouthful. Up close, the fizzing water sounded like fat frying. I looked down into that volatile mixture of liquid and ice; down on to the pip-shedding, pop-eyed, swirling slice of lemon.

He asked, 'Does your husband know?'

'Philip,' I said: I felt that we should say his name, that this was his due, and I felt that if we were to have this conversation, then it was important to be clear about absolutely everything.

'Yes,' I answered: somehow, I realised, he knows.

'And what does he say?'

'What is there to say? I think that he thinks that I'll settle down.'

'And what do you think?'

'I don't know,' I said, 'do I.'

Neither of us spoke again for a moment, but I wanted to say, *Go on, ask me another*. I was ready for more. Never having spoken a word of this, here I was, replying to his questions with no hesitation. And of course I was, because I had had the answers for a long time. There is nothing that I do not know about my situation, about living with someone and keeping up appearances but longing to be somewhere else, anywhere else. Oh, yes, I am an old hand.

His next question was, 'And for how long have you been thinking of leaving?'

But this was wrong, I knew instantly that this rang untrue, and I knew why: I have not been *thinking of leaving*, during these bad years. Thinking of leaving is not what I have been doing. I have simply been thinking of *not being where I am*. I have nowhere to go. I have no reason to go, and every reason to stay. Mine is a perfect life, courtesy of a perfect husband. Leaving is unthinkable.

I said, 'Three years.'

'Three years,' he did not seem to flinch, he seemed to be mulling this over. 'How long have you been married?'

'Three years.' I was the one who flinched. 'We've been together for seven.' Seven minus three leaves four. I looked around for the waitress, then smiled for her to come and take an order. I wanted so desperately to avoid mention of those four years; four years when Philip and I were happy, the four years of my life when I was happy; four years that are lost to me, that I have lost. I have lived three years on ice. What would Jacqueline have given to have had three extra years of life?

Edwin said fairly cheerfully, or at least with some vigour,

'We've been married for six years. We've been together for seven. We married because Vivien was pregnant.'

Vivien. Momentarily I was baffled, because he had said that they had no children; but I realised what had happened in the instant that he explained, 'She miscarried.'

I said, 'Oh. Oh, I am sorry,' and I was.

'I expect that a pregnancy seems a bad reason to marry, but I'm not sure what a good reason would have been, for me. I didn't want us to marry, I didn't see that marriage would make a difference, but that was what she wanted, and why should I refuse? In the end, she miscarried before we married, but . . .'

'Yes,' I said quickly, to save him from having to say.

Much slower, he admitted, 'That would have been really rather heartless.' Then he resumed, 'And if that was important to her, why should I refuse to sign a piece of paper and have a party? I mean, we were together, and we seemed to be going to stay together.'

He had not mentioned love, but perhaps that was a given.

'I was thirty-three, and I suspect that there's something about reaching thirty-three, that round number.'

I said, 'It's not a round number, Edwin.'

He frowned. 'But you know what I mean. It looks round.'

Thirty-three plus six: he was thirty-nine, he was only thirty-nine, only eight years older than I am. I had thought that he was much older because of his less than full head of hair, and because he looked so resigned. Yes, that was his look: one of resignation. Also, I should have allowed for my habitual over-estimation, my tendency to assume that grown-ups are so much older than I am simply because they always were.

He finished with a sudden, cheerful, 'In seven years, we've never had a crisis.'

I did not know what to say, whether to congratulate him or to ask, *Why? what have you been doing?* The waitress whirled to our table, and I blurted, 'Coffee?'

His mouth opened and closed, he was undecided, and looked as if he would remain forever undecided.

I heard the impatient shuffle of the waitress's shoes, and requested, 'Two espressos, please.' She turned on her heel, literally, causing a squeak.

He looked up, puzzled. 'I don't drink espresso.'

'A double for me, then.'

'Why did you marry Philip?'

'I don't know. No reason.' I meant, of course, no specific reason like pregnancy: and this Edwin seemed to understand. I meant no reason other than the usual ones such as that Philip asked me and I was in love with him. Are they reasons? do they explain? I have been thinking, yesterday and today, and now, if I do not remember *why*, I do remember *how*: I know how it happened.

This is how: Philip had said, 'Marry me,' as a little joke – no, a little dare – and in the same vein I said, 'Okay, then.' He was serious, though, and so was I. This had come out of the blue, we were whoozy in slapdash evening sunshine. He was lying in bed, our bed, and I was sitting on the edge. There should be a word for the edge of a bed, that crucial, pivotal place. I was leaving him, but not quite back in the world. The warmth of him was on my skin: a sensation of blood-warm water. He was propped on one elbow, he had been drawn up in my wake, but I had a sense that this was as far as he was coming: he would stay there for a while, happy with my body-heat wrapped into the bedclothes. His smile was dazed because he had been dozing; he was smiling because he had been trying to persuade me to turn back, but knew that he could only do so a few times and that this was the time he had lost. His little dare was a diversional tactic: I had to stay a moment longer in order to answer.

I answered, and he had what he wanted. I married him because he was good and good-natured and he had faith in me and he loved me, and I loved him for that. Looking at him looking as if he had never before set foot in the world,

I was thinking, *You're perfect*. Marrying him must have been the right thing to do. The problem is that somehow it was wrong *for me*: the closest I can come to what is wrong is that I married Philip because of him, not because of me.

Edwin and I were in the coffee shop for two hours and we never did have any cake; cake did not happen. Perhaps we never paused for long enough to make a decision of the magnitude required by the cake display. I was stoked with coffee, that raw, black bean juice, and he sipped his way through several pots of camomile tea. Finally, the conversation moved from the state of our respective private lives to the only person our lives have in common: George. Edwin explained that he had finished interviewing George; he will not be returning to my town. When we said goodbye, he wanted to know if I would be in London next week.

I said, 'Possibly.'

I have no plans; but conversely, there is nothing to stop me.

And now, nearly a whole twenty-four hours later, Hal and I are patrolling our territory. Ahead, a poster announces a *fun run*, surely a contradiction in terms. Beneath, a small, bedraggled, handwritten poster pleads for the safe return of a missing cat. The pitiful inventory of charms concludes with, *She might be hiding*.

Cloud, today, is thin and broken like the milky residue of bubble bath on cool bathwater.

Earlier, Hal was sunbathing on the carpet in front of the window. On cloudy mornings, he will follow me around the house, staring into my eyes; sometimes whimpering and going to the door. He is stilled by sunshine: this morning, all that I heard from him was the occasional sigh.

Once I said to Philip, 'Hal's sighs are so human.'

He looked sceptical.

I had to explain: 'Well, I mean, do cats sigh?'

Across the park is the blind dog, a very old red setter,

florid, with eye-catchingly fluorescent cataracts. The dog's habit is to lumber from the path – her ribboned coat an autumnal grass skirt – and stagger in circles as if preparing a bed. Then she sits, cautiously, and sniffs, extravagantly: dredging the air for scents.

'She's happy,' her owner reassured me, when we first met them. The owner – unlike her dog – is a youthful middle age. 'That's all she wants to do.'

What else *can* she do?

Usually, Hal tries to be sociable and the setter tries to reciprocate, bumping into him time and time again like something on water. The first time, we two owners laughed kindly over this sorry display of compromised dogginess, this cobbled-together bottom-sniffing.

While apologising for Hal's enthusiasm I had turned towards him.

Behind me, the woman said, 'I'm sorry, but I don't hear very well; I lip-read.'

Immediately I realised that I had indeed been listening to the indistinct speech of someone who is deaf.

She sees me, now, and waves.

What a coincidence, seeing her here. Working in my garden, today, for the third consecutive day, is Carl, Jason's cousin; a cousin in need of work – odd jobs – for the summer months before beginning a college course.

'What's the course?' I asked Carl, on his first day.

'Signing.'

'Painting them?'

He laughed. 'You're thinking of sign writing. I'll be doing sign language.'

On Carl's first day, Philip called to me from the kitchen when he arrived home: 'Poppy? Why is there an Adonis in our garden?'

I called back from the hallway, 'Better than a gnome.'

Joining him at the window, I said, 'He isn't an Adonis; look how skinny he is.'

Philip smirked, and went from the room singing, *She was thirty-one, I was seventeen.*

Carl's job is to clear the back of the garden, the patch which Philip has always avoided. Philip stays close to the house, pruning and planting. Behind, beyond the pond, is an area decades-deep in brambles and rubble. In many ways, we took on too much when we took on this house: a house that was big enough for three, but dilapidated enough to be affordable. *A knock-down price*, says Philip: *they paid us to knock it down.*

When Jacqueline was here, we had no energy for DIY; but since she has gone, we seem to have even less.

The clearance is heavy work for Carl; heavy work in heavy weather. The unrelenting sun is a problem for him. His back is the colour of cinnamon. All day, he is dressing and undressing, putting on and then pulling off his T-shirt, each rise and fall of the neckline tousling his hair.

From Jason, I know two facts about Carl: at the end of last year, he separated amicably from his girlfriend of five years; and he is twenty-seven. He has the kind of face and figure that will never slacken. God's own bone structure.

I was never beautiful, but seemed to have whatever was needed: I had whomever I wanted. Perhaps there were beautiful bits of me; perhaps I was beautiful in bits, and had enough to do the trick. Whatever I did have will now have faded. Not literally, unfortunately: my hair is as weal-coloured as ever, and my skin still glows like freshly-sliced pear flesh. But I cannot be a patch on what I was. I cannot shake the feeling that I am nothing, nowadays; I am scuttled bones.

Whenever Carl catches me watching him from the window, he smiles. That smile is far from self-conscious, or reluctant. It is sheer smile. I remember an expression that was favoured by my mother: *There is no side to him*. Whenever I look away, he comes with me, his image burned on to my eyes. Asleep, I dream of him. The dreams come in the mornings, when sunshine strokes my eyelids. They are close to daydreams. Too close. They are sexual dreams, dreams of sex, vocal sex; more sexual, somehow, than any sex that I have ever had. In these dreams I am not me; I am no one else, but not me. I am no one. I am desire: something fed into a vein, distilled, heavy but slick, treacly, deadly, pure.

When the dream drains away, I am beached in my bed. And for a time, the real, everyday world is beyond me. Coming to, dry-mouthed but damp everywhere else, sloppy with sexual desire, I am rudderless, a mess of limbs and linen. Then I begin to be aware of Philip. He is turned demurely away into his doze. He seems so far away, borne on his tidy half of the bedclothes, waiting patiently for the turn of consciousness. For him, sleeping, dreaming and waking are not the exertions that they have been for me. Across the expanse, he is unrecognisably-shaped and I take a moment to make sense of him. If I reach to touch him, he is dough-warm and calico-clean.

It's nothing, it's physical: this is what I tell myself, whenever I look at Carl.

I feel like Samantha in *Bewitched*, acting the model housewife and coping with a contrary nature.

Carl is scrupulously cheerful, as if to be otherwise would be to do me a disservice. He called me *Mrs Summerfield* until I impressed upon him not to do so. Early this morning we had coffee together. Having brought my coffee into the garden, I called: 'Come over here, have a break.' He had already done over an hour of hard work.

'I'm fine, honestly, Mrs Summerfield.'

'Don't call me that. And I mean that.'

'Sorry. Forgot.'

'Come over here.' He is younger than I am, and I am paying him: I suppose that I can issue orders.

He came over, smelling of grass.

I looked down at my tray, at my cafetière. 'You want some water or something?'

He, too, looked at the cafetière. 'I don't suppose you have any spare coffee?'

'Oh, sorry: I didn't think you'd want a hot drink, that's all.'

'But there's something about coffee in hot weather.'

'Yes, isn't there. I drink far more coffee during the summer.'

'Me, too. And the treaclier, the better.'

Treaclier. I laughed. 'Yes.'

I went to the kitchen for a cup for him. Returning, I asked, 'Has anyone ever asked you that question: if you were on a desert island, what would you pay five hundred pounds for? Has to be a food, or a drink.'

'No,' he raised those eyes of standard, boyish blue; he was smiling, 'No one has ever asked me that.'

Philip says that I am *a one for creature comforts.* I suspect that I am made of them: take my creature comforts away, and nothing remains.

'Tobacco isn't allowed?'

'You're a smoker! I didn't know.'

'Ex-. But once a smoker, always a smoker. Nothing to do with addiction, everything to do with pleasure. Ideal for a desert island. And you?'

'Well, when I was asked, I thought I'd say chocolate but found that I went for coffee, and that was a surprise. The same reason, I suppose: I live on coffee but, until then, I'd thought that I was simply addicted, that coffee was a mere addiction, not a . . .' . . . a what? 'Not a . . .'

'Passion,' he said.

'A passion, yes.'

I had some physalis on the tray – an attempt to break the habit of chocolate – and as I offered him the plate, he asked, 'What's your favourite fruit?'

'Depends what for.'

He raised his eyebrows: *explain.*

'Blackberries for ice-cream, I think. Apricots for juice.'

'Apricots . . .' he pondered.

'Yes, try it. Papaya for texture. And, oh,' of course, 'oranges for their smell.'

'Oh, yes.'

'And raspberries for . . .' but the best I could do was, 'for themselves.'

'Unadulterated.' He popped a physalis into his mouth. His eyes widened slightly with the first bite. Perhaps he had never had one before. But perhaps their flavour always comes as a surprise.

'So, they're your passion,' he said, when he had finished his mouthful. 'Raspberries.'

'Well, they have a rival: strawberries, but only for the one that's just right, the perfect one in every punnet. There's always that one, isn't there.'

Smiling away over the garden, he muttered, 'Oh, Mrs Summerfield.'

'Don't –'

'I was joking, that time.'

QUICK, SLOW

Yesterday morning, I went upstairs to Philip's study to look for the phone number of a particular builder who had done some work for us. Searching through his desk, the drawers, I delved into a slurry of stationery, bills, insurance policies, bank statements and passbooks. Inside the deep bottom drawer was a box, a shoe box, which contained postcards, cards, and letters. I looked at the postcard on the top of the pile. *Poppies Against the Night Sky*, a painting by William MacTaggart. I knew that the card must have been from me, although I had no recollection of writing it. I did not want to read it. Instead, rummaging, I confirmed my suspicion that all the cards and letters were from me. I read none of them. I had had no idea that they had been kept there; I had had no idea that they had been kept. I had forgotten that they had ever existed. They were sloughed skins. But there they were, boxed: raw, sweet sentiments, layered with pretty pictures and become rather dessicated. I returned the card unread to Philip's makeshift treasure trove, replaced the lid, closed the drawer, covered my tracks. I wonder if the writer of that card is as dead to him as to me. Does he miss her?

He is home early today because for some reason – I forget why – he is going into work tomorrow, Saturday. When Hal and I set off to come here to the park, he was cooking. His unexpected return was not my only surprise, this afternoon. Earlier, as I opened the back door, returning from a stroll down the road with Hal to the bakery, I glimpsed a figure in my kitchen. My breath boomeranged into the reverse of a scream.

The silhouette enthused, 'That's the kind of response that I like.'

'Drew!'

Drew, who lives in London: sitting in my kitchen, reading a newspaper. I closed the door behind me. His smile shone with crammed, angular teeth. Leaning back in the chair for a yawn and stretch, he lowered a hand for Hal, who went warily to investigate the fingertips. As he looked down to Hal, a halo of sunshine slid around on his black hair. The ends of the hair were closer to his shoulders than when I had last seen him.

I demanded, 'Where did you come from?'

'The *front* door.' His other hand gloved one of mine and he pulled me down so that he could kiss me. His lips were cool and papery on mine. I suspect that he knows I am made uneasy by his aim for my mouth. And that is why he persists. These kisses do not come from the old days, our student days, when we were flatmates. In those days, if we had kissed whenever we met, we would have been forever kissing. I cannot remember when our lives became separate enough to require these bridging kisses.

'The front door was *open*?'

'No, I used the key.'

'The *key*?'

'The spare, under the brick by the drainpipe.'

Discovered. The best I could manage was, 'It's not by the drainpipe.'

He steadied my gaze with his own – those eyes of no particular colour, but dark – and revised, sarcastically, 'Okay, let's say six or seven inches away from the drainpipe.'

'And, anyway, how did you know that I was going to be back?'

'Oh,' he smoothed a curtain of hair behind one ear, 'you never go far.'

I slapped the loaf on to the table.

'Don't be cross with me,' his tone was impeccably even.

'This is like something from an Iris Murdoch novel.'

'I wanted to see you.'

'You could have rung.'

'You haven't been returning my calls.'

Suddenly I remembered the last one, last week: a simple, *Call me, Cupcake*. I slid on to a chair, lowered my elbows on to the table and my face into my hands. 'Don't take it personally.'

'I won't.' His smile was slow, considered.

I closed my eyes. 'I've been so – oh, I don't know – unorganised.' As if I had had a lot to organise.

'I know.' A momentary silence, before he was explaining, 'I'm on my way to a site visit ten miles up the road.'

'Oh,' I opened my eyes, 'work.'

'Yes. I don't spend every minute of my working life striking an artistic pose over a drawing board in a studio in Clerkenwell.'

'No, you dirty your hands occasionally on the steering wheel of your company Audi.'

I rose to go to the kettle. 'So, is this a one-off, or will you be over this way again?'

'A couple of mornings over the next couple of months.'

'Oh, well then,' suddenly this was fun, 'you can come here for coffee, we can have breakfast, I can buy some brioche.'

'I work with men in hard hats: I don't eat brioche.'

'Would you be emasculated by the odd blob of apricot jam on a croissant leg?'

'The coffee will do nicely.' From his pocket he took a small, pharmaceutical-looking packet, printed with a name which suggested nicotine chewing gum.

I nodded towards it: 'I thought that you gave up when Oonagh was born.' Three years ago?

Delving into the packet, he glanced upwards from beneath one eyebrow. 'I did.'

'So why the gum?'

'Why not?'

'But you're supposed to use them to help you to give up; you're not supposed to use them all the time, for years and years.'

He mimicked, 'Supposed to . . . not supposed to . . .' and slotted two pieces into his mouth.

'And how are those blissfully smoke-free babies of yours?'

'They're beautiful and they make me laugh: what more could I want from my girls? Oh, except for some sleep, for a few hours each night. And patience, twenty-four hours each day. Don't believe a word if you receive one of those newsletters at Christmas telling you that Oonagh took her Duke of Edinburgh Gold Award before going off to do VSO in Belize, and that Caitlin has set *The Songs of Innocence and Experience* to her Grade Eight violin pieces. The truth is that Oonagh has an aversion to toilets, and Caitlin screams unless she's attached to her mother.'

'And how is Sarah?'

His head tipped backwards in a soundless laugh. 'Put-upon.'

He never talks of Sarah without affection. The apparent success of their relationship is intriguing. Drew had been involved with so many consciousness-raised, sexually-confident, clever-clever women, and then suddenly there was Sarah. They met when she came to work behind the bar in one of his haunts, never having worked anywhere but pubs and shops. Within a couple of weeks, there was an unplanned pregnancy, which was surprising because Drew never makes mistakes; and then, more surprisingly, the decision to marry. But although their domestic lives are necessarily interdependent, their social lives seem to have remained resolutely separate. I rarely see her; but whenever I ring to speak to Drew and she picks up the phone, we perform the full range of pleasantries with enthusiasm. I love to listen to her Scottish voice, the slides as impressive as those of a trombone.

Philip came home half an hour or so after Drew had arrived. Drew and I had giddied each other with gossip:

friends in common, other friends, in-laws, property prices. Drew greeted Philip with a kiss on both cheeks. Now, while I am here, in the park, he is watching Philip cook. He had wanted to know what Philip was making; Philip had explained that what appeared to be a pancake was going to be a roulade.

Drew laughed, 'Rolling your own.' But then, suddenly and defensively, 'Listen, you two, I grow my own basil, these days.'

I made the mixture for ice-cream; the bowlful is chilling now, in the fridge. Some local friends – a couple of couples – are coming for dinner, this evening. I make puddings; puddings are all that I make. The icing on the cake, in this household. While I was stirring the syrup into the cream, and Drew was nosing over my shoulder, Philip said, 'I love that recipe.'

I barely heard him over the whoomphs of the wooden spoon in the mixture, the muffled knocks on the bottom of the bowl.

'I love the simplicity,' he was saying, 'just the strawberries and cream, a little sugar and balsamic vinegar.'

'Vinegar?' Drew sounded affronted, and close to my ear.

I said, 'Nothing's quite as sweet as you think it is.'

He laughed. 'No one's quite as philosophical as you are.'

Philip mused, 'The sour with the sweet, and all that.'

I tapped the spoon a few times on to the rim of the bowl, then passed it to Drew. He dipped it into his mouth, and as the wooden lip slid back into view, I explained. 'The vinegar brings out the flavour of the strawberries. And you know strawberries: some of them do need coaxing.' I was speaking over his protracted groan of pleasure: the proof is in the pudding. He went to replace the spoon in the bowl, so I had to swoop, snatch the handle, tick him off: 'Saliva *digests*, Drew; didn't you know that? That's what saliva's *for*.'

'Oh, and I thought –'

'– Drew, don't.'

He was amazed, amused. 'You don't know what I was going to say.'

'Coming from you, and concerning a bodily function? Bad news, whatever.'

From across the kitchen, Philip enthused, 'So strawberry-ish.'

I said, 'So real that somehow it seems fake.'

Drew said, 'Post-modern strawberry ice-cream.'

Putting the bowl in the fridge, I complained, 'Ice-cream is underrated in this country.'

Drew despaired, 'Oh, everything is underrated in this country.'

'Except self-denial,' I said.

Which made him laugh.

I did ask Drew if he wanted to come with us to the park, but he declined. I felt that I should ask, but knew that he would say no. So, here we are, Hal and I, alone together as usual, side by side, accompanying each other on our separate strolls, like an old couple. And we have just passed the impeccably dressed old couple who are here most days in their small parked car, asleep. As always, she was in the driver's seat and he was sitting directly behind her on the back seat. They do not always sleep. Sometimes she holds in her kid-gloved hands a floppy book and a pencil: puzzles, crosswords, I presume. Sometimes he stares ahead through the windscreen. But the purpose of the daily trip seems to be to sleep, because on the rare occasions when they are awake, they look furious, cheated. Why do they come here to nap? I went to parks, in darkness, in cars, when I was a teenager. Odd, to think how I slid into those deserted parks under cover of darkness alongside someone else. Odd, to think of once having been so purposeful, so physical. So purposefully physical.

Whenever I see the old couple, I ponder their relationship: perhaps she works for him, drives him here, because why else the bizarre seating arrangement? They seem to be of a similar age, but of course there is no need for her to be younger than him in order to work for him, to care for him. I am a poor judge, though: to me, old is old; I could be looking at an age gap of ten or even twenty years and I would not know. I have doubts that their relationship is professional, I see no semblance of good form in those faces.

So the homeless man is not the only person to sleep here. And as well as the old couple, there is the courier. Every morning, Hal and I pass a parked van, the windscreen of which displays a sign, *Courier on delivery*. We had been passing that van every morning for weeks before I realised, one morning, that what I was seeing when I glanced through the windscreen was a person, asleep. What I was seeing was a figure, reclined and wrapped in blankets: formless, feature-less, but the repose unmistakably that of sleep. Suddenly, I was uneasy: I felt caught out, as if *I* had been observed, as if it were me who had been seen. Self-conscious, I was anxious to be quieter, although that was scarcely possible. I wanted to mark my respect. And so, nowadays, I tiptoe by the van, marvelling at the ability of that person to sleep visible, to turn so thoroughly and apparently peacefully from the day-time world of dog-walkers, childminders, council workers.

Yesterday evening, I was driving along this side of the park on my way back from the station. The drive home from the centre of town is so familiar to me as to feel choreographed: a five-minute journey made from precision-timed turns of the wrist, and a balance of braking and acceleration. No steps up and down the gears: my car is, regrettably, an automatic. I love driving. I love the necessary, narrow, but unremitting focus on the minutiae of the windows and mirrors: the whole busy world reduced to blips on my screens. I love that I cannot go forwards without constantly, simultaneously look-ing backwards. Driving is made of judgements of distance and speed, the very two elements by which I am so floored in my earthbound life. But on wheels, on a road, I am fault-less. When driving, I am nothing but eyes, hands, feet, all in perfect co-ordination, and all-powerful. I have never had a moment of panic or fear or even of doubt when driving; in no other circumstances do I ever feel so safe.

Driving, I am transformed into someone decisive and able. My father used to say, *A moment of hesitation is a moment gone.* Sometimes he said, *A moment's hesitation and you're dead. And so's the other bloke.* I learned to drive to his constant refrain, *Anticipation.*

Driving is in my blood. My father drove even as a child; his family – his father, grandfather, uncles, older brothers – were mechanics; they cared for engines, composed them, cleaned and coaxed them. My blood hums with, and thrills to, this particular competence.

Sometimes I think that this is all that there is to my blood: this most unnatural of activities seems to come to me more naturally than anything else. More so than the activities that are supposed to come naturally, such as eating, walking, sleeping. I am never so alive as when I am driving. And never so happy: the world shrunken, scrolling, passing beyond me; my machine responding to every mere touch. Sometimes, arriving home, I turn and do another lap, or go to the motorway to speed and watch the speedometer, to relish that immediate, utterly uncomplicated relationship between the downward push of my toes and the smooth rise of the needle.

My father used to say, *The faster your car, the faster you're away from trouble.*

This is a fast car.

Sometimes, driving, I sing:

> *You may not have a car at all,*
> *But, brothers and sisters, remember,*
> *You can still stand tall.*
> *Just be thankful*
> *For what you've got.*

When I arrive home again, I stay for a while in the car, perhaps listening to the radio, and gazing through the windscreen: I love to be there, in the street but not in the street; home, but not home.

Yesterday evening, when I was driving home along this edge of the park, the radio was playing the Chopin nocturne that is the theme tune to my memories of childhood ballet classes. The classes' pianist was our teacher's elderly mother. That piece of music – strangely, only that piece – recalls for me the slippery, bouncy sensation of wooden floorboards beneath my soft shoes; the smell of the church hall, balmy with beeswax; the blaze of Victorian windows, numerous, high and viewless, and faintly mysterious with blinds, ropes, hooks, like sails. The pianist was so old; I wonder, now, how old she was. I remember her face and no others, not my teacher's nor my peers'. That old face looked so resigned, was expressionless. And terrifying, for some reason: terrifying in retrospect, not at the time. Perhaps I am troubled now by her phenomenal agedness, or by the almost muscular expressionlessness. Or perhaps by the anomaly of such a bearing in a roomful of supple, self-conscious little girls. She was old in the way that perhaps women of my generation, later generations, will never look old: the white perm, the unsoothed wrinkles, the standard-issue specs. To her Chopin, we did our pliés and stretches, each of our movements deliberate, slow-motion, expansive; each of her notes roping us into a sequence.

My drive was interrupted when I had to stop at the zebra crossing; a crossing that, close to the park, is rarely used, particularly during the evenings. There was something unusual about the pedestrian, too: a girl, a young woman, in pale and therefore illuminated clothing. Then I realised that it was the way she was moving that was confounding me. Her move across those black and white keys was unbroken into steps, wiped of the numerous tiny groundings that would indicate motion on foot. And so she seemed to be moving above the crossing; the movements seemed fluid, drawing low luminous arcs in the deep dusk. She crossed quickly, taking perhaps two seconds to reach the far side, and as she did so, I realised what I was seeing: she was rollerblading. I stayed still for a moment, wishing that I could do that, watching her sweep away into her disappearance.

Closer to home, around the corner, I passed George's house: the windows solid, swollen, with curtains and lamplight. I imagined him there, behind them, beyond them, settled down into an armchair. He seems to stay home in the evenings: the mentions of telly programmes, conversations with his wife, phone calls to and from the sons and grandchildren, all of these indicate that he is home in the evenings, absorbed. And how unlike the daytime, when he seems alienated from the house, seems compelled to be elsewhere, even if no further than the garden. The old story: during the daytime, the domestic interior is not his domain; never was. He once told me that his wife alone brought up the children: that was her job, he said. A simple division of labour, to him, to his generation. And her labour continues, flourishes: I see the fruits whenever I visit the house. But his labour is no longer required. He was early-retired, no doubt on excellent terms; about which all he says, dolefully, is, *Can't complain*. I know how that feels: to be unable to complain, to be sick with a distress which seems groundless.

I drove on, passing the bus stop. There, once, George told me how, habitually, he will look over any queue in a disinterested way for what he refers to as a *villain*. 'The clue is the cigarette,' he told me, 'an extremely thin roll-up, no one can roll as thin as a villain can. A skill perfected in prison, because of the baccy ration.' He once, and only once, admitted to me that he had become unhappy at work in his latter years. Instinct, he said, had become officially devalued, disapproved of; whereas in fact instinct was everything, he claimed. 'But nowadays,' he told me, 'in order to do the job, a policeman has to, well, justify everything, explain everything . . .' he began to flounder with this, his own explanation.

I said, 'Account for.'

'That's the word,' he said. Then added, despairingly, 'Impossible.'

As I drove by the bus stop, I was thinking that I had better see him soon. Lately, he has asked, and asked: asked me to lunch, asked me to tea. Once, he assured me, 'There's nothing improper in these invitations, you know.' He was laughing, but serious: I could see that he was anxious, that this was serious to him. Even if instincts are crucial to him, he is a stickler for proper conduct. I suspect that he has an instinct about me. I suspect that he suspects he is missing something, that something or someone is missing.

A couple of days ago, I rang Edwin. The answerphone was on, and his taped voice invited me to leave a message for Edwin Robinson or Vivien Blake.

I began, 'Hello, Edwin,' but then heard the clatter of his receiver being raised and his voice, untaped, unsurprised: 'Sadie, hello.' We exchanged pleasantries, he made solicitous enquiries about my last journey home from London, and I explained that I was returning again in a couple of days: faced with a run of friends' birthdays, I had several presents to buy. I asked, 'Would you like to meet for a quick coffee?'

'Quick, slow, I'd love to.' I could hear his smile; his smile is easier to hear than to see.

'But are you sure? I don't want to stop you from working.'

'Oh, you're the very last person I'd hold responsible for that.'

We arranged to meet on the steps of the Museum, as before.

As soon as I replaced the receiver, an image of his wife came to me. She came unbidden, and with considerable force; I had never before had such an immediate and clear vision of someone unknown to me. There she was, suddenly, in my mind's eye: tall; her hair, black and short. Her skirt, short, in a classic Chanel check; and her other clothes, black: the slinky polo-neck, and opaque tights. She had presence. She had confidence. She was self-assured, self-contained, substantial, centred. Yes, centred: I knew nothing of her but I could tell that she was central to her own life in a way that unfortunately I am off-centre to mine. She wore that life as an aura, a life that complemented her in the sense that mine fails to work for me and even seems to go against me, trips me up. She was everything that I am not: I am made of brittle, bright surfaces; I deflect, I am all glare, I am something smashed.

I wondered how she had been conjured. Perhaps from her name, on that tape? In her name there is nothing lispy or choppy, as in mine. Hers chimes regularly and then finishes on a single, distinct note. There is nothing frivolous about her name, unlike mine. And hers has a sense of old Englishness, of connections. It is not a name I would want, not a name I find particularly attractive, a rather alien name (I know no Viviens) but all the more intriguing for that. Perhaps she was conjured by both names spoken together in Edwin's usual low, sure tone; no chirpiness, and clearly enunciated. The two names together made a perfect refrain; they balanced. I was impressed by the ease with which Edwin said them together, and by the respect which he gave them. Yes, of course, my imagined Vivien was quite simply the kind of wife Edwin would have; measured, doleful Edwin.

And from that message, I could tell that they live the kind of life that people are supposed to live: busy, productive, fulfilling, earning them leisure and nurturing a vital undercurrent of joy. I knew that their answerphone serves that life. I imagined them strolling into an airy room and, with a casual press of a button, retrieving messages which, untroubled, would declare themselves as from family, friends, work. My own answerphone is idiosyncratic, demanding, rapidly becomes unmanageable with messages which, when I release them, are tiny but overwhelming irritations, like flies.

Yesterday, so that I could go to London, I took Hal to Dodie. I found her, months ago, listed in the phone book as *Animal Nanny*.

'Title of a porn film,' Drew claimed, when I told him.

Her daily charge is barely more than a typical babysitter's hourly rate. She is helped by her husband, Joe, who, according to her, is *retired sick*, but who, to me, looks absurdly healthy, always scantily clad and deeply tanned. Yesterday he answered the door, in his bathrobe, in the raucous company of twin Westies, a beagle, an Alsatian puppy, an elderly character who looked like a fox, and the family's own dejected dachshund. He had the family cat in his arms. 'Hal!' he enthused. 'My fave!'

'Bet you say that to all the dogs,' but I knew that he was genuine. Hal and Joe do seem to adore each other. Dodie complains to me that she is forever finding them together on the sofa. The house rule is, *No dogs on the sofa.*

Apparently Joe's defence is, *Well, he looks at me . . .*

And Dodie's reply is, *I look at you, a thousand times a day, but you don't do as I want, do you?*

Behind Joe, upstairs, I could hear Dodie shouting, good-naturedly, presumably to one of the children. She once said to me, 'Four kids and two husbands, one of them an ex-, of course; ex- since I discovered that I was one of his two wives, and I'll tell you all one evening over a bottle of wine,' an invitation for which I am on tenterhooks.

Handing over Hal's packed lunch, I said, 'You look busy today.' Hal was obviously of the same opinion, backing away from the bundles of fur and noise. Guilt burned me like a blush.

'Oh, we're always busy, but there's no one in this lot who's a problem. I mean, except Maud, here.' We both looked down at the beagle. 'But don't ask,' he said.

* * *

I arrived early in Bloomsbury and decided to pass the time in one of the coffee bars. As I came through the doorway, I saw that Edwin was inside. He was sitting, his back to me. A woman was with him, but leaving, standing and pushing her chair into place beneath the table. I knew that she was Vivien even though she was nothing like how I had imagined her. She was so directly in contrast to how I had imagined that I had to try hard to quell a laugh. I knew that she was his wife because of how she was cheerfully chattering, constantly and without checking with him, her gaze everywhere and nowhere. She was taking for granted the fact that she could talk and he would listen. And he did; his attention did not move from her face. This real Vivien's hair slithered around on her shoulders and down her back, was layered to look a mess and dyed dark blonde, the colour of overripe bananas, bananas on the turn, turning mushy from the inside. Framed by all that hair, the face was solid. She looked pleased, as if life was better than she had expected, although only just: the look was a mix of celebration and relief.

Edwin's face held his pale version of a smile. His glazed expression could have been one of tolerance, or fondness, or perhaps both, each shoring up the other. I could not see if he was blind to her or saw her only too clearly; I did not know which could explain that peculiar look on his face. He was stiff as she moved, as she pushed that chair, gathered her bag and mac. Still talking, she leaned forward and picked fluff from his lapel: and so, for a second, she seemed to be talking to the fluff. Then they kissed, a chaste kiss, a peck, and she was off. I stepped back into the doorway but need not have worried that he would see me because he had picked up a book and his glasses and was reading intently. She came towards me, aiming for the door. I was impressed by how she was propelled forwards by sways of her wide hips; I wished that I could walk like that, so carefree. She was wearing something blue, navy blue, a dress, buttoned and belted, nothing special; I noticed no more than the colour and the presence of those faintly fussy details. As she passed me, and I held open the door for her, she looked at me and smiled, a perfunctory smile but nonetheless pleasant. Her eyes were blue; no, their borders were blue, her eyeliner and mascara. The eyes, I think, were no particular colour; dabs of internal fluid and external sky. She wore no earrings.

She looked at me but did not see me: me, in my linen shift of ghostly grey, my hair tied back by a piece of muslin, my eyes behind my wraparounds. When she had gone, I waited for a moment or two, lingering in the doorway and by the counter, the rack of newspapers, before I removed my sunglasses and crossed the room to Edwin. 'Look who's here,' I said, which, of course, could have referred to him or to me. 'I was early, I was coming in here to kill time, to read the newspapers.'

Looking up, he removed his glasses without moving his gaze from mine; his eyes seemed to stay magnified and glassy. 'Don't let me stop you.'

'Don't be silly.'

'You can read them to me. I've become appallingly ignorant of current affairs.'

'No, that's what Jeremy Paxman's for.'

'But he's so abrasive. And that makes me panic. So, then, I don't pay attention.'

I laughed. I cannot remember when I last read a newspaper.

He placed his book face down on the tabletop, rose as I was sitting, and followed me, bending to kiss my cheek. 'If you'd been a moment earlier you could have met Vivien.'

I wondered if he ever called her Viv; somehow I doubted it. I wondered if he would ever call me Poppy; and doubted that, too.

'We were having lunch. She's been wanting to meet you.'

I bet she has.

So, he has told her that I exist.

On the table, in her place – my place – was an almost drained glass of Coke, the remaining ice propping up a straw, the tip of which was fatty and florid with lipstick; and a plate on which was a droopy, dressing-damp lettuce leaf, a couple of slivers of tomato, and the crust of what had been a sandwich.

'We try to have lunch together once a week.' There was nothing in front of him except a teapot, cup and saucer.

'*You* didn't try very hard,' I said.

'That's because I have to face dinner this evening. Vivien has her weekly trip to the pictures with the clan and then, as usual, I have to meet up with them for a meal. And, let me tell you, they do nothing by halves.'

'She's Scottish?'

He frowned, puzzled.

'You said *clan*.'

'Oh,' and something like a laugh, 'no. There are lots of them and they're fearsome, that's all.'

That's all?

'How many?'

'Actually, what am I saying? Only two, and one of those is a half. But somehow they give the impression of being rather more.'

'Someone married again, somewhere along the line?'

'Again and again. Her father. There's a half-brother who's much older, in his fifties. Big brother isn't invited to the weekly weepie: strictly for the sisters, this pics fix. You could say that at least Vivien's father had the decency to marry all those women with whom he fell in love. Vivien's brother has always had mistresses.'

Decency and *mistresses*: words to conjure with; words from an old language, a dead language, faintly familiar and res-onant. He said them in a manner that was both clipped and fluent. I wanted to hear him say them again.

'The second marriage resulted in Vivien and her sister; then there was a final marriage, and a baby.'

'Baby?'

'Well, Judith.' He frowned, 'Vivien was thirteen when Judy

was born, which makes her . . .' he frowned harder, over his computations, '. . . twenty-seven.'

And makes Vivien forty.

'Judy seems the grown-up, though; perhaps that's because she had the happy childhood. Nowadays she's all Dolce and Gabbana and proper job.'

'What's the job?'

In the corner of my eye, I saw his wince of self-recrimination. 'Why did I say *proper* job? One of those *fake* jobs, PR or something.'

'Proper *salary*.'

'*Improper* salary.'

'What does Vivien do?'

'Works for the council. In housing. Four days a week. Hates it.' He pulled the small stainless-steel teapot towards him, checked the contents. The hinged lid fell back down with a yap. 'I don't know why she stays there. Well, yes, I do: she stays because she feels that she has no choice. But, you know, there *is* a choice. I tell her to have . . .' he paused, opened his hands, palms upward.

Children?

'. . . a *break*, or something. We can afford that; we afforded all those years of my PhD, and so now we can afford her turn. She should retrain.'

'Does she see her father?'

'Dead,' he was pouring the remaining dribble of tea into his cup. 'Ten or twelve years or so.'

'Mother?'

'Spain.' He took a sip of the tea: peppermint, judging from the scent. 'Runs a bar in Spain. That's where she took the girls, when their father divorced her. They'd had an Army upbringing, nomadic, and they ended up in Spain for a couple of years. Vivien had nowhere that she could call home.'

No: on the contrary, she had *here* that she could call home. A place of which she could dream, and to where she could run. How precious and powerful that sense of home must have been. I had nowhere else.

Almost jovially he said, 'Her mother has worked her way through a succession of fairly unsuitable men. We never quite know who we'll find, whenever we go over there.' More cautiously, he added, 'I don't think that she has ever recovered from having been abandoned.'

'Does anybody?'

A momentary pause, during which he tidied the teaspoon on his saucer, and then he said, 'You're right: in a sense, it's in the definition of the word, abandoned.'

'Depends what you mean by the word *recover*, though, I suppose. I mean, we all *do*.'

'Yes.' Then, 'Do you have any brothers or sisters?'

'I'm an only.'

He failed to hear, or misheard: he looked baffled.

'I'm an only child.' An odd expression. I listened to the echo inside my head: I'm *only* a child; I'm *only child*.

A small lie.

'You?'

'One sister, Clara, younger, we're not close.'

A definitive statement. So why did I persist? From a weird notion of politeness? Or to usher away the pause? 'What does she do?' The ultimately trite question; my most loathed question. All the talk of jobs had gone to my head.

'God knows. She's an accountant or something.'

'*Or something*?' Strange how an expansion can in fact serve to belittle.

'Some kind of accountant', and he smiled, rising to this. 'Apparently, there are different kinds. Chartered . . .' but here he stopped, flipped his hands into the air with hopelessness, '. . . surveyed?'

I laughed. 'Certificated?'

'Should be.' Then he asked, 'Do you still have parents?'

As much as I ever did. 'Both.' Bizarrely, whenever I think of the house in which I grew up, all I see is what my mother used to praise as the *wipe-down surfaces*. She doted upon those surfaces, they were indeed always wiped down, and quite unnecessarily because there had hardly ever been anything on them: they were for wiping down and looking at. She hated mess, she hated clutter. Whenever she was cross with me, she would call me a *waste of space*.

'And you?'

In a flash of irritation he whirled around, away, and was complaining, 'That waiter still hasn't come . . .'

'I know,' but I looked, too; compelled somehow to follow him.

'My mother died,' he was saying, as I turned back to him, 'eight years ago. She had cancer.' The tone was pleasant, slightly higher or lighter than usual so as to move above and around the fact of her death.

The words that came to mind were, *Over and out*.

My response will have been inarticulate, inadequate: *Oh dear*, or, *Oh God*, or, *I'm sorry*, in some combination.

He had already moved on: 'Her death didn't unite Clara and me. On the contrary. Her absence is between us, if you know what I mean.'

I said, 'I do, yes.' *Oh, yes, I do*.

'Not very Hollywood, I'm afraid. But, anyway, that's enough doom and gloom for now.'

So, we had coffee and no more doom and gloom. Eventually, I said that I should do my shopping, which, I was determined, would take no more than a couple of hours. He suggested that if I was thinking of having a break afterwards, before I went for my train, then we could meet again. I agreed; and when I turned up back at the café at the agreed time, five o'clock, he was there with two coffee cups on the table in front of him, one of which was covered with its saucer. A little later, he accompanied me to the station.

My visual memory has recorded that moment at the station when we said goodbye as the same as every other that I have spent there: the glaring expanse of white floor; the banks of fast-food counters, barricades of telephones, carousels of timetables; the apparent chaos of hundreds of people on precise, individual trajectories. Edwin and I stood still in the middle of all this and, miraculously, no one bumped into us. Standing there, facing him, I was aware of how much taller he was than Philip, and of how far he was from me, but, in a sense, too, how close. Imposing, perhaps. I was reluctant to lower my heavy bag to the floor, which would hold me there; but once I had made the move and done so, we were both relieved.

I think that he said, 'Well,' and that I said the same.

Then he said, 'Lovely to see you, as ever.'

I will have replied appropriately: probably, 'You, too.'

He asked me if I would be in town again soon. 'Because if you are, I'll leave my books and come for a coffee, if you twist my arm, a little.'

I said, 'Good luck with the clan.'

'The clan?' A wince. 'The clan. Oh, God.'

That was all; that and the kiss, his cheek surprisingly cold on my lips.

Whenever I pass through that station and reach the place where we were standing, I will know. My whole body will know. Shutting my eyes will not allow me to side-step that memory. But none of this was clear to me until I was on the train and sitting down, taking my book from my bag, opening then closing that book and turning to the window. My only thought, then, was a loud, clear, dolorous, *Oh, shit*. Because suddenly I knew what had happened. I had fallen in love. The realisation tightened on me like an unbidden squeeze of a hand over mine. Something had happened between us and we both knew, and both knew that we knew. And knowing can never be undone; never mentioned, perhaps, but never undone. The book stayed in my lap and I stayed staring from the window, shocked into thoughtlessness, suspended through the suburbs.

When I arrived home, yesterday evening, Philip said, 'Nice to see you so cheerful.' He was concocting a curry.

I said, 'Am I?'

'Mm.' He was intent over the steaming pan.

I told him that I had done some good shopping, and had had coffee with a man whom I knew through George: Edwin.

I had to tell Philip something of Edwin, if only the fact of his existence. I could only keep so much secret.

'You and George,' sighed Philip, indulgingly. He had begun to chop some coriander. 'What's he like?'

'George?'

'No, not George; I know what George is like.'

He knows only what I have told him.

'No, this new man of yours; this Edward.'

'*Win*, Ed*win*.'

So, I told him about Edwin, told him plenty and made him laugh. For a few minutes in the kitchen, Edwin was someone we could share; and, marvellously, for those minutes, sharing was fun again. But the more that I told, the more I craved to hear: Edwin's name said in our kitchen, in the hub of our domestic privacy, was a violation which I was compelled to commit. Remaining unsaid was that Edwin and I had met up once previously: a secret at the time, and now sealed into that secrecy. And something else: that I had fallen in love with him. The falling in love was for me to deal with; would pass. Philip could be spared, never knowing that I had failed him in this new, worse way.

I was surprised, then, when he laughed, 'A thirty-nine-year-old balding academic: no competition.'

He should have been right.

I was careful to laugh in reply.

But I thought, *How little you know me*. And felt both sad and victorious.

This morning, as I surfaced from sleep, opening my eyes to familiar lemon walls and ivory ceiling, the air was ablaze and breathless with sunshine. The full-blown sunshine had come early, while I was asleep, and saturated the calico blind, settled all over the room. I woke, as ever, on my back, and all around me this brilliance was somehow both a dead weight and utterly insubstantial, like water. Like water, too, somehow leaden but alive with movement. For that instant, as my eyes opened, there was nothing else in the world; not even me, I was simply eyes in which there was this light.

And then something happened; what happened was that I remembered; remembered Edwin, the absence of him. His absence sliced through the moment. The day before me was stretching away into other, similar days, a whole summer of them. Then the summer would curl into autumn and die away into a bedraggled winter. And I would spend some of those days elsewhere, sometimes in other countries, but on every one of them, wherever I was, I was going to find Edwin gone. I lay there and they pressed down upon me: days and days, a lifetime of them.

Now, here in the park, hours later, I remain awed by the ferocity of that recognition. Why had I not closed my eyes again and hoped to die? I know why: because the sheer force of the feeling turned me over, upwards. Made me want to live. And another reason: I had a sneaking suspicion that his absence from my life would not be the whole story. Lying there, I was consoled by the fact that he existed and that I had found him and he had found me. That was enough. That was a start.

DEAD GIVE-AWAYS

✦

Today, cleaners are working in the park's public toilets. Beside the door marked *Ladies* they have, as usual, propped their own sign: *Warning! possible male cleaners.* But this morning a piece of paper is stuck over the *possible.* 'Good to have that confusion cleared up,' I say aloud to Hal.

Ahead of us is a huddle, a commotion involving the elderly, wonky-hipped daily Alsatian-walker, her Alsatian, and one of the many uniformed gardeners, the man with the palsy. His palsied, inflexible facial muscles give him a fixed expression of surprise: his eyes, too wide; mouth, rounded. His steps fall short and shatter into shakes. Last week, late one afternoon, I saw him leaving work, hurrying towards town, looking thrilled. I had assumed that the job was everything to him, I had never considered the likelihood that, for him, as for most people, a job is just a job. I had assumed that he was here because of someone's kindness or obligation. On sufferance. I should have known better. Surely, of all people, I should have known better.

Like many of his colleagues, he has been working here for years; many of the faces are known to me from my occasional outings here with Jacqueline. In those days, they were employees of the Parks Department. Then, compulsory tender brought new overalls and trucks emblazoned with the logo *Ecoservice.* The logo, in green, is linked to the council's corporate signature by the proclamation *In partnership.* A partnership, presumably, in that one organisation pays and the other makes the profit. To my untrained eye, the gardeners' daily duties look staggeringly, wantonly destructive: digging up flower beds, chopping into bushes, razing the lawns. All around them are heaps of soil veined with vegetation, and paths hazardous with disembodied claws of branches. By the end of each working day, though, the park is orderly again; impeccably flowered.

The mutually respected convention is that we, the park-users, never acknowledge them, the gardeners, and vice versa; no one acknowledges our co-dependency; this specious boundary between work and pleasure is unimpeachable. No fraternisation. So, I am dismayed to see the Alsatian-owner aiding and abetting the gardener to throw a tennis-ball for her dog. The old Alsatian is a burly animal with a bear-like tread. He is all shoulders. Dour, he prowls rather than runs to retrieve the ball. Hal, ahead of me, is sensibly wary, steering clear. He knows from experience that for this Alsatian, retrieval is no game but a serious business. For this Alsatian, retrieval is everything. He requires nothing except that the ball is thrown; distance is a drawback. For his purposes, this man, with his weak throw but excessive enthusiasm, is ideal. In return, the Alsatian performs the expected but impressive display of uniquely canine skill: moving as the ball takes to the air and faultlessly tracking the trajectory.

And this exacting little exercise is enough for the man. More than enough. His eyes and mouth are even wider than usual, the mouth unfurled into laughter lavish with spittle. These skidded laughs and wobbly lobs rebound on him; he is shaking more vigorously and comprehensively than I have ever seen anyone shake. Obviously, this is new, for him: he has never before played fetch; somehow, so far, this minor, particular pleasure had been overlooked. And now, whenever he raises his arm and takes aim, a sliver of that unfamiliarity flares and falls away: he is learning fast. Beside him, the woman is whooping encouragement and congratulations. As I pass by, unnoticed, but nevertheless feeling conspicuous, the phrase that comes to mind is *out of hand*, although of course this is anything but: everything, here, is utterly *in* hand.

In one weakened hand, in the holding and letting go of a small ball, there is enough grace and power to make one fractured and foreshortened action into an airborne skein; to rein the instincts of that lion-like animal and tickle a woman so hard that she cannot catch her breath.

Yesterday, Edwin came here for the afternoon. On my way to the station to fetch him, I wondered if I would recognise him. Odd, to realise that I had so little visual memory of him. For the thirteen days since we had seen each other, he had been a voice on the phone; that was all I had known of him. But what a voice: low-pitched and subdued, incongruously intimate for someone unrelentingly formal. Driving up to the station, I thought of how, whenever he phones me, my name is the first word he says, following a drawn breath . . . *Sadie, hello* . . .

In these pauses, he is very much there; he is there in his frequent, split-second, finely-timed withdrawals, moving forward via these inaudible purrs. His laugh is usually a single note, not dissimilar to a smothered cough, and detectable in the words that follow; the words lowered and quickened. On several occasions, lately, that single note has been made of more, like a stone skimming over the surface of water.

A week or so ago, he gave me a second phone number on which to call him: his new line, for the fax machine. No one else would think of using the new number, he said, other than to fax, so he would know that the caller was me. This was said as if we were going to have some good, clean, harmless fun. And, so, lately, I have been unscreened, and answered; answered immediately, unheard. He answers with a *Hello* stripped of a question mark. Usually I say, *It's me*, and usually he replies, *Hello, you*.

For two people who claim to have almost nothing to do, we are almost always doing something, or, rather, dealing with something; there seems to be plenty to discuss.

'How was dinner with Vivien's cousin? were words had? was wine thrown? was the car towed?'

'Kind of you to ask, and the answers are yes, no, yes respectively.'

'Oh. Oh dear. No dry-cleaning bill, though.'

'For a date with Vivien's cousin, this was a roaring success. But did I say yes-no-yes? That should have been yes-yes-no.'

'Wine *was* thrown?'

'Spilled, officially.'

'Spilled *officially*?'

'Did they deliver your bath?'

'Who?'

'Well, the bath-delivery men, I suppose; I don't know, who else delivers baths?'

'How did you know that I was having a bath delivered?'

'How do you think? You told me.'

'Did I?'

'Well, how else do you think that I'd know?'

'Good luck with the dentist; I don't know how you do it.'

'Do what?'

'Well . . . *go*.'

'Oh. Every couple of months, I've eaten my way clean through my teeth. With my tastes, it's more a case of the dentist giving me the odd pass to the outside world.'

On this last occasion, he had said, 'Let me know the damage,' and I took him at his word, called him a couple of hours later, one side of my face still saturated with anaesthetic.

I whined, 'For all I know, I could be dribbling and leering.'

'There's no harm in the odd little dribble and leer.'

I complained, 'Have you ever tried putting on lipstick when you've no feeling in your lips?'

'Well, now that you mention it . . .'

I had hoped that lipstick would cheer me up, perhaps even

hasten my return to normal. I had had the necessary props: a mirror and a hand. All that was missing was sensation in and around my mouth, the mere passive focus of my attention. Nevertheless, that numbness had flummoxed me, and so I was smudged. To Edwin, I bemoaned the numbness, the choice between numbness or pain, life's chief insoluble dilemma.

His laugh was a dropped stone. 'Speak for yourself; I'm overwhelmingly partial to numbness.'

I laughed too, and thought, *Oh, I bet you were; but not now, you're not; because of me, you're not.*

If there is absolutely nothing to talk about, we manage to talk endlessly about nothing, about how we have nothing to do. Long, languid conversations, begun by his . . . *So . . . how are you?*

My answer is that I am bored. Hot and bored. This heat is making heavy weather of everything, particularly of the activities that are usually the most effortless: too hot to eat, to sleep. A couple of days ago, he asked me what I do if I cannot sleep; how I contrive to creep up on elusive sleep. Luckily for me, insomnia is unusual: I relish sleep, holding each day to the promise of eventual oblivion. I live to sleep rather than sleeping so that I can live. I am uncompromising, craving a pure strain of sleep unsweetened by dreams.

I had to warn him, 'Well, this will seem odd . . .'

He was listening hard. His listening is unlike that of other people, which is hazy with their own anticipation. I gave him my odd answer: lately, whenever sleep has slipped from reach, my mind's eye has delved for the hands that I saw some time ago in an exhibition of photographs taken by James Abbe in Hollywood in the 'twenties. I dwell on the composure of those hands. If sleepless and unsettled, I run those calm, calming hands through my mind. Abbe's stars, long-dead if not also long-forgotten or in freefall to being forgotten, were like stained-glass saints, luminous, absurd but brazen. The eyes were headlamps; the bow-mouths buttoned, like kisses unblown. But within that exhibition of glorious faces, clothes, nakedness, I was drawn to the hands; not the hands that were occupied with parasols or cigarettes or some staged gesture, but those that were draped like kid gloves in laps. However useless, the hands were never overlooked; in Abbe's photographs, nothing escapes the pose; for him, hands counted. Only Fred Astaire's were invisible, tucked into his folded arms. Beside him, his sister's hands were a picture in themselves. The caption read, *Fred and Adele Astaire for Gershwin's* Lady be Good *London, 1926*. Black-haired, black-eyed Adele faced me, serene, her features drawn so high by her cheekbones that she had an illusory smile. Her brother, darkly and plainly dressed, gazed at her. Contemplative, he was unrecognisable.

From time to time, one of us will discover, later, that we did have something to say, that there was something forgotten. Or something happens. And so then we will ring again, sometimes to leave a message and have the call returned. And so the calls can stack up, and divide up the day. Routinely, we speak during the morning, prior to Hal's mid-morning walk, or perhaps in the hour or so following Hal's walk, which is known as *before lunch* although neither of us has lunch; only Hal has lunch. Then sometimes there is also a call during the afternoon or even the half-hour or so that we seem to refer to as *last thing* which means five-ish, just before our spouses return home. During the working hours of the weekdays, I never stop listening for him. If I am in the garden I tend to mistake the warble of a wood pigeon for his voice speaking through my answerphone; I rush indoors, but find silence.

Occasionally I hear voices on *his* answerphone: we are speaking and I hear the distant ring of his other phone followed by a voice being taped. I can never resist asking him who is calling. Sometimes he simply says, *Work*. Several times, though, the reply has been, *Vivien*. He never responds to the work calls. Sometimes he leaves Vivien to drone, but occasionally he leaves me abruptly with an assurance that he will call back in a minute, which he never fails to do. Several weeks have passed, now, since we were planning when we could speak to each other again and he remarked, 'Vivien's home on Fridays'. That was all that he needed to say; his meaning was clear: *Don't call me on Fridays.*

Four or five days ago, he said, 'Could I come and see you next week? It would be nice to see you; and nice, too, to have a day away from London.'

I agreed, assured him that any day would be fine.

He said, 'I've nothing much to do, next week; I'll make sure that I have a free afternoon.' Free afternoon? I have a free life.

But later, Annie rang to tell me, 'Next week, I'm going to skive and come over to you for a good, lung-chafing laugh.'

I had to tell her, 'I don't know when I'll be around.'

All that she could do was echo, 'You don't know when you'll be around?'

Flustered, I said, 'Yes. No.'

And she demanded, 'Explain.'

'Casey's passing through, sometime, and we're going to meet up.' So, there I was, all of a sudden, lying to a friend. Lying to a friend, now, as well as to Philip. Mere mention of Casey, my ex-, was enough to distract her.

'God,' she enthused, 'Casey. He's passing through, eh?'

For a moment, I thought that she suspected me.

But she laughed, 'Makes him sound like something swallowed.'

In the end, yesterday was the day that Edwin chose to come and see me. Having parked the car in the area marked *Drop off and pick up*, I went into the station to look for a man whom I remembered only as wearing grown-up man's clothes and having grown-up man's hair (that is, a lack of). Not much to go on. Giving myself up to the crowd, I was unable to anticipate even the shape of the man who was going to come up and claim me. I remembered once having registered that he was taller than Philip but this told me nothing because most men are taller than Philip.

What on earth had I been doing when I was falling in love, to make Edwin no more than a shadow in my memory? I remembered that line from Donne: 'Some lovely glorious nothing did I see'. Edwin's darkness in my mind's eye is a considerable presence, dense and physical, recalling for me the odd sensation of focusing on my blind spot. When I was a child I learned that trick by which pencilled dots on a piece of paper are made to disappear, to be replaced by a nothingness, a blankness that is small and hazy but palpable. I was captivated, compelled to move the piece of paper back and forth in front of my eyes, to tease invisibility from my visual field, to see my own blindness. Whole hours were spent sliding between one state and the other, sighted and blinded. I knew what was happening, I understood the mechanics: those dots were coming into focus on the sliver of retina that is seamed with the optic nerve, a nerve without which vision would stay uselessly in an eye like goldfish in a bowl. Perhaps the expression that *love is blind* refers not to oversights which have to be made so as to fall in love with someone, but to that someone's blinding fall on to a crucial nerve.

What of those who claim that love has come to them solely via letters or even e-mails? I am a sceptic. Likewise, for love at first sight. But who am I to say? Someone who claims to have had that very experience is Casey: up-front, down-to-earth Casey. And with respect to me. His story was always the same: *You were strolling down the corridor with Jacqueline, laughing.*

To which I would say, *And . . .?*

And he would simply shrug and smile, finish with a flourish, an eddy of celebration and abdication: this was his party piece, for the private party that was our relationship. I had no doubt that I had been there, strolling and laughing, as he says; but if he did fall in love with me, then and there, I had to know how, why. What clinched his love for me? the strolling? the laughing? And Jacqueline, she was there: did she have a part to play? would I have been laughing or strolling differently – less lovably, somehow – if I had been in that corridor with someone else? Why me, rather than blonde, blue-eyed Jacqueline? And what of the corridor, even? was there something about my being in a corridor? a purposefulness to me, perhaps? Casey, though, did not want to know, and could never understand why I had to know. I could never understand why he had to *not* know. That was just one of the fundamental differences between us, perhaps the only one over which we ever reached a truce: I stopped asking.

A couple of weeks ago, during a phone conversation that was at least a couple of months overdue, Casey said, 'I'm missing that laugh of yours.'

I recalled how, once, my neighbour had said to me, 'Every time I hear that full-bodied laugh of yours through my wall, I can't imagine how someone like you can conjure up something like that.'

Someone like me? I have not always been someone like me, someone like this; which, of course, Casey knows. And is that why he made something of my laugh? Nowadays when strolling in a certain manner is something that I can no longer do, was he trying to protect me from the fact that, for him, my slinking had made the moment?

Or, now that Jacqueline is dead, did he feel obliged to remove her from the picture? Now that I am never in corridors, looking purposeful, did he decide to foreground that laugh? Absent as he has been, how was he to know that laughing seems to have become as impossible as sauntering, as enjoying the company of a best friend, as looking forward to working?

Nevertheless, I played along; saying, 'Oh, so, it was the laugh.'

His own smile was audible in his reply: 'Who knows? Not

everything can be explained away, Poppy; some things just *are*.'

That was when I realised: I had never wanted an explanation. I had never wanted the moment explained away. What I had wanted was for him to tell me more: more of what had happened to him when he glanced down that corridor and saw me.

When we separated, nine years ago, I suggested, rather caustically, that he must have been mistaken: whatever he had seen must have been a trick of the light. He said no, the moment was not re-filed: not under *lust*, or *light, trick of the*; still under *love, in*. But the whole file was marked *dormant*, he said, because we had agreed that there was nothing more that we could do, that we were fundamentally unsuited, that a future together was impossible. I was grateful to him for that: for not doing the denial that ex-lovers so love to do; for not diminishing me.

Why did *I* fall in love with *Casey*? Somehow, he passed his state of mind on to me. It was as if I had taken him up on something; as if he had thrown me something so that there was nothing for me to do but catch. He appealed to me, in both senses of the word. There are words that could have been invented for Casey: *maverick*, *chancer*. Once upon a time I would have included *no-hoper*; which, in an earlier time, would have been *ne'er-do-well*. And all of this shows on his face: he has a good old-fashioned twinkle to his eyes. One of my mother's expressions is *Johnny-come-lately*: I have no idea what this means, but suspect that it applies very nicely to Casey. He was a *barrow-boy*, someone *made-good*. All good reasons to steer clear of him, but of course that was the catch: they were also, mysteriously, precisely the aspects that made him compelling. These days, Casey is a *wheeler-dealer* whose deals do not concern wheels. He is a dealer in Amsterdam.

Not what you think, he always likes to joke: Casey, the rough diamond, is in fact a diamond dealer.

Someone has to do it, he says, never quite joking.

Philip is good-looking but I have no particular memory of physical, sexual attraction having been crucial to my falling in love with him. I have always adored that he smiles even when he is sleeping; but for me to have known, I must have been sleeping with him, and so love must have been well underway. Whenever I look at him, I dwell on his mouth; whenever I think of his looks, of how he looks, his mouth is the feature that comes to mind. The lips are thin and firm. Such a mouth gives him an intentness and a resistance that is uncharacteristic, and perhaps I like that; perhaps that intrigues me. His constant smile happens around rather than on those lips: he simply dimples. It is a mouth which promises considered kisses. I am forever quelling a faint urge to tease his lips with mine, to ease him, open him up.

Looking for Edwin, I was looking for a pair of stunning eyes: the blue of those eyes, I remembered. I recalled his hands, too: his white hands, the sole unclothed or unshielded part of him. What I recalled, though, was their conspicuous lack of features. Slim but unbony, prototype hands, piano-player's hands. Unmarked, unscarred, unadorned.

Annie loves a man's hands; hands are often what she loves about a man. I knew that she would say of Edwin, *I don't know what you see in him*.

She once said of a soon-to-be ex-lover, 'He leaves me so cold that when I'm in bed with him, all I'm thinking of is Ovaltine.'

A man known to us from then onwards as *Ovaltinie*.

Waiting for Edwin at the station, leaning on to the barrier between concourse and platforms, I looked down on to my own hands. Extremities, exposed, they show my age, my ageing.

Philip seems entranced by my ageing, by the prospect of the two of us growing old together: that, for him, is our future. My hands show me as older than I am, they seem to belong to an older woman; showing me as I will become, they are an anatomical fast-forward. The skin has slackened over the spindly, splayed, vein-slopped bones. My ring is rose gold, but worn and dulled. Of all of me, my hands are most in the world: taken up by the world, taking on the world. Everything begins and ends with hands, with holding.

Holding hands.

To have and to hold.

I looked up, and half-way down one of the platforms was Edwin, coping poorly with the crowds, stepping into other people's paths. Focused on me was his quizzical and rueful expression, the one that passes for a smile. He was dressed in his habitual dark, heavy clothing, making no concession to the weather. I was in silk, a sleeveless top and shorts. I love silk for the counterbalancing of climatic highs and lows, cool in the heat and warm in the cold.

As we walked to the car, I looked more closely into his eyes, determined to gauge their peculiar power. From my surreptitious forays into his glance, I saw how the dark-blue irises are distinctive: textured, deepened, they have the quality of crushed velvet. Keeping such gorgeous eyes hidden from the world must require considerable restraint. I wondered why; why give so sparingly of oneself?

He asked if we could go home so that he could have a tour of what he referred to as *the work in progress*. He was very taken with the house, walking ahead of me from room to room with an expression that was lighter than any I had seen from him, that was opened up even though it was my life that was opening up to him. He said several times in a tone of amazement, 'But isn't this nice!' When he had finished the tour, he admonished me: 'Sadie, you had me believe that this house was a tip.'

I countered, 'Okay, well, for example, you can push your fingertips into the frame of that window behind you.'

He was unconcerned. 'This house has *charm*.'

The house of beautiful things, as Annie says. Sometimes,

coming into one of the rooms, she will remark, happily, dreamily, *Oh! the house of beautiful things*.

The house of things, certainly: so very many of them. And she and Edwin should see the loft: stuffed with charm. Charm among the rafters. This is a house in which the emphasis is on things rather than furniture. Philip and I have never spent money on functional items; or not seriously, not serious money. My mother's ambivalent praise is that we *muddle by*. And, yes, the house is shabby; but, I suppose, extravagantly so. I have noticed that friends' children seem to love the very aspect of which my mother disapproves: the clutter. For children, there are objects to pick up, to hold, to move from place to place, and everything has a sense of a story, like a whisper that is hard to catch. And this is the reason why I love the house: everything in this house has a history, and each of these little histories is mine. The clutter in this house is almost all mine. Perhaps men do not have *things* in the way that women do; or, their possessions are pieces of equipment, technology, and Philip has precious few of those.

Fern once complained to me, 'Have you noticed? – whenever a man starts living with a woman, he brings nothing but a sports bag, he doesn't even have so much as a cushion.' *Cushion?* I relished my vision of a sports bag bulging with a cushion; a man wrestling a cushion from a sports bag and glancing around for the perfect place for it.

I accrue, I am unable to lose the objects that I should, in time, lose. The attrition that seems to happen to everyone else quite simply fails to happen to me; I defy gravity, the peripheral details do not drop away.

Edwin was taken with Hal, too. On our way to the park for coffee, he remarked, slightly hushed with wonder, 'Hal adores you.'

I said, 'He's only human. But seriously, he's a dog and that's what dogs do; that's the point of them.'

I had decided that I wanted a dog when I noticed how

they wait outside shops for their owners: anxiously watching, craning. I had thought, *I want someone to look for me like that*.

Edwin said, 'I'd love to have a dog.'

'Oh, you were brought up with one?' Since having Hal, I have learned that people who were brought up with dogs seem forever to hanker for canine companionship, but those who grew up dogless seem never to consider the possibility. There is no such divide regarding cats, who sometimes even choose their owners and always require little from them. Cat-ownership is less conscious.

He said, 'No.'

I was going to tell him that he was unusual, that he was the exception proving my rule, but then suddenly I was struck that *I* was an exception: *I* had crossed the divide. Moreover, I had thought that I was someone who disliked dogs; but in fact I adore them. My life would now never be complete without one. How was I so fundamentally mistaken about myself, and for so very long? And what if I had never discovered the truth? How nearly I never did.

When we arrived at the park, Edwin told me that he had to be home by six. He emphasised, almost pleaded, 'Six, no later,' and I had to reassure him that I would return him to the station in time for an appropriate train.

Then he tried to lighten the mood by saying, casually, quite jauntily, 'My turn to cook, this evening.'

The problem, I knew, was nothing to do with cooking. The problem was that Vivien did not know that he was here. This gave me no thrill, nor any misgivings: her ignorance was nothing but a fact, the interpretation of which I deferred. What made the impression was his caution, which seemed excessive, counteractive, clumsy, smacking of something to hide. And so I suspected that, before now, he had never done anything like this; this deception. I wanted to tell him that he could be half an hour late and cook something simple. Instead, I asked him what he was planning to cook, and, sure enough, he had no plans: 'Oh, I don't know; pasta, I suppose.'

I was trying to make up for the inconvenience that I seemed to have become, I was trying to be helpful when I said, 'Use dill in the sauce; if you're having a tomato sauce, use dill.'

Looking into the distance, he seemed to be giving this some consideration, echoing, 'Dill.'

Then I saw the tail end of a smile. 'To tell you the truth, I had intended to use Sainsburys.'

'You can still use Sainsburys; Sainsburys will have dill.' *Herb of the month*, on my last shopping trip. Currying favour. A response, perhaps, to poor performance in herb sales figures. 'You'll need a clove of garlic fried in olive oil, a tin of chopped tomatoes and a carton of creamed tomatoes, then a tablespoon of honey and one of dill. That's the basic mixture; you can add onions and fresh tomatoes, of course.'

He mused, 'Aren't you clever.'

'Yes, and that's only cookery: perhaps by the time we reach that far bench, I'll be on to quantum physics, and I'll blow your mind.'

'Oh, I don't doubt that. I would never have thought of dill.'

'No one thinks of dill; everyone thinks of basil and oregano.'

'But you were thinking laterally.'

'Literally: dill is a couple of bushes along from oregano in our herb garden. I'll pick you some when we go home.'

'No.' Expressionless, but unequivocal. Not until the word was spoken did I hear the preceding drawn breath. That word trailed its reluctance as a stealth bomber gives its roar the slip.

Neither of us faltered, we continued walking side by side, to our different rhythms. As if nothing had been said. But something *had* been said, and now someone would have to say something *else*. From the silence I understood that the someone would have to be me. I simply said, 'No, I suppose not.' Because he was not supposed to be here; he was supposed not to be here. A mere wisp of tickly, tasselly dill was a danger: unpackaged, free-floating, it would be inexplicable – where had it come from? – and there was to be nothing inexplicable, there were to be no loose ends. And this dill was the least of it: from now on, the whole world would be made of dead give-aways. There was to be no trace of any of this, of us; there was to be nothing to lead back to us having been here together.

Lulled by our footsteps, moving on down into the park, I thought: *Yes, this is how it is, this is how it has to be.*

I was certain that I could cope.

Eventually, I added, 'Well, as I said, Sainsburys will have dill, but you might have to settle for dried.'

We completed Hal's constitutional without further reference to the trickiness of the situation, and then retired to the café in the park's rose garden. The café is a round Victorian building which, George once told me, was constructed for the Great Exhibition, somehow brought here, and then accommodated the hospital's overspill during the First World War. I cannot imagine the one round room – wooden-floored and French-windowed – crowded with casualties and nurses. Whenever I try, all that comes to mind is a sole, khaki-clad man with a heavily bandaged head – ostentatious, extravagant bandaging, a kind that is nowadays never seen – tended on the terrace by a woman with the dress and deportment of a nun; their shared business the body, the bare minimum of which is visible.

When George and I had last been there, we had differed over etiquette. I had attempted to pay our bill, recalling for him that he had paid on the previous occasion. His resolutely-voiced objection was, 'I do realise that it's different for your generation – you've all been to college together, you've been hard up together – but I'm afraid that I simply cannot have this any other way.'

Yesterday, though, with Edwin, I was the hostess, and I led the way with our tray through one of the many French windows on to the terrace, to a table in the shade of one of the stone pillars and the canopy of vines. Our view was a haberdashery of beady rosehips and velvety pompoms. In the middle of the garden is a stone statue of a child-sized Roman centurion, his weight on one hip and a hand on that hip. I remembered how, one morning, the crook of his arm was draped with a teatowel until the gardeners arrived to restore his dignity, such as it is.

'Are we likely to come across George?' Edwin leaned back in his chair and contemplated me; his eyes, finding mine, lacked the characteristic flinch. A second or two must have passed, during which I relished the unrestrained blue of those irises; a second or two before I realised that what was unspoken was, *We are in this together; whatever it is that we are in, we are in it together*.

'Very unlikely.'

'And anyway we can say . . .' but, thinking, frowning, he paused to reach for a paper serviette, dabbed at a small spill-age of milk on the tabletop, and never finished the sentence. Instead, glancing above his head, he said with a faint note of surprise, 'These are vines.'

I said, 'I know.'

He looked at me again; the same look, but then the sugges-tion of a smile. And suddenly I was the same: on the verge of a smile, for no reason that I could fathom, which was quite dizzying. I said, 'Sitting beneath these vines, I can imagine that I'm in France.' The fruit above and around us had remained immature, however, and looked like frogspawn.

'You'd like to go to France?'

I laughed. 'I think I'd like to *live* in France.'

'Would you?'

I backed down, as ever. 'Oh, I don't know.'

He began pouring his tea. 'But what if you did have children?'

I was puzzled. 'What if I did?'

'What about school?'

'What about *school*? What *about* school?'

'You'd have to deal with that dreadful French system.'

I was incredulous. 'Do I have to think about that *now*?'

A raised eyebrow, but no smile.

'Don't you decide what you want to do and then deal with the problems?' I teased him, 'That's how you do it, Edwin; that's how you do life.' But then, following a silence, I said, 'Isn't it?'

Still, there was no response.

I returned him to the station in plenty of time, and we walked the length of the train. He was in the doorway of the front carriage, on the step, when he leaned down to kiss my cheek. His hand was on my shoulder. The kiss, like all those that he has ever bestowed on me, unlike any that I have ever had from anyone else, was quite startlingly cold, tingling on my cheek. He said, 'Let's speak tomorrow.'

I said nothing, there was no need, because of course we would speak tomorrow.

When I arrived home, Carl was sitting on the doorstep. He smiled as soon as he saw me, and held me in that smile while I came up the path; that unwavering smile; unshadowed, uncomplicated. A smile for which the only word is winning. And duly, although I had been dismayed to see him there, I was won over. However, he greeted me with, 'You look as if you've seen a ghost.'

I gave a feeble, 'Oh,' a mix of apology and dismissiveness, and became busy with my keys.

'The heat?'

'I suppose so.'

'But you look cold.'

'I do?'

He was frowning, concerned, and scrutinising me. 'Pale. Shaky.'

I smiled as I pushed open the door. 'I'm always pale.' *And always shaky.*

Hal had been overjoyed to see him, and was head-butting him; Carl was reciprocating with extravagant ear-fondling. I had to make quite an effort to usher them inside.

'How long have you been here?'

'Not long.'

'But how long would you have waited?'

'Oh, I don't mind waiting.' Then he said, 'I saw your car. You had someone with you. That, and your direction, made me think you were on your way to the station. So I reckoned that if you were coming back at all, you'd be back soon.'

I was surprised: surprised that he knew my car; surprised that I could be seen so clearly from the roadside. I muttered, 'Friend from London.'

And he exclaimed, 'They *do* that, don't they?'

'Do what?' I was hanging up Hal's lead; the chain whip-lashed, tinkled on the wall, which made me shiver.

'*Descend*. Muscle in on our little rural idyll.'

'Oh, yes,' and I laughed with him, but harder because suddenly I was thinking of Annie: untouched by the rural idyll aspect, but nevertheless muscling in.

In the dimness of the hallway he handed me something; my hands were nowhere and closed but suddenly something was in them. It was a punnet, smaller than for strawberries except perhaps for the English variety, the delicacy of rose-bud-like English strawberries. My vision strained against the shade and I saw the clotted, blued red of raspberries. These nubs were nestled on the verge of mush, they were in their ephemeral prime. As a reflex, I inhaled, and there was the scent: overly fruity but with an underlying menace of acid. Quite unlike the candy of strawberries. I recalled the sensation of my tongue pushing up on to my palate; the instantaneous rupture and disintegration of the fragile, dry, blushed skins; my sucking down the small yield of juice. And beyond the raspberries was the scent of Carl, which was not dissimilar: faintly musty and sour.

'Oh, thank you,' I breathed. The dado rail was digging into my back; I straightened.

'Pleasure,' he replied.

I invited him to join me for raspberries, coffee and sunshine. He took two deckchairs into the garden and settled in a puddle of shade. When I arrived with the tray, he was stroking Hal, who lay surrendered on the grass. In spite of myself, I followed his hand with my gaze. Each stroke, although rhythmically consistent with the former, was somehow fractionally longer than I anticipated. The fingers were extraordinarily long and bony but balanced so that no sole bone was more prominent than another. The build of those hands was transparently purposeful: they were made to move, to be put to use. Odd, then, that what came to mind was flowers: the symmetry and androgyny of flowers.

Then I checked his eyes, for comparison with Edwin's, and saw that they were star-blue. Once, when I was a child, my grandmother pointed to some flowers and said, 'I've always wished that my eyes were that colour.' I remember that they were mauve, an odd colour for eyes, an absurd colour for eyes, a colour that is not for eyes, not an eye-colour. I was troubled, moreover, by the existence of a wish for my grandmother. I had never before heard her mention wishes, I had been unaware that she *could* wish: surely she was too old, surely this was far too late for wishes? How could she have any notion of life as other than how she had lived for so very long? And what a wish: girlish, but absurdly embedded in old-age; so inconsequential, for a wish that had come through the years with her. As a child and teenager, I scattered wishes on to early stars and blown candles. When did I stop making wishes? None came true, but perhaps that is the nature of them: if they had ever been at all attainable, I would already have had them. Fate is made of saving graces, because if they had come true, I would have had rabbits, ponies, bikes, cars: a host of unmanageable livestock and unwieldy machinery.

Oh, and a fair number of unsuitable lovers, too. I would have been forever under pressure and overwrought.

Beneath Carl's hand, Hal was in a swoon, eyelids slack. I love his eyes: hazy, muddy, utterly incomparable to the shutters that are cats' eyes. For some reason – going back to his puppyhood? – he likes his eyes hidden, his head covered. He loves to nose into the crook of my arm. And then we tend to stay cuddled, losing track of time, our only interruption any strand of my hair that falls over him, on to or even merely near an ear: the ear twitches until one of us moves. He is made of reflexes. I could have told Carl how to make him roll over, how – where – to nuzzle behind an ear: an acupuncture of kisses.

Carl looked up at me. 'You don't burn, do you?'

'Burn?'

'Sunburn.'

'Oh.' Unlike him, I was sitting in sunshine. 'No.'

'That's odd, isn't it?' Still looking at me, he kept on with those thorough strokes.

'Is it?' By now a little too warm, I closed my eyes to make my own private shade.

'Odd because you're pale, I mean.'

I opened my eyes, gave him an exaggeratedly caustic smile.

'Nicely pale,' he revised.

'*Nicely pale?* Oh, that's horrid, Carl; that's an insult.'

'Okay . . .' he retracted, and mused, uncommittedly, '. . . beautifully pale.'

I reached for the raspberries. 'And that's a contradiction in terms.'

'Is it?'

I swiped my free hand through my hair, complained, 'There's nothing pale about *this*.'

'Poppy red,' he said.

Napoleon banned the colour known as poppy red because the craze for it would have bankrupted his court. Red was the most durable of the old, natural dyes in Napoleon's time, and therefore the most expensive.

'My nickname's Poppy.'

'I know. I heard.'

Heard Philip.

He asked, 'How long have you two been married?'

'I don't know.' And this was the truth, at that particular moment. *Too long.* I was too weary to add up the years; all those years. So I stayed like that – eyes closed, question unanswered – until he changed the subject.

At the end of the day I did have some colour; or, when I undressed, the skin that had been clothed was even paler than the skin that had been exposed. The clothed skin looked bleached, stripped, reminding me of the virgin skin beneath my wedding ring.

My second journey, last year, was in December, and again I did not want Philip to know: that, I knew. I chose a week when he was going to be away at a conference. If he had known what I was planning, he would have been happy for me, and I did not want him to be happy for me. I knew that I would have his blessing, but I did not want to be blessed: that was precisely what I did not want. I had to be free of that. And if, later, he discovered that I had been away, there would be careful questions and copious understanding from him and I was so sick and tired of being asked how I was and of having to think of a reply. I simply wanted to *be*. I simply *wanted*. And during that December, my one overwhelming physical need was for the sun, for warmth, for natural warmth on my body. I craved my skin oiled and steaming.

Not until I was on the plane did I realise that because I did not want Philip to know, I would have to avoid any touch of colour. The crucial privacy, the irreversible secrecy, would preclude that which I wanted above all else: sunshine on my skin. So, I had to settle for warmth, sunless. I stayed indoors or in shade during the days, only went into the open at dusk or in darkness. And I found that I loved what I had settled for; what I had settled for became all the more precious. Warm nights are so much more special than warm days. English warmth almost never stays beyond sunset.

In the vast Atlantic blackness, Venus was a gaudy gem; and in the gloom-swallowed sea, the terrestrial illumination of the neighbouring island's coastline looked like a dropped necklace. Every evening, I walked around the small harbour: the reflections of streetlamps, broken on wavelets, showered over the lapping water like fireworks. The hush was haunted by the rhythmic rising and subsiding of the many moored leisure boats. Their creaking could have been the calls of odd birds. They moved in unison, giving the illusion of being joined.

During the daytime, I watched the sky from my balcony, the occasional length of faint cloud ribbed like tyre tracks in snow. And there *was* snow, on the mountain: craning from my balcony, I could see the distant brilliance of the summit, the unseasonable persistence of snow. In the other direction was the sea, on which, one morning, for a while, there was something that confounded me: something as amorphous, unbounded, and insubstantial as a shadow, but faintly luminous. It was too extensive to be a shoal of fish. The effect was that of moonshine. Eventually I noticed the cloud: what I was seeing on the water was the reflection of a cloud; something intangible reflected on something scarcely more material.

Every day when the sun began to sink, I would cross town to the beach, going against the returning crowds to take my place on the shadow-chilled sand with the few other lone die-hards, all of us aesthetes come to see the sea. The sun's last, lateral rays skimmed the navy waves on the brink of breaking and tipped them turquoise. They broke surprisingly tidily on to the shore. When the sun had drowned, I would return to the garden of my apartment block for a swim in the recently vacated pool; so recently vacated, sometimes, that the surface was shivering with exhaustion. I loved to be the last swimmer of the day to grace that water.

I was the last person of the day in the gardens, too: the paths, lawns and poolside paving deserted briefly before the evening processions. Processions of people who, hours earlier, were scattered sun-dazed and barely-clad, but by seven o'clock were showered, lotioned, dressed, restored as family members, friends, lovers, and heading to social engagements in bars and restaurants. During that half-hour before seven, the sole trace of everyone else in the darkening garden was the scent of cooking, simple self-catering: the elemental smells of sizzling oil and toasting bread. From time to time, I glimpsed a few solitary people on balconies, looking down on me as they idled with a drink or cigarette. But I was unbothered, because what was there to see? I was mostly submerged; I was nothing but small splashes.

To those fellow holidaymakers of mine, I must have been truly unfathomable: alone, and indoors during the day to the tinkling of Thelonious Monk; then coming into the cooling gloom in my Esther Williams costume, quite covered up, to exercise the paced crawl of a racer through the remaining thirty minutes of light. To finish this daily, dusky swim of mine, I would roll on to my back and play dead: me stilling the water, and the water stilling me. Once, facing the darkness that was dropping from a lightening, dawn-blue sky, I saw a bird which seemed unusually high up; so high that any move-ment was undetectable. And there we were for a couple of minutes, the two of us, reflections of each other, relishing our separate, darkening blues.

So, for several evenings, I was the last person in the pool; but then, on the final few evenings, there was someone who came later. I heard the late swimmer for the first time when I was on my balcony, towel-drying my hair and tightening my tastebuds with sips of wine. From the pool, beyond the palm trees, came not the pitter-patter of a child's splashes, nor the roars of a drunken dare, the sizzling of a quick cooling down: no, what I heard were the very sounds that earlier I had been making, an echo of my own swimming. I shuddered to think of that drenching, the giving up of a body to unlit water. But her measured and relentless crawl was a tune that I knew: a sure, faultless turning through her arms of the quicksand of water. I was certain that the swimmer was a woman: the composure, the thoroughness; a conscious, controlled, slow taking of physical pleasure. And every evening, from then on, I listened for her, needed her to take me with her through the dark water, and she never disappointed me.

For my return to the airport, I boarded a minibus which was then delayed. From my incandescent window I saw the maid reach my apartment, unlock the door and disappear into my shady hallway. During the quarter of an hour of the delay, she reappeared from time to time to retrieve various tools of her trade – mop, broom, cloths and sprays – from her trolley. For a while I detected the motion of the mop in the hallway, the undulation of the darkness. Then she brought my bedlinen into the sunshine and threw the bundle on to a pile of others: the invisible configurations of my mild, dream-drawn perspiration were screwed up and dumped with similar etcha-sketches. Finally there was the bin from the bathroom, the contents of which were tipped into a black plastic sack: the flecks of toenail clippings; the tufts of cotton wool on which were faintest smears of my facial oils; and the slip-knots of hair that I had eased from the teeth of my comb. Then, when every last trace of me had been removed, cleaned up, wiped away, she slammed the door behind her and, whistling, hauled her trolley to the neighbouring door. I had been watching my own disappearance.

Watching the detectives.

What I learned to love during that week was the solitude; what I rediscovered was sheer physical pleasure. And all the time I was visited by memories of another holiday, a week in Spain when I was seven years old. My most potent memory was of the pool: so many threads of sunshine in chlorine-sharpened shallows, mescalin-like. This intoxicating water was my domain; my parents were complicit in their own exclusion, they were beached on loungers, listlessly watching over me. All day, for days, I waded around the shallow end, the water lapping my shoulders in a continual, delicious confusion of warmth and chill. And then suddenly, one day, one moment, I was swimming: my soles and arches were stirring water. I remember that I screamed for my father, presumably some version of, *Look, Dad, no feet*. My memory of his response is word-perfect: 'We have lift off.'

For all my love of pools, I had been a little late to learn to swim, a little later than my friends; disappointingly late for such a water baby. I was too cautious. But then, days into that holiday, when I was slightly sunstroked and further dizzied by exertion and exhaustion, swimming simply happened to me. Elusive but ultimately instantaneous, and therefore magical.

Presumably anything learned is never unlearned: over-looked, perhaps, rather than unlearned. I can remember, over a quarter of a century ago, gazing from our car on to the hoardings and billboards of our local high street and thinking, *Soon I will learn to read, then I will know what all these words say*. I knew that the world would become full of unsaid words which nevertheless made sense. I must have been on the brink of literacy: I knew *what* written words were, but not *how*. The anticipation was such that the memory has stayed with me ever since; but just as memorable, for me, is my patience, my confidence.

With one exception, every memory of that Spanish holiday, twenty-five years ago, involves the swimming pool. The exception has me sauntering down a road, fixated by the gigantic billboards: for the first time since I had learned how to read, there were words that were completely beyond me. I knew how to go about them, how to take them from the squiggles and translate them into sound, but they remained mysterious, pure sensation in my mouth. During my days in the pool, I made a good friend, a girl whose name I have forgotten, a German who knew some English and taught me a few words of her own language. I learned to say *mein bruder* for *my brother*, and was tickled by the similarity. She had a sister, so I learned *meine schwester* too. I would love to know where in Spain I was, for that holiday, but there are only two people who know, and how can I remind them? *Mum, Dad, do you remember that holiday, the first time that there was just the three of us, you two and me; the very last week when everything was okay?*

Carl was disturbingly close to the truth with that remark: *You look as if you've seen a ghost*, because falling in love was a phenomenon from long ago, and in which I had even ceased to believe. I am spooked by how this has stolen up on me. Until recently, my life was . . . was *what*? My life was as usual, was running vaguely to plan. Not *my* plan – I had no plan, which was the problem – but *some* plan, the general plan, the generally accepted plan. Home, husband, and a likelihood of children: mine is a life that could be deemed *perfectly acceptable*, to use a phrase that seems, to me, to be a contradiction in terms. Now, suddenly, everything is different. There was a moment when I realised that I had fallen in love with Edwin; but that moment of realisation, on the station concourse, was a mere echo of the split-second when I fell, the split-second between everything having been as usual and everything being different.

TRIPWIRE TENSE

If Edwin's plane took off on time, five minutes ago, then he
is now in the air above me, he is somewhere in this high-
summer air. His plane is making one of the several scratches
that are thin but definite and spectacular on this blue enamel
sky. Gone into thin air, he feels closer than when he is in
London. In Donne's words, 'Like gold to ayery thinnesse
beate'. During his five airborne minutes, there will have been
times when there was nothing in him but the thought of me,
both the memory and prospect of me. Because that is what
happens when a plane climbs: the world is turned upside
down, the wide world magicked away into a mere two dimen-
sions; so that, suddenly, the only real world is the inside of
one's own altitude-sodden, light-headed head. And what is
thirty-three thousand feet but a single foot stacked thirty-
three thousand high? A distance that is finite, more precisely
computable than any that has ever separated us. A foot is a
little more than a hand-span: thirty-three thousand of them,
linked; each holding nothing but air. There is nothing between
us, now; just air. Throughout the rituals of ascent – the vigilant glare of no-smoking signs, the drop in pitch of the engine,
the release of brakes on the hostesses' trolleys – Edwin will
think of me; he will sense me with a certainty as absolute as
gravity.

Edwin and Vivien. As they pass over me, close to the speed
of sound, I am dwelling on the armrest between their two
seats, their twin seats; taking absurd comfort from the
thought of that armrest. A beaker will be in his hand;
his glance sliding down the alcohol-oily plastic. The

imperfections of the rim will be rough on his lips. Lately, he has been drinking too much, we both know that; he has told me. I suppose that she knows, too. How can she not know? The drink will be whisky. In his other hand he will hold an itinerary, which they will peruse together. Take those props – itinerary, alcohol – away, though, and I am certain that he is thinking of me, that the whoozy blue of his own private sky is made of me.

Ahead of me, Hal is indulging in a minute or two of aimless running, digging into a stretch of distance, flinging yards of park behind him with every bounce of his hips. In the rush of air, his eyes are watering and his mouth is open, which looks to me like laughter and in turn is making me laugh. At home, his yawns make me yawn, and my laughter makes him wag his tail, which makes me laugh harder.

An hour ago, I was driving Hal home from his annual immunisation when Edwin rang me from Departures. I knew that it was him before I had answered because no one else ever calls my mobile phone, which was intended by Philip for emergencies. Sometimes Edwin calls as soon as we have finished a conversation on the other phone: the immobile, terrestrial, domestic phone. He calls because he has remembered something, wants to add or ask something. These brief, inconsequential calls are the closest that we have come, so far, to sweet nothings. Sugar to my ears.

You don't have to say anything and you don't have to do anything. Not a thing. Or maybe just whistle.

The first time that he ever called, moments after I had given him the number, his excuse was, 'Just checking.'

I said, 'Checking what? my batteries?'

The second time, a day later, he told me that Vivien was taking his phone for the day. 'Just to warn you,' he said, 'because if you'd have called me, you'd have been surprised.' No, I thought, *she would have been the one who was surprised.*

And so, an hour ago, I retrieved the phone from my bag, and, with a 'Hello?' summoned the characteristic understated '. . . Sadie, hello.'

Bizarrely understated in the circumstances, in my circumstances: a double roundabout and four lanes of rush-hour traffic. I said, 'I'm driving, and, believe me, I'm in a lot more danger than you'll be when you're speeding down that runway.'

He is a nervous flyer. His unconvinced response was, 'So they say.'

'Yes, and they don't know that I'm driving one-handed on a double roundabout.'

A hollow silence, the sound of shock; then, 'That's where you are? now?'

'That's where I am. Now.'

A faint, hesitant, 'Are you coping?'

'I'm *steering*.' The first time I have ever been pleased to be driving an automatic.

'Stop. Go.'

Stop, go?

'Hang up . . . switch off . . .' he was flustered, afraid for me.

'Oh,' and despite my predicament, I laughed, 'No. No.' I was going to hold on to him; I was holding on to that voice for dear life.

As soon as I was on a straight stretch of road, I checked, 'Are you okay to keep speaking? Where's Vivien?'

'Duty Free.'

'And are you okay?' What did I mean, this time? okay with Vivien? okay to fly? okay to go so far away from me for a fortnight?

'I think so. You?'

'Think so. Are you okay to fly?'

I heard the answer as, 'I will be, when I've had Valium.'

'You have Valium?'

'A *dram*; I said, *when I've had a dram*.'

'It's nine in the morning.'

'Not where I'm going.'

'No, where you're going, it's even earlier.'

'Still night. Late night. Whisky hour.'

Then he said, 'Look, yes, I suppose I should go.'

I said, 'Yes,' and of course I did, because what else could I do?

He checked, 'But you're okay?'

'Well, let me think, because a whole moment has passed since you last asked me.'

A sliver of a pause before, 'Anything could have happened.' He sounded genuine. I was surprised by the surprise in his voice, the sense of wonder. This was the first time that I had heard him worried by more than conduct, that I heard him vulnerable to other fears, to the kind of fears that I have.

I was touched, and smiling, and I knew that he could hear the smile, 'Well, nothing did; nothing did happen.'

'Good.'

'And I'm fine. I'd be even better if you weren't going away for such a long time.' This daring of mine was another surprise: I had come close to a declaration.

'Two weeks,' he said, which deflated me, but then, within the same instant, reassured me. He said, 'You'll see me in two weeks' time.'

'Yes, I will.'

'Yes, you will. So: until then, then.'

When we said our goodbyes, I could so easily have said *I love you*, and perhaps I should have done. I wanted to, and anyone else would have done. But I am not anyone else. He is not anyone else. The unspoken, between us, is a deep fascination, down into which we stare. Somehow I knew that he did not want those words said. His own withholding had a hold on me, was a hand over my mouth. All I can think is that he worries that, if spoken, love is diminished.

* * *

Before we went to the vet, I did some housework, washed the kitchen floor, crawling on my hands and knees and ending up doing a kind of doggy-paddle in the slick of soap-slippery water. Then, later, in the bathroom, searching for a bottle of limescale remover, I heard the doorbell. Creeping up on the front door, I peeped into the spy-hole. Inside the tiny lens, Drew's nose – which never, under any circumstances, from any distance, looks small – was swollen to awesome proportions. His nose, I would know anywhere.

When I opened the door, he kissed me and mused, 'You smell of . . .'

'You don't know what I smell of, do you? You mean that I smell.'

'Limescale remover,' he said.

I realised that I had the bottle in my hand. He never misses a trick. I chucked the bottle into the air and enjoyed the slap back on to my palm. 'No, I *will* smell of limescale remover, in a minute.'

'No, you'll smell of coffee.'

'We can't go into the kitchen.' I was leading him into the front room.

'Why not?' I heard his mouth slide into a smirk, 'Who d'you have in there?'

'I have *water* in there, Drew. All over the floor.'

'Lucky water.'

He folded down on to the sofa, his bones cracking like wicker. 'So, why the water?'

'I've been washing the floor. Not very glamorous,' I admitted, sitting opposite him.

'Perhaps you don't look glamorous, but I can tell you that you do look *something*, with your hair pinned up and falling down like that, and colour in your cheeks, and a smudge on the tip of your nose.'

I rubbed my nose.

He laughed. 'The nose was a little elaboration; allow me my little elaborations. What's your new, mystery smell?'

I came clean: 'Brasso.'

'Why? What do you have that's brass?'

'My bed.'

'Ah, the bed, your Lay-lady-lay bed.' He leaned forward, intent. 'I never thought that you'd have to *polish* a brass bed.'

'Constantly. Like the Forth Bridge.'

'They *polish* the Forth Bridge?'

'You know what I mean, Drew.'

Years ago, some mornings, when Philip had gone to work, I would return to the bedroom and delve for his scent in the bedlinen, the tracery of folds.

For a while, Drew and I gossiped, leaving time for the kitchen floor to dry.

'How's home life?' I thought to check, at one point.

'Exactly that, I suppose: homely, lively.' His tone was jaded.

How different from mine: home life, still life.

'Trouble with the girls?' I asked.

'Is life ever anything but trouble with girls?'

One trouble, surely, that Drew has never had. 'Seriously, Drew.'

'Oh, it *is serious*. Double, double, toil and trouble.' But when he told me, the trouble with Caitlin seemed to me to be the same as ever, the same as the trouble of any baby, the screaming and sleeplessness. Oonagh's trouble was rather more singular, focused on a helium balloon that she was given at a birthday party: she has such a terror of losing it, of letting go and losing it to the sky, that she has shut it in the cupboard beneath the stairs.

Eventually we ventured into the kitchen and I made coffee. As soon as I sat down with my cup, Drew decided that I needed a massage: braced behind and over me, he was wringing the muscles in my shoulders.

'You're so tense,' he hissed his exasperation down into my hair.

I was flinching. 'That's because I hate this.'

'But it's necessary.' He pressed a thumb very hard on to one shoulder, screwed his thumb down into a pebble of muscle.

'*Ouch*!' I twisted in his grip, which only seemed to tighten. 'I've been washing the floor; of course I'm tense.'

'That's not why you're tense.'

I said nothing.

Then suddenly he protested, 'You've folded your arms! Unfold them. I can't do this when your arms are folded.'

I did as he said.

He mused, in time to his kneading, 'All these muscles. Stubborn little muscles. You're all shoulders. Holding you back. Holding you down. You should do more exercise; there should be more of you; you should build up some proper muscles.'

'Oh, yes, and where are yours?'

'I don't need muscles, I have charisma.'

Unfortunately there was some truth in this. No muscles, but a big head.

By now I had no pain from his hands, and was drawn into each slow, careful, circular stroke. My body loosened for a deep breath, but his hands slid inwards to the base of my neck and the air flattened in my throat.

'Do you and Philip still have sex?' His question was warm and comforting on the top of my head.

'Sometimes.'

One complete stroke before, 'That's no answer. Everyone has sex sometimes. No one has sex all the time.'

So I gave in, gave him an answer: 'Not often.'

With the next stroke, he said, 'But, of course, it's quality rather than quantity.'

Silence from me. Because, no: no quality.

The less sex that Philip and I have, the more perfunctory. Physical contact is a language to which we have become unaccustomed, and the nuances are beyond us. I suppose that we get by, we both aim to take what we need and sometimes we succeed; one or both of us succeeds, sometimes, I suppose.

On and off. Hit and miss. We make do; we do not make love, we make do. Sitting there beneath Drew's insistent, kneading hands, the phrase which came to mind, from which I could not wriggle away, was *state of disrepair*. Those words describe how we are, Philip and I, in bed. And bed is where we are whenever we touch; out of bed, we never touch more than in passing. *State of disrepair* has the appropriate sense of something ragged, uncared for, and sliding towards that moment – unidentifiable, unquantifiable – beyond which there is no hope of return.

Disrepair, a mere consonant away from *despair*.

Drew asked, mildly, 'And do you have sex with anyone else, ever?'

'Who?' I turned around, turned on him, muscles like hackles.

Reeling, he laughed, 'Well, I don't know. I'm only asking.'

'And the answer's no.'

I changed the subject, or the focus: told him about Annie who, in her own words, *has someone new*. How would that feel: to be someone's someone new? I am Philip's *someone old*. Whenever I say *someone new*, I want to sing,

> *And you'll see me*
> *with somebody new,*
> *I'm not that stupid little person still in love with you.*

The version inside my head is the laid-back, low-key Cake version, the Lou Reed-ish vocals, *I should have changed my fucking lock.*

I told him that, because she has someone new, Annie has cystitis and thrush, too. Yesterday, she went to the chemist without realising that she had two separate items on her prescription, and was unable to afford both. In the queue behind her was the father of one of her Girl Guides, and he funded the shortfall. I said, 'There's chivalry for you.'

'If rather misguided.'

I would love to be able to talk to Annie about Edwin. But how could I explain? How could she understand? This is so far from any experience of hers: this unarticulated, unacted-upon adoration.

The sunshine, today, has brought lots of people here to the park, and almost all of them are eccentric in some way. We, the British, spend so much of our lives indoors that we have no flair for being in public. Almost everyone is either over or underdressed, and utterly devoid of poise, either hurried or slumped. No eye-contact anywhere, of course; and every-where parents noisily anxious over children. Everyone here has either too little or too much self-consciousness.

The tennis players are the exception. Approaching, I can see that all of the courts are occupied, but as usual there seem to be no games in progress. Occasionally there is an arc of an arm, a pop of a ball, but most of the players are strolling, circling one another, chatting, a few prowling solitarily around the perimeter fence. All of them are coddled in layers of clothing – hitched, rolled, tied – and bands, bandages. On the path in front of me, heading for the courts, is a boy whom, over the years, I have seen around town at all hours with a can of lager in his hand and a lack of focus in his eyes. Good-looking, mid-twenties, but a sleazy mess. Today, he has an expensive-looking racket in his hand. He is swinging that racket as he strides purposefully behind a conservatively-attired, middle-aged man, probably his father, who is simi-larly equipped. All the tennis players here have a studied insouciance that bewitches me. I cannot help but stand for a while by the fence and watch them, their protracted practice, the fine-tuning of their bodies. I love to see that resolute sloppiness yielding suddenly to a flex or stretch, to a tense on to tip-toe; those muscles suddenly tripwire tense.

Walking across the park towards me, with his dog, is the man whose injuries, I suspect, come from a motorbike smash. My supposition has less to do with his age, late twenties, or the length of his hair, or, on cooler days, his leather jacket; more to do with the location of those injuries. Bikers injure their fingers, legs, and head: Drew told me.

In that order, he used to say; *You start small.*

Drew worked as a despatch rider in London during his years as a post-grad student.

According to him, DRs – that was the term he used – anticipate between four and six scrapes each year and a serious smash every thirty thousand miles.

'We obsess about injuries,' he told me, once, all those years ago, 'It's a major topic of conversation: what we couldn't live with, where we'd draw the line – where we'd want the line to be drawn – and then how we'd want the end to be quick.'

I remembered where I had heard this before: racing drivers' talk, which was talk that I heard during my childhood.

Drew was lucky, he retired before his time was up. This man's leg injury is shocking: the limb is bowed, giving the illusion of odd, unilateral rickets. His head injury is invisible, but on the one occasion when we spoke – exchanging pleasantries about our dogs – the extent was obvious. He seemed unable to know when to stop, unable to know how to let me go. As I was backing away, unavoidably brusque, I wondered if he craved my company because he saw me as a kindred spirit: a fellow sufferer, struggling around the park, time on my hands, a dog for company. I wondered if, in his opinion, we were bonding. But no: within that same instant, I saw that he, of all people, was oblivious; he, who could have seen what was wrong with me. He is what my mother would call, *Too far gone*, or, *Not all there*. And now, because of that – because of his social clumsiness – I do as I have done ever since that occasion when we spoke: I avoid eye-contact. And so he limps by, unseen. But unbothered, too, mercifully, because ever since that initial encounter, he has shown no recognition of me.

Drew has a nose for indiscretions, and this morning, walking around the park, I am haunted by that nose of his. His hands, too, but differently, literally, physically: the ghost of his touch on my shoulders. He has probed and made tender the hardest muscles I have; the muscles that hold me up. That expression, *Someone new*, has brought to mind for me another, *Someone else*.

Perhaps the most difficult question to have to ask of one's lover: *Is there someone else?*

During my marriage ceremony, the words that made an impression on me were not our vows but the registrar's decree, *The exclusion of all others*. Philip and I had a civil ceremony. That word, *civil*; the other connotation, *polite*, *restrained*: that was exactly how our wedding was. Philip and I are both polite, restrained people, as are our friends, or the few friends who we invited to the wedding. Annie did not come; she was invited but had glandular fever.

The exclusion of all others: I was prepared for the *sickness and health*, which was exactly what Philip and I had been doing so well; but I was shaken by that *exclusion of all others*. When the words were said, I wanted to stop the registrar, because I was absolutely sure that there was a question to be asked, although I did not know what.

Exclusion. Absolute, decisive. A burning of boats. During the past decade, I have excluded so much from my life, and had so much excluded. Suddenly I am so very tired of exclusion. The *sickness*, on the other hand, is no problem. If marriage is the decision of with whom to spend one's dying days, years, then I made no mistake when I married Philip: Philip, for dying, every time. Good, gentle, capable Philip, like a brother to me. I was glad to place myself in his hands; and that is where he wants me. But life is more than days of dying. What is my life other than all the days when I am not dying?

So, today, and always, this *exclusion of all others* haunts me, troubles me, taunts me, has done so ever since the registrar spoke the words and broke the spell, because before those sing-song words of hers, and my on-cue acquiescence, I was confident, or willing, or something, I was *something*; I was someone who somehow *believed*. And then she spoke those words and my faith dissolved, went with the words as if washed away into water.

... *the washing of water, by the* Word: a refrain that I remember as belonging to the old ceremony, the traditional service that we never had. Oh, I had it easy, and *still* failed. And failed instantly: never off the ground, my faith dropped away in front of all those people on my wedding day. With my back to all those people, all those eyes on my back, my exposed shoulders, blades, I realised, *I cannot do this*. Or, *A day will come when I am unable to do this*. Three years later, with Drew's hands moving on my shoulders, I recalled the certainty of the realisation, as unequivocal as the scorch of cold water. By going ahead and marrying Philip, I betrayed him; as I do every day by staying.

... *hereafter for ever hold his peace* ... Drew, today, neglecting to hold his peace; Drew, the stirrer. I have no peace to hold. There is no word for what I hold, for what holds me. *Doubt* is nebulous, to do with gnawings, ranklings, nigglings. Self-doubts are what are had – or have been had, or will have been had – by the people who were watching my back for those few minutes on that day three years ago. And self-doubts are all that are had by that kind of person, a person who attends weddings, a person of basically good faith: doubts, yes, from time to time, and even misbehaviour, but these people come through. Even if they fail in the conventional sense, by divorcing, they married with good intentions. And will remarry. They want to be married, they believe in marriage. They mean well, are well-meaning people. And I am not. I stood there, on that day three years ago, and went ahead, married Philip, even though I knew how I was flawed and would ruin his life. Standing there, sensing all those eyes on my back, I saw myself for what I was, what I am: a disgrace.

Faintly dizzied, I sit down on a bench. Hal is reluctant to move far, and undertakes an intricate sniffing of a flowerbed. To what, precisely, did I agree, when I married Philip? how do I fail him? Did I promise never to love anyone else? No, of course not. What I vowed was never to love anyone else in the way that I love him. Why was that a problem for me? Me, who never loves any two people in the same way; me, who knows that there are as many kinds of love as there are people. No, love was never the problem; I am being disingenuous: everyone knows that the exclusion refers to sex. If I was appalled by the prospect of exclusion, then surely the problem had to be this: the sex, with others, lack of. But was it? for *me*? me, who could count my previous lovers on one hand and was happy with that? No, surely sex was not the problem.

Whatever unsettled me at the time, the problem now is that I speak to someone other than Philip on the phone several times every day. The problem is the content of those conversations, which is nothing: nothing but the minutiae of every moment. I seem to live every moment so as to tell Edwin. My experience of every moment and my articulation of that experience are indistinguishable. *Intimate* comes from the Latin for *innermost*. Edwin has most of me, the inner me; he is in all my thoughts, the thought of him is in all my moments.

On some days – the good days – I am happy to think that all that we share are words, and that words are mere musical breaths. So, no harm done. And on those days, I am hopeful that we can go on loving each other in our unmarried, undeclared way. Because that is all that I want: to have this, to hold this love as it is. And is that too much to ask? considering all the love that has been lost from my life? Surely I can keep this one, small love, even if only for a while. I am not asking for the happy ending.

Somehow even now I know that my love for him is not the marrying kind; perhaps because I am already in the perfect marriage, perhaps because I have had enough of marriage. I do not want to marry him, to live with him, to take on a mortgage with him, to load and unload the dishwasher with him: no, none of that. This is not that kind of story, with that kind of ending. No, this is a love affair, and love affairs end; they have a shape – that is the beauty of them – which entails an ending. I am braced for the ending. I have never been so brave. In time, Edwin will leave me cold: even now, I know that, and even know how. There will come a time when I will loathe what I now love of him. He is so hard to love: pompous, ripe for taking a pinprick to; and closed away. And married, of course; hard to love not least because he is married. I love him in spite of himself. Philip, on the contrary, I love *because* of himself. Philip, unlike Edwin, is lovable.

Hal is sitting beside the bench now, his manner rather formal: ostentatiously in attendance. I close my eyes, lids rosy with sunshine. On bad days, I smart with the unspoken condemnation of the whole world because this love of mine for Edwin is bad in anyone's book. The final taboo, even, perhaps: there is no word for this unacted-upon in-love; this not-quite-adultery. Edwin and I lack the excuse of sex, the most excusable sin. And then public sympathy is reserved for those who go public, who acknowledge their separate relationships as youthful mistakes and try again: this is the acceptable version of the love story of two people who are married to other people. So, we can either stop, or own up, stand up, come clean, grow older and wiser. The only other ending is comeuppance; the sticky end.

Before all this, the problem for Philip and me was passion, good old passion, good old-fashioned passion: the lack of, in me. I have never had a moment of passion for him. Isn't the word Latin, meaning *to suffer*? For me, there has been no suffering in this relationship. Falling in love with lovable Philip was easy, suspiciously easy. Every moment of every day, I feel the lack of that passion, cumbersome like a numbed nerve. I have no idea whether he knows this, nor whether he lives with any similar wound. I have never known how he feels. He says that he loves me. So, I know *which* feelings he has, but not how they feel to him. If feelings were truly palpable, if I could reach into him and touch the love that he feels for me, I suspect that my fingertips would stop on an unrecognisable substance; the sensory data scrambled in a fundamental, physical confusion, just as a burn comes to fingertips as a blow. Philip and I are made of different mettle. Take away our home and our history, and we have nothing in common. And I have nothing. Worse: I seem to be losing whatever I had inside my head that made the world make sense. I am a stranger in a strange land, becoming stranger still.

Why did I marry? I married so as to have a family; to have Philip as family, which, as my husband, he is. I know, now, the question that I wanted to ask the registrar: *What if I fall in love with someone else?* And now here I am, falling. A falling is unstoppable. I suppose that I could unplug the phone, return the letters to sender, and refuse to see him. And so, it is for this, and only this, that I take responsibility: my refusal to turn away, which would be as pointless as trying to turn from the sky.

This morning, when I had watched Drew drive away, I went back into the kitchen and – as a mild, momentary distraction from the troubles that he had stirred – perused the open newspaper. I turned the page, turned listlessly, unintentionally, into the Lonely Hearts columns. This never ceases to bring me up sharp: that there are people who regard love as something for which they can browse and into which they can enter by transaction. And there was I, suddenly, unwittingly, a spectator once again while stacks of anonymous participants declared themselves as keen to share their pleasures in music, films, pubs, walks, bikes, and meals.

I saw that one woman had specified *WLTM socialist* and of course I thought of Casey, that eighties' entrepreneur, riding roughshod over my political sensibilities; and me, in love with him nevertheless, perhaps all the more so because of my surprise, the perpetual surprise. Love has to take me by surprise, take me over; that element of chance is essential; the haphazard. Fate has had the say-so in love; I have never had a say in who I have loved. I have to be hapless, disorientated, my whole world and all my faculties on hold. Haphazard, hapless happiness. Perhaps love is all the better if contrary to my better judgement; because all my life, in all other aspects of my life, I have followed my better judgement and now I am nowhere. Fate has slapped me around, but has been kinder in love; I have been lucky in love. I have always turned up gems. Up until now.

The woman who *WLTM socialist* described herself as *slender, spiritual, but energetic.* Could I say that? would I say that? What would I say? what am I? I could be said to be slender.

An odd word, *slender*: she is *slend*, I am slend*er*.

. . . *but energetic.* Is *energetic* a drawback?

In an adjacent column, a man announced that he was an *ex-comedy writer.* How strange, to advertise one's failure. Or was this a different take on *GSOH*? an offering of credentials? A few adverts below him was a *one-time actor, composer, writer*; someone significantly come down in the world. Is this a new trend, defining oneself in terms of what one once was? In such terms, I am an attractive proposition; the only terms in which I am an attractive proposition. My only problem would be the choice of where to start; I am spoilt for choice. I am an ex-carer. And before I became an ex-carer, I was an ex-goldsmith: a claim that not many people could make; an eye-catching ex-identity. I am an ex-lover, of course, a few times over: I am a few ex-lovers; par for the course. An ex-sister, too, I suppose. Unless I am careful, I could soon be an ex-wife.

I went from the kitchen into the hallway to fetch the old book of *Common Prayer* from the shelf. Its role in this household is decorative; but up close, under inspection, the leather-bound volume was dismayingly unattractive. I had been taken in by that gold; that thin, disintegrating gold. Even the gold of the title was a disappointment, flaked and dimmed, and the brown of the binding lacked an olden-days' hue, was unweathered, unfaded by sunshine; the leather devoid of nuttiness, homeliness. The book had probably never been in my hand for longer than the five minutes, twenty years ago, when I was skipping home from church, from our school's end of year service. The old books had been offered to us because the new, modern edition had arrived. My friends went home from church via school, where they fetched classroom goldfish and hamsters, offered holidays to tame mice and stick insects. I had been forbidden by my mother to bring home anything live, so, instead, I provided sanctuary for a prayer book. When I turned up with my gold-leaf treasure, she complained, 'I'd rather have had the terrapins, and that's saying something.'

Twenty years later, holding the book again, I was struck by the unpleasantness of the shape, the pudginess. My fingertips anticipated a lip to the cover, an endearing upwards warp; but the cover clamped down. I opened up, looked down the list of contents, looked for weddings, found only *The Form of Solemnisation of Matrimony*. No laughing matter, then, according to this book; no cause for celebration. *Solemnisation* has no connotation of, say, cake.

'At least let me see to a cake,' my mother had said when Philip and I chose to forego what she referred to as *the trappings*. This offer of cake concurred with her frequently-voiced complaint – complaints were all that she ever voiced – that, *People need feeding*.

The other day I related this story, with that quote, to Edwin, and his comment was, 'Faultless political philosophy from Mother Summerfield.'

I said, 'All those years, I was nothing to her; but then, as soon as I was due to appear in public, if only for my own tiny wedding, she wanted a role.'

'Several platters of them, I imagine,' he said, 'with a variety of fillings.'

I remember how I was adamant: 'No cake, no cutting, no photos of any cake-cutting.' I had in mind what a caterer had called *reception pastries*.

Philip said, 'My vote's for French Fancies.'

To my mother, I tried to explain: 'We don't want to do much, and what we do want to do, we want to do differently.'

She muttered, 'Story of your life.'

In the prayer book's list of contents, the chapter following *The Form of Solemnisation of Matrimony* was *The Order for the Visitation of the Sick*. I am certain that I have only ever seen the word visitation in connection with angels. And so *Visitation of the Sick* implied to me that the visits are by the sick: their coming unanticipated and unannounced; their appearance otherworldly, a shimmer of shivers, a draping in dressings. And ludicrous though my vision was, I suppose that there is a sense in which the everyday world – the big, bold everyday world – is merely visited, always unpredictably, by what the book calls the sick; the injured, the damaged, the lost and disappeared.

Further down the list was *Forms of Prayer to be used at Sea*; and this, I found irresistible.

Those captivating words, *at sea*.

Go to sea: do people still *go to sea*?

I turned to the section, began to read the enchantingly entitled *Short Prayers in respect of a Storm*. They were shocking, even repellent, in their lack of sophistication. Pleas for mercy, for salvation, they seemed little more than screams; noise thrown on to, into, much louder noise. How had anyone ever had faith in these frantic incantations to save them from storm-swollen seawater? But then how do I know what would help, facing death by drowning?

I turned the pages to the wedding words. This was what I had intended to do: discover the meaning of marriage, according to this old book. What I discovered from the first paragraph was that marriage was to be undertaken *reverently, discreetly, advisedly, soberly, and in the fear of God*. That was the how. Then came the why. Firstly, *the procreation of children*. Secondly, *as a remedy against sin, and to avoid fornication*. Thirdly, *mutual society, help and comfort*: even that, I no longer seem able to manage. The vows stipulated a *forsaking of all other*. Closing the book, I pondered how a *forsaking* differs from an *exclusion*. An *exclusion* is a simple exercise in boundary construction, a clinical excision. A *forsaking* is an abandonment. If I were to stop seeing Edwin, I would be forsaking him.

Hal and I have begun walking again and are now beneath trees. From between trunks I glimpse a car travelling too fast down the tarmac drive that borders the park. Even more worryingly, a dog is giving chase: to a fanfare of his own barks, he bounds from one rear wheel to the other. Hal is too close to this commotion, to those wheels. I am hurrying over varicose roots to take hold of him. But the car has stopped. The driver, a man, is craning through his opened window, and yelling; the yells are directed towards another dog, one I had not seen, who has been exploring the base of a distant tree. The passenger door opens and the chasing dog leaps into the car. And I realise: this man has been walking his two dogs; this is how he walks them, by driving ahead of them around the park. The second dog has returned now, and jumps into the car. The door slams. I am near enough to see the clenched face of the driver, and, behind him, the blank faces of two strapped-in toddlers.

Yesterday, when Edwin and I were having coffee, we somehow strayed into a swapping of stories of exes, of first loves and successive, disastrous loves: love-life-histories; all told easily, for fun. I refrained, on grounds of delicacy, from telling of the man in the café where, earlier, I had had a coffee. I had only just taken my cup from the counter to a table when the man burst into the room from the toilets, accompanied by an anxious, aproned man. The lively man was the elder of the two, middle-aged, tall and broad, black, dressed in a multi-coloured kaftan. And he was euphoric, kissing the aproned man – noisy, emphatic kisses – while declaring in a bona fide American accent, 'I love you. I love you, man. You hear me? I love you.'

The aproned man – whom I surmised to be the manager from the gravity of his expression and deference of the other members of staff – was appeasing, twittering, nodding, his ponytail bobbing. Although the troublesome man's principal fixation was the manager, he was keen to express his appreciation of us few others in the room, calling, 'Hey, I love you, you people . . .' and turning around, reaching to bestow his touch upon various tables. Inevitably, within a few seconds, he had made his way around to me. 'Hey, lovely girl . . .' He leaned down towards me. I was prepared. I smiled – a contained, clipped smile – and appealed, saying very quickly, 'Could I just read this?' I opened the leaflet that I was holding: programme notes from a photography exhibition.

'Sure! Sure, baby.' Perplexed, his attention slid away. Having ruffled my hair, he moved across the room, and drew a chair up to the table of a more unfortunate, less assertive woman. She looked Japanese or Southeast Asian. Although I was unable to hear her words, I heard an accent and saw her incomprehension, her diligent courtesy.

The manager neglected to pursue him, staying instead to whisper to me, 'I'm so sorry. He's very drunk.'

You don't say.

'He's been to a reception at the embassy around the corner.' The manager's expression was blank, shocked, his tone one of desperation for my approval. 'He's quite famous, you know.

Musician. I don't know his work but some of the staff here do.'

I thought, *What difference does that make?* I wanted to say, *Yes, he's drunk, and no, he's not a bad soul, but he's harrassing your customers and we came here for peace and quiet so it's your job to eject him.* In the face of such inadequacy and embarrassment, though, I froze. And then, from across the room, I heard the words of the drunk man to the foreign woman; mildly-spoken words, polite and interested, as if he were passing comment on the exceptional weather: 'You know, I've never fucked a Japanese woman.'

Weary, all that I could think was, *Nor have I, but I don't tell the whole world.*

I was remembering this when Edwin remarked that he had assumed that he would never fall in love. The words were, 'I never thought that I'd fall in love'; the tone carefully conversational. As he spoke, he was gazing into the bowl of demerara that was between us on the tabletop, and idling the lip of his dry, unused teaspoon into the mound of golden grains. I could hear quiet crashings of sugar and steel. On his downturned face, I detected fragments of a smile within his habitual and ever-vigilant frown; and a resultant, mild discomfort. Silently, I was picking back over his words, unteasing them, the tense of them, trying to follow his thread: did he mean me?

'No?' was the best I could do. I was genuinely puzzled. Never falling in love was incomprehensible to me. Love is my lifeblood, even though against the grain, my ingrained solitude.

'No. I didn't think that falling in love was for people like me.'

This time, I was appalled, by both the exposure and the inadequacy. Poor, poor Edwin.

Falling in love is hard and rare, but I am perverse. Anything unlikely, and only anything unlikely, will happen to me. Everything easy, on the contrary, fails to come easily to me.

This is so fundamental a trait of mine as to seem physical, biological; as if I had been born wrongly polarised, like someone born with a heart on the wrong side. And just as if my heart were on the wrong side, my perversity is so scrupulously compensated for that no one will know, until something incidental exposes me.

I can count on one hand the times that I have been in love. How can my life have been taken up and taken over by so few falls? The first time, I was twelve, and the impetus was sex, that primary mover and shaker. He was brimming with a sexuality of which he – a twelve-year-old boy – was barely conscious. My body hungered to shoulder his burden. The obsession lay within me for two and a half years, the two years before I made my catch and then the six months of reciprocal, repressed passion. For the initial two years, I was nothing more than a presence in his life. I made sure that I was there and that he knew that I was there. What else could I do? Beyond that, I was at his mercy. When my love was requited, I was both surprised and surprised by my surprise. Now I can see that I did not think that the falling in love of someone like him was for someone like me. *Ask no questions*: this is how I feel whenever someone falls in love with me. Or, how I did feel, until now, until Edwin. How could someone like me fall in love with someone like him?

When I was first in love, I took six months to see the light. What I had loved was that he was articulate and ambitious; he was what my mother called *a character*. What I had overlooked – love being blind, me being young – was the kind of character he was: a nasty one. A couple of years ago, on a train, I saw his ghost. My journey was local, the train very old and barging creak-raucously along a track that was crowded by high-summer, overblown hedgerows. Bowed over a book, I was drowsy on the dust and gloom of the carriage's upholstery. As the train slowed – mechanisms moaning – for a whitewashed and flower-frilled station, I glanced up and saw a crowd of schoolkids on the platform, as incongruous as a crowd of extras. They were homeward-bound, released and reckless; uniforms slack, allegiances tribal.

The older I am, the earlier in the day schoolkids seem to leave school, and this was only mid-afternoon. As a dozen or so crashed through my carriage, I was braced, determined to continue reading. But, immediately, they were irresistible, the spectacle unmissable. I made myself invisible by appearing to be absorbed in my book, but, furtively, I was agog. Near to me was a knot of boys fringed with girls: three boys sitting together, and six or seven girls sprawled over surrounding seats. The boys were bantering, quipping, loud. The girls were louder, laughing and eager to be entertained, their shrieks tinged with a girlish mixture of goading and scorn. One boy took on the role of jester. He was smaller than his two friends, and sharper, working harder for attention; he played to his crowd, and blazed with adrenaline. I had an overwhelming sense of recognition: *I know you*. I saw what they saw in him – his boyish charm – but with no warm wash of nostalgia. Being older and beyond his spell, I saw through the charm that, in time, he would lose, and it was not a pretty sight.

Now, from nowhere, comes an inkling that perhaps I am wrong, that a fall in love is in fact no fall, no simple happening. A fall would prompt an instinctive resistance, a correction, probably an over-correction. And it is life that happens; not love. Life, not love, has been happening to Edwin, hauling and bumping him through the years. A fall in love is no swoon, no loss of consciousness nor even of poise, no ungainly and momentary loss of footing. A fall in love is supremely conscious, involving every nerve-ending: a dive, and then a bathe. It is a following through of a hunch; sometimes a hard-nosed following through, requiring not merely heart but guts. Yes, to me, this time, this supposed fall of mine feels like a surfacing; both instinctive and somehow also the hardest work, the only work in the world.

* * *

Ahead of me, something involving Hal is happening: he has come to a stop in front of a little boy; the boy – five, six or seven years old – is standing still in front of him. Hal is nosing into the air around the hand that the boy has extended towards him. My pace picks up, and I counter little-boy-blankness with a grown-up's emphatic smile. He is speaking to me, announcing, 'I'm not frightened, I'm not frightened.'

I agree with a glad, fond, 'Oh, he's an absolute baby.'

'But he's big for his age, isn't he?'

This brings me up sharp; I hear the echo of brittleness in that initial bravado. His blankness is grave, his hand lifeless. He *is* frightened. How careless of me to have taken him at his word. I slide my cooing towards Hal and touch his head, turn his attention to me, encourage him to come away.

Yesterday, Edwin asked me if I was afraid of flying and when I said no, he wanted an explanation.

I laughed, shrugged, suggested, 'I have absolute faith.'

He seemed delighted with this. 'That's quite something, for a cynic.'

Yes, quite something. A lie, in fact. The truth is so much more extraordinary, though, and, sitting there with him, I suppose that I wanted to be ordinary. I wanted to be *me*. I wanted to be simply the person who was sitting with him; I wanted him to be sitting with me simply *because of me*. With everything that has happened to me, sometimes I feel that my life story is bigger than I am; that I am less than the sum of everything that has happened to me.

The person to whom I most recently told the truth about flying was a stranger, a fellow passenger on a return plane journey from Nice. I did so because I wondered if perhaps she needed the story, if perhaps she could make use of me. She was terrified, and there was a chance that what I could tell her would reassure her. Not that there was anything wrong during the flight. On the contrary. For me, one of the main joys of air travel is sunshine – the unbroken sunshine when the plane is above cloud; the cloud-cover, so dreary from below but stunning from above, dazzling in that sunshine – and during this journey of ours from Nice, the clouded sky was gorgeous, perhaps because of the time of year, perhaps because of the time of day, perhaps both. Early on, there was broken cloud, which could have been ice floes on a sea. Later, nearer England, we seemed to be moving above an expanse of virgin snow. The sun-drained horizon became tinged like a bitten red apple, the colour of the broken skin bleeding into the flesh. And in the dusk and then darkness, the white light on the tip of the wing beneath me was our own star, accompanying us; our very own evening star.

The crew was jovial, the pilot as overbearing and unctuous as the worse kind of DJ. I love crews, even the most glacial British crews. Over the years I have seen all kinds: lackadaisical Italians, leaving drinks in hands during landing; French, demonstrating emergency procedures by prancing down the aisle and twirling, co-ordinated, as if on a catwalk; and the gaggle of giggling stewardesses behind me during take-off from Dublin, unaware that I was able to overhear them fantasising over one of their passengers. I love how the name badges on male crew members, unlike those on the women, seem overfamiliar: *Jeremy*; *Craig*. I love the women's time-warped make-up: sixties' eyelashes, and what looks like fifties' pan-stick. I am held in thrall by the poorly-disguised weariness of crews, the peculiar physical strains of their weird work: radiation, dehydration, disturbance of diurnal rhythms. I am fascinated by their outlandish routines: the schedules, the hotel rooms, the parties. For all the prim uniforms, theirs is a rock and roll lifestyle; they are the roadies of the air.

During our flight from Nice, the pilot had been encouraging audience participation, telling us what we could gaze down on. As a consequence, there was almost a party atmosphere; spirits were high. During the final slow-motion minutes of suspension above a world that was becoming overwhelmingly recognisable, my fellow passengers were craning towards windows in awed enthusiasm, their comments audible to me despite my pressure-muddled ears: *Look, that's a train* and *Is that the M23?* Each voice sounded an authority for the moment of recognition – *Look, that's a train* – and then deferred – *Is that the M23?* – before a pause, a mutual, respectful search for more. They behaved as if this were crucial: the pilot's job was to land the plane; his passengers', to appreciate and reassemble the world.

I love everything about flying, I was born to it. I even love the words, names, *Hawker-Siddeley* and *Gypsy Moth*; even the newer ones, *Boeing, Lufthansa*. I thrill to those ritual utterances, *Doors to manual* and *Commencing our descent*. I relish the history, how the earliest pilots were – in the words of my father – *the pop stars of their day*. Young, beautiful, daring. Lindbergh, known in Britain and the States as *Lucky Lindy*, in France as *Le Boy*. The stunning Dorothy Spicer, the first woman to possess all four certificates in aircraft engineering.

My father's unfulfilled ambition was to be an aeronautical engineer. When I was little I loved to hear him say the word, which I heard as *aero-naughtical*. Then, when I was perhaps six or seven, he used to take me to a local airfield – *airfield*, an odd word, field-of-air, how wonderfully unlikely – to watch the planes; those flimsy, noisy, wind-grizzled planes. And there, once, he told me the story of the airfield's erstwhile owner and his love affair with a woman known as Blossom. 'Not her real name,' he added.

I laughed. 'I know that.' As a Poppy, I understood.

According to my father, Blossom was titled. The man was her flying instructor, and they fell in love: that was what my father said, relating this as a fact. She was married to someone else, though, so her admirer took the honourable course of behaviour – that was what my father said – and went away, sailed for South Africa. Honourable, yes, but wrong; he realised that he had made a mistake.

A terrible mistake, were Dad's words.

So, he came back. She divorced, and they married. She learned the trade, and they became one of the most formidable partnerships in the history of British aeronautical design.

There's romance for you, my dad said.

He was joking, but I have never overcome the notion that romance involves – what? – a bi-plane? a turning of the world upside down?

My father was never an aeronautical engineer but – happily, nearly as good, in his opinion – he was a motor-racing mechanic, working on Formula One cars. For many years of my childhood, he was travelling, flying to destinations around the world, and occasionally we joined him.

My mother says, *Dates weren't what they are now*; this is what she says of the time when she was pregnant with me. And perhaps she was genuinely mistaken, but perhaps she lied, declining to declare the advanced state of her pregnancy because she was afraid to be alone. She flew to be with my father and I was born on the plane, on an airborne plane. This was what I told the woman who was sitting next to me on the flight from Nice, the woman who was so obviously terrified as we came in to land. I said that surely the chances that I would die on a plane, too, were minuscule. I do not know whether I am right, but I believe so. I have no idea whether she believed me, nor whether I was any comfort to her, but she listened, and by the time I had finished, we were down.

The bizarre circumstances of my birth only began to have an effect last year. The tradition is that anyone born mid-air is entitled to a lifetime of free travel on planes. When I flew to Nice, I did so because those flights were available on the dates when I could travel; Nice as a destination was unimportant. Not that I failed to enjoy the city. I spent four days there, staying in a small hotel. What did I do? The usual. Lived. Pottering around the old town and market, popping into bars for coffee, collecting pebbles from the beach.

For a whole year from the day of my return, I never once left the house without my passport. I was determined to be able to leave whenever I wanted to do so. I was addicted to leaving, to getting up and going, and my free flights fuelled that addiction.

RUINOUS BLUE

❧

'I'll call you,' Edwin said, yesterday, when I stood up to leave.

I said, 'Yes,' but simply for something to say, to sound a response; a grace note. For me, calls were an irrelevancy; the future was far from my mind, even the near and small-scale future of phone calls. Standing there, across the table from him, I was quite simply suspended in my leaving, my leave-taking. Busily picking up my bag and packing away my purse, inside I was utterly still, calm, laid wide open so as to absorb as much as possible from the final moments with him. I am never less than very happy in his company, even during moments of leaving; perhaps especially during them, these moments that round our time together and contain the promise of more.

He is the one who is always keen to establish the day when we will meet again. His planning has become a habit, with which I have learned to fall in.

He will worry, *The week after next, then; probably that Tuesday*. And, automatically, I will say, *Uh-huh, okay, the Tuesday*; thinking, *We'll see*, and *Why worry?*

But on this latest occasion, yesterday, he turned his attention not to when we would meet but to when he would call me, saying, 'Friday,' which was uncharacteristically decisive. And then, even more decisively, even less characteristically, he said, 'Morning.'

And that was when I understood; that was when we had our understanding.

The understanding was that tomorrow, Friday, is to be when we start the new system, the system which we had, an hour earlier, discussed and decided upon: our new, Vivien-proof system. Vivien has to be fooled, from tomorrow morning onwards. Not that either of us said the word, *fooled*, nor anything even faintly similar. We took no pleasure in the decision: on the contrary, having to have the discussion was unpleasant. In a sense, though, Vivien was not our focus; we were talking about how to keep our current level of contact, which is jeopardized, now, by her feelings on the matter. By Edwin's feelings for her feelings. Vivien is not my concern: as simple as that, in this complicated situation.

And that is what I want to explain: *Vivien, you are not my concern*. To think otherwise would be presumptuous; I do not know her. This is not personal. Sometimes I want to ask her, *Do you understand? Do you understand why I am doing this to you?*

Not *not* doing this. Because surely she wonders. I would wonder, if I were her. But if he chooses to fool her, then I follow his lead; I have to. Because his lead is my only clue: I know nothing of their relationship other than whatever he shows me.

I want to say, *Oh, Vivien, please don't expect me to put someone else first; not again, not this time, not in love.*

My concern is Philip. But he knows nothing, because I am invisible to him. Last year, I flew abroad seven times, and he had no inkling. Edwin asked me, yesterday, if Philip needs to be fooled, although, of course, those were not his words; he asked, anxiously, 'Does Philip see *your* bill?'

He had been bemoaning that fact that Vivien had never before looked for their bill.

I thought, *Ah, yes, but she's no fool*. And, *Anyway, how do you know?*

Because how do we know what they do, those closest to us, to keep close to us? How do we – the restless – know the mechanisms, the mysteries of how we are held in place?

The answer was that the phone bill is mine, the one bill that is mine. I explained, 'I'm the one who talks.'

He gave me a pained, cautious, melancholy smile, and said, 'Not too much, I hope.'

What was I to make of that? Only minutes earlier, downcast and subdued, he had said, 'I've reassured her that she has nothing to fear from you. I've made it clear that you are no threat to her,' adding, 'and, of course, that's quite true.'

My first thought was, *Is it?*

My second, *It's not.*

His gaze had come to mine when he said *that's quite true*, but there was no look, there was a conspicuous absence of a look. He intended the words to be taken – what is the expression – at face value? as read? As the truth.

And this made no sense to me. I wondered whether Vivien believed him. No, or not for long; she is no fool; she is on to something.

I wondered, *Am I mad?* Mad, no. Nor naïve. He must think that both of us – she and I – are stupid. Looking across the table, I almost pitied him: his pathetic hope that what he said was true or would become true because he said so; his pathetic hope that there was an escape from all this, that the escape was so simple. I could have pitied him if this had had nothing to do with me. But he knew my feelings – oh yes, he knew; how could he not know? – and here he was, disregarding them. We were at sea, so very badly at sea, and he had had a chance to unfurl a lifeline, a chance to say something – Vivien had given him that chance – but he had failed even to test the water before jumping feet first into denial.

I forgive you, I thought, *but only this once.*

'She bears you no malice,' he was saying: those were his words. I doubt that they were hers; I cannot imagine her saying *I bear her no malice*. I wonder what she did say. And I wonder what she feels.

I have to take him at his word, I have to follow his lead. The new system is that he calls me, but replaces the receiver within two rings. I dial 1471 to check that he was the caller, then I call him back. So, our calls will be confined to my bill; and when the bill comes, he says, he will settle up with me.

He will call me tomorrow morning. The meantime is dead time. I am spending this morning with Hal, on a longer walk than usual because there is nothing else to do and because yesterday I dumped him on Dodie, the nanny, so that I could go to London.

Edwin – newly returned from his trip – had called me from his office.

Following pleasantries and summaries, I had exclaimed, 'Three weeks since I saw you!'

'And a day. Are you up in town again soon? this week, at all?'

Suddenly I was impatient with this pretence of ours that I came to town for purposes other than to see him. I said, 'I'll come up today.' Time for a gesture, I reckoned.

'Oh, don't do that:' the tone was kind.

However kind, I would have preferred to have heard, *Yes, do that*. Or, better still, *No, I'll come and see you*.

I was dismissive; I said, 'It's no problem.'

'It's a long way.'

'I said, it's no problem.'

'Are you sure?'

'Yes.' *Aren't you?*

He told me that he had a meeting but would come to the station, would try to meet me from the three o'clock train; if he was late, I was to wait.

So, I rang Dodie and begged her to take Hal, then drove him to her house; said hello to her, goodbye to him. Then I drove back into and across town, spending ten or so minutes in stationary traffic and as a consequence missing the train. Plan B was a rush across country to a station on an adjacent line. There, fifteen minutes later, I was scuppered by the barrier to the station car park: *Exact money required*. Leaving the car, I rushed into the station to join a formidable queue at the ticket office. In the end – ticket bought, coins obtained, and car parked – I reached my train with less than a minute to spare.

And then, made shaky and queasy by the rush, I had the thought, *Why am I doing all this*? This came as a shock; this was the unthinkable. I had assumed that I would do anything and everything for him, but suddenly there I was, thinking, *Why am I doing this driving, this travelling, why am I suffering the expense, the exhaustion*?

No: what I was thinking was, *Why me, alone*?

What had come to me was the supremely uncomfortable realization that he would never do this for me. Worse, somehow, was that he had never asked this of me. So this – all this rushing to see him – was my choice. Some choice. But that was the deal. Some deal. One person always has to make more effort than the other, to move a relationship onwards.

Sitting down on that train, I was struck by my tiredness: an ominous tiredness that I suspected to be beyond the reach of sleep. When I arrived in London, he had been there for ten minutes, he had arrived on time. He seemed irritable, said that he had come away early from the meeting, had taken a taxi across town.

This morning, Hal seems unenthusiastic for this extra time in the park. Initially, he was intent upon doggish business – working his way along the hedgerows, in detail, in depth, adding his scent at seemingly precisely-calculated intervals – but now he is trotting absent-mindedly beside me, on automatic pilot. A return home means lunch, to him; his mind, now, is on lunch. I know how he feels. Perhaps we should go. Suddenly I recall the awful occasion when he was so desperate to go home that he led me to the park gates. He had ambled over to a collie, and then there was a noise as he whirled away: a scream, a sound that I had never before heard from him, unlike any that I had ever heard. He raced towards me, still screaming, as his attacker closed in on him; and by then I was screaming, too, but for the owner to take control. My words, I remember, were, *Do something. Something*, because I had no idea what would stop the collie in its tracks. All of a sudden, everything was under control; the collie was under control, being chastised by its owner. She – twenty-something, dumpy, dour – did not ask after Hal, did not even look at me. I was trying to comfort Hal and check for injuries, my hands both soothing and exploratory. We were breathless and shaking, and he seemed, in turn, to be trying to comfort me: certainly, he was keen to oblige, to be held. But he was slipping free, again and again, to circle me. The fear had not subsided but had backwashed into the new calm and turned into embarrassment. We both wanted to move on.

So then he began to lead me home, scampering ahead of me for a few paces at a time and then pausing, pointedly, for my approach. Never before or since have I seen such clear intention from him. He has clear needs, of course – he is made of them – but in hope of their satisfaction, he will ask, cajole, or beg. This leading across the park was the only occasion when I have ever understood him to be telling me, *I am going to do this and I want you with me.*

This morning, the park is damp. Earlier, the air was downy with drizzle. A shock, to remember rain: to remember that there is rain in the world; to remember that this world is the same as the sun-starred one of recent months. A dip in the summer, and a corresponding dip in my mood, today. The path ahead is blued with puddles. All I can hear is the desolate, protracted howl of a descending plane. My mood is bruised. My only laugh so far today has come from the sandwich board on the corner of my road, on which was written, in chalk, *Fresh continental hand-tied*: only when I saw that the board belonged to the florist did I surmise that this referred to a kind of bouquet rather than a sexual practice.

And this makes me think again of Drew, who was drinking beer in the garden with Philip when I arrived home yesterday. I had not expected to come across Philip, let alone Drew. Philip never leaves work before seven.

'What a dress!' Drew called across the lawn.

They were drunk: Drew, expansive; Philip, laid back. *Flying on instruments*, to use my father's expression.

Stepping from the doorstep, I was now even more weary than when I had come through the front door. Behind me, indoors, warbled Radiohead:

> *Such a*
> *Pretty house.*
> *Such a*
> *Pretty garden.*
> *No alarms*
> *And no surprises*
> *Please.*

I made myself smile in greeting to Philip, which was difficult for a number of reasons: the clutter of bottles on the tabletop; the fact that, in all our years together, he had never come home from work before seven to drink with *me* in the garden; and, oddly, that he had no idea where I had been. Glancing at the bottles, I tried to calculate: how long had the boys been there? how drunk were they?

'What a colour! Makes a change from your usual widow's weeds.'

Philip announced, 'New dress.' He could have added, *Like several others*, or, *She's been panic-buying in Liberty*. But he asked me, 'Been anywhere nice? Would you like a drink?' The elevated mood, diligent politeness, carefully-enunciated words: Philip, drunk.

Suddenly I was grateful to Drew for being there; thankful for not being alone with Philip. I prompted, 'Say hello to Hal.' Poor Hal, overlooked, literally. Both men looked beneath the table, Drew lunging with extravagant strokes, Philip offering a pat.

Then Drew was back on the subject of the dress, blaring, 'It's *short*.'

'No shorter than my others.' This was probably untrue. My gaze was still on Philip; to him, I replied, 'Town,' which could have meant our local town, or London.

'Cerulean blue,' Drew discerned, hoping to compensate for the crassness of his previous remark.

To him, I said a pleasant, 'I suppose so.' To Philip, 'Would you mix me a martini?'

Drew cackled, 'You're a one,' which could have been a reference to the dress, the trip to town, the drink, or all of them; neither Philip nor I asked for elucidation.

As Philip and I passed each other – him, heading for the house, me, joining Drew – he dabbled fingertips on my forearm. The gesture was a combination of greeting and apology, but failed to touch me, and, worse, irritated me. I told him, 'Just pass the vermouth over the glass.' When I had settled into a chair, Drew leaned from his own to kiss me; his steadying hand on my thigh. I was faintly surprised by that hand, the heaviness, the warmth; the sensitivity of my thigh.

As he came away, he moved his hand just enough to ripple the material of my dress, murmuring, 'Is it silk?'

'It is.'

Without taking his eyes from mine, he reached for his bottle and drank. I saw him swallow three times, saw the three full pulses of his throat.

I laughed, quietly. 'Don't be lewd. This isn't the time or the place.'

He replaced the bottle on the table, his wetted lips opening and disappearing in a lupine smile. 'Well, you name the time and the place.'

I have known him for a long time, I know what to do with him: distract him; change the subject. My suspicion is that the women who know how to deal with him are the only women to know him for a long time. I said, 'Do you know, blue's my favourite colour,' the colour of safety, 'and it's most people's favourite colour. Red is the favourite of adolescents,' the colour of appetite, of instant gratification, 'but then there's a change to blue; did you know that?'

The smile was unchanged. 'I didn't.'

'Well, now you do. What are you doing, here?'

'Knocking off from the working day in style, in your lovely garden. Old friends and cold beers: what more could I want?' He laughed. 'Cool beers and cool friends.'

'And what does Sarah want? does she want you home?'

He laughed again. 'Would *you*?'

He had a point.

He said, 'She's busy.'

I went to say, *Oh*, was intending to ask why she was busy; but then he was saying, 'Always busy.'

'Oh: My-wife-doesn't-understand-me.'

The smile, this time, was different; tempered.

I said, 'Philip's never home this early.'

'Well, I rang up my buddy and – hey presto – he was here for me.'

'So, tell me, am I interrupting boy talk?'

'Boys don't talk.'

He reached again for his beer, and I raised a hand, indicated for him to pass the bottle to me when he had finished. After a mouthful, I said, 'Talk to *me*, then. Tell me something.'

He ran a condensation-dampened hand through his hair, strands of which fell forward from his fingers. 'I had a rather tasteless erotic dream, last night, after I'd watched *The X Files*.'

'*The X Files*?'

'Yes, there was a – what's the word? is it *succubus*?'

'Okay, I think that's quite enough.'

'No, I'm serious. And, anyway, you asked.'

'Yes, and I should have known better.'

Then I had to ask, 'Is there a difference? Are there taste*less* and taste*ful* erotic dreams?' If Philip has ever had an erotic dream, he has never told me. And my dreams of Carl: are they tasteless?

Drew's hand was on my thigh, again; but this time, brief and avuncular. 'There is; there are, darling.'

'If I didn't know, then I've only had one kind,' I mused, 'and if I've only had one kind, then I don't know *which* kind.'

'You know the answer to that: you're going to have to tell me – and tell me *everything*, because you'll never know which details are going to be important – and then I shall give you the benefit of my very considerable experience.'

I gave him a look pitched somewhere between scepticism and contempt.

His response was, 'Sensible girl. For my own good, I know. I'm fine with other confidences, you know that; but as soon as I know someone's sexual fantasies, I'm in trouble. Remember when you told me that Claudia told you that Michael likes to be dominated?'

'Unfortunately, I do.' At the time, Drew barely knew Michael and Claudia; but later, somehow, through a connection that had nothing to do with me, they became friends.

'Well, ever since then, whenever I'm with Michael, I'm terrified that I'm going to find myself dropping some telltale word into the conversation, unconsciously: you know, *spank*, or *thigh-high boots*.'

'Is that likely?' I contemplated him. 'Yes, that's likely.'

He asked me, 'Who were you meeting in town?'

'No one.' I spoke nonchalantly, but a rush of prickles took me by surprise and transformed me: I was damp, I was covered by a film of dampness; I imagined a marine sheen.

'You can fool some of the people some of the time.' His tone was resigned.

I had nowhere to go; I recall that as my immediate thought, in those words: *I have nowhere to go*. He had me cornered. He knew something and I realised that I was too tired to come up with a denial, to think of a lie, to carry through a lie. And this was a relief. For the first time, there was nowhere that I wanted to go. I wanted to tell the truth; I wanted to have this – all this; this situation with Edwin – made real. I could have said, *We speak to each other every day, by way of various routines and codes; we see each other every time I'm in London; I tell him everything and I think of him every moment and I'm fairly sure that it's the same for him.*

I could have asked, *What do you make of that?*

And he would have laughed and said, *Nothing.*

Or would he?

I said, 'It's not what you think.'

In that same tone, he said, 'It never is, is it?' He reached into the jacket which was draped on the back of his chair and extracted a packet of cigarettes.

I watched him slide one cigarette from the others and place the tip between his lips, then delve again into the jacket for a lighter from which he snapped a flame.

Echoing his tone, I remarked, 'I thought you'd given up.'

He removed the cigarette, and closed his mouth. Smoke tumbled from his nostrils, and he closed his eyes. Then his lips relaxed and his eyes opened. Looking at the cigarette, he said, 'It's not what you think,' before turning to me with an uncharacteristically slight smile.

Suddenly Philip was with us, one hand a blaze of glass, alcohol, ice.

With the same smile, Drew said, 'My friends don't understand me.'

Philip chided, 'We do, you old bastard.'

'Oh, we were talking about someone else, I was paraphrasing someone else.' He looked away, over the garden. 'Oh, no, *I'm* understood very well, I think.'

So, I am going to have to talk to Drew. How odd, to know, now, that this will happen: I will tell someone; or, I will tell someone *something*. When? When Philip is not around: that much, of course, I do know. Lately, he seems very much around. He has been very much around so far today: another lieu day. This morning he had maps and guidebooks all over the living-room floor. Coming in from the hallway, I stood looking down on them, Hal trod on some of them, and Philip, crouched over one of them, looked up and said, 'We decided that we'd take another week or ten days because Lanzarote was so early in the summer, remember?'

'Oh, yes. We did.'

The maps dizzied me. The books wearied me: the clever, angular graphics on the covers. Also on the floor was his work diary, open; various rotas marked in coloured pens. Extracting a week from those lurid lines is always quite an undertaking, for him; arduous, fraught. Whenever he does, his aim is to please me. If not for me, he would be content to take the occasional couple of days at a time, between the holidays of his staff. All this – the tangle of motorways and sleep-overs – was for me. I had to turn away from his upturned, hopeful face.

The Lanzarote trip was in May. May was in the time before I knew Edwin. A now-unimaginable world. What did I do, then? How did I survive? Perhaps survive was all that I did. What do I remember of that holiday? Nothing. Nothing awful. I spent every day on the poolside, reading unconvincing novels: they were peopled by characters of a kind that appear only in novels, They Came From Planet Fiction.

We were in Lanzarote because everyone had said, *You need a week in the sun.* An up-market, upbeat version of, *You need a nice cup of tea.* What I needed was a life. Philip said, time and time again, *You've had a long winter.* Poor Philip, unaware that my seven trips abroad had given me a winter ablaze with illicit sunshine.

I do remember Shannon. A barely toddling baby, she was white noise, unmemorable, but I remember her name, said over and over by her parents every day on the poolside. I never saw them smile. The woman scowled. I never heard the name of their son; they seemed only to give him instructions concerning his sister: *Let Shannon go with you; Don't do that to Shannon; Watch Shannon.* I never heard them speak to each other except to make childcare arrangements:

negotiations which had a surprising, marked lack of unpleasantness; had, instead, a tone of thankfulness. *I'll go, and take him with me*; *You take Shannon for her feed, then bring his sandals down*. Shannon – emitting shrieks of indignation from behind her dummy – was the only one who seemed happy. I remember the time when the boy wanted to be taken to the pool but his father wanted to lie in the sun and had tried to persuade him to do likewise. Having failed, he closed his eyes and endured a probing with endless chatter, culminating in, 'If you threw a jellyfish from the balcony, would it be dead, I wonder, Dad?' Those were his actual words: *I wonder*. 'Would it be dead forever?'

His father, resolutely shut-eyed, managed, 'Yeah, it would.'

'Why?'

'Because when you're dead, you're dead.'

Philip, looking up from the maps, continued, 'And Lanzarote was just for relaxation. This time, we could *do* something. And we're too late to be organising much, so I reckon we should drive, then do whatever we like.'

Oh, Philip, what would we talk about, trapped together in a car for all those hours and days?

His work, I suppose: he could – would – talk about work. I used to love that talk, the characters. Perhaps this is my imagination, but nowadays he seems to talk only of his managerial problems. And what will I talk about? Nothing; I have nothing to say; or, nothing I can say to him. He will talk to stop my silences, to cover for me. I fought an urge to ask *Philip, what is happening to us? What are we going to do?* Neither of us knows what to do. He can do nothing.

He said, 'We could – I don't know – drop in on Jess and Rob?'

His parents' friends in the Dordogne: good hosts; good cheer. I am afraid of a week or ten days away from Edwin, another stretch of time when I will know nothing of him, when I cannot know what he is doing, what is happening to him, what he is thinking, feeling. Days when I am blind to him, when I am blind, following everyone else from drink to drink, conversation to conversation, meal to meal, then following Philip to bed, into a darkness deepened by his thorough sleep.

'Or Susie, because Toulouse is nice and she's always said that she'd love to have us. Or your friend Peter, of course.'

'Oh, Pedro,' in Barcelona, with his wife, his kids: fun.

No: fun, if I were someone else, anyone else. I will be no fun, blind and bothered by the silence of the phone. How did this happen, how did I become no good to anyone but Edwin?

His tone had changed, quietened, when he said, 'We've years to make up for; all those years when, you know –'

'– Yes –'

'– Jacque was around.'

Yes, yes; no need to have said.

'And now we're free to do whatever we want,' and the smile, measured, was both permission and persuasion.

Did he still believe that her presence had hampered us rather than held us together?

There was a time when Philip and I had fun; when fun was all that we had. Even when we had problems – work, money – the texture of our shared life was wondrous. Even doing the laundry was fun: who would believe that? We moved into our own house and had our own washing machine; suddenly we were the kind of people who had a brand new washing machine. Together we discovered the machine's intricacies and idiosyncrasies. Usually we hung the laundry before going to bed, on a clotheshorse in the hallway. In bed, I could smell that beguiling cleanliness, a sheer absence of us from our own clothes.

As for doing whatever we wanted, there was plenty that we wanted to do; in fact, there was everything, we wanted to do everything. And now there is nothing. Is it that we have done everything? There was a time when I loved Philip so much. There was a time when I loved Philip. Loving him, now, is like singing a song to which I have forgotten the words: I am humming, and hoping. No, worse: loving him is like being with someone to whose face I cannot put a name; I am bluffing, and on tenterhooks for clues, and beneath the tenterhooks is frustration and panic for both of us.

He was murmuring, 'I'll do whatever you want. You had a rough year, last year, I know.' Then he said, 'There's the rest of your life, Poppy. Your whole life. I'll be here for that. I want to see you through. You had your problems, but, well, your problems are my problems.' Then, 'Are you okay?'

I had sat down, not next to him but in an armchair. 'Oh. Yes.' And, quickly, I reached to the floor for a book, the book that was nearest to me, which had *motoring* in the title. I opened the book, randomly, read aloud, '*Not easy.*' which was one line within a table of similar comments.

'What?'

'What *is* this?' Turning back, I saw, 'It's *Mountain passes.* Oh, look: all of them! Details on all the mountain passes in Europe,' which was something to which I had never given a thought, but there they all were. They were all there, in Europe, up in the mountains. '*Thirty-two hair-pin bends.* And, *Many well-engineered hair-pin bends*, isn't that wonderful? Isn't there something wonderful about that? And this one is *Just negotiable*. This one is *Pic*, presumably that's picturesque.' I checked in the key. 'Yes. And this one is *Pic but tr*. What's *tr*?' To the key, again. '*Treacherous.*'

'Poppy.'

I looked at him.

Slowly and definitely, he said, 'You'll have to tell me.'

I wanted to ask *Tell you what*? but I did not dare.

Just as slowly, he clarified, 'You'll have to tell me what you want to do about this holiday.'

In an identical tone, I said, 'Oh, yes, I will do.'

Later this morning, following all that talk of the holiday, Philip wandered into the kitchen and said to me, 'You know what?'

'What?' I was drinking coffee and skimming the newspaper, pondering the newspaper's promise of *A look behind the headlines at the issues affecting you and your family*; thinking, *How do you know what affects my family? How dare you presume to know anything of my family?*

'You've not been playing much music, lately.' He sounded puzzled, looked puzzled, as he half-smiled and perched on the stool. 'There's – oh, I don't know – there's silence around you where I'm expecting music.'

This silence of mine is not unheard of. Occasionally, for weeks, all the music I have seems either inconsequential or self-conscious, mannered. Unmusical. Whenever I am in this mood, even Bach is noise. The choice between noise and silence is no choice. I suffer the silence; I yearn for music. A silence of this nature is a mere absence of noise; a noise of which, somehow, I remain aware, like a metaphysical tinnitus.

I returned Philip's smile, explained, 'I'm in that mood when I'm not in the mood,' and went into the living room to look through the CDs. I stood there, savouring the pianists' names; I love their names, a music by themselves: Sviatoslav Richter, Vladimir Ashkenazy, Mitsuko Uchida, Artur Schnabel, Andras Schiff, Alicia de Larrocha, Radu Lupu, Dinu Lipatti. Still, I made no choice. I would have liked the choice to be made for me; I wanted to be surprised. So, I switched on the radio. A male, Radio Three voice enthused, 'I think you have an early Strauss recording for us, today,' and another male, Radio Three voice replied, 'That's absolutely right, Peter, I do.' I turned off the radio. Philip came into the room, and exclaimed, 'All those CDs of ours that we never, ever play! You know what we should do? We should make ourselves play them. We could plan to play one every evening.' Then, mock-darkly, 'Mind you, I can think of quite a few evenings when I'd be coming home very late.'

I laughed. And that was when I spotted a CD I did not recognise. 'What's this? Is this yours?' The title was, *Sounds of the Rainforest*.

He replied with an overly casual, 'Oh, yeah.'

'You bought this?'

'Oh, *dead* cheap,' was his defence. 'Thought it might be nice. Might relax me.'

I was touched. There, in my hand, was something of Philip of which I had known nothing. He had been shopping and had seen this CD; he had had ideas, notions, hopes for this CD, all of which were foreign to me. He had made a decision, or perhaps given in to an impulse, then carried home his purchase, pleased. And had he been pleased when he listened? or disappointed? Had he forgotten this CD, since? How did he feel, now, about that little, long-ago decision or impulse of his? Involuntarily, I said, 'Oh', my free hand momentarily on his arm.

'What's that for?' His smile was uneven, unsure.

I winced. 'Hard to explain.'

Tentatively, he said, 'Ah, one of those moments; they're the best ones . . . Well, I *think* so.'

I kissed his cheek, reassured him, 'Yes, they are,' and had to leave the room before I cried.

I am in a bad way, today. Having a bath, this morning, was a bad sign; a bath, rather than my usual shower. Having a bath is more drastic than a lie-in or return to bed. Staying in bed is a delay; having a bath, a disappearance. In water, I am beyond the reach of the world; the real, dry world. I can be called from bed – for the post, the phone, breakfast – but am less likely to be expected to leave a bath before I am ready. Bathing is an experience, there is a lot to accomplish, not only the rituals – lotion, talc – but, of course, washing; I cannot leave the bath until I have washed. And drying, of course: I cannot leave the bathroom before I have dried.

This morning's bath was a distressing experience, though, despite the pampering and solitude. The drawback of water is transparency. My body was on display. I did not know where to look. Our bathroom is small; the bathtub, of course, smaller. Bathrooms exist for tubs; tubs, for bodies: my body was inescapable. And vile. How had I never noticed how vile? Spindly, pallid, and hairy. *Downy*: I suspect that I am supposed to say I have *down*; I could say that I am *slender, fair and downy*. Do other women have this down? this much down? How much down can I have before I become no-nonsense hirsute? And stubble: stubble, whatever I do and however often I do it. Perhaps I could cope with shins, but I am undermined by hair in unexpected places: my toes, for example; the gilding of hair on the tops of my toes. These follicles are fault lines in my keeping up of appearances.

This morning I found a few clotted-looking veins shadowing my calves: ageing means that my insides are toughening and working their way to a thinning surface. I am going wrong. My surface is busy with moles: all small and pale but a thorough splattering. To add insult to injury, I seem to suffer, now, from asymmetry of the nipple. Is it too much to ask for symmetrical nipples? Also, I have a cyst on the back of my neck, and what if Edwin ever feels that? A lump that is pea-sized, of raw-pea-consistency: fluid-filled, tautened, prone to infection. Philip is unphased by flaws; on the contrary, he welcomes them, indulges them. But Edwin? Cautious, heavily be-suited Edwin? No. I could never be naked near Edwin. He would be horrified. His distress would distress me. I am certain that his body is no improvement on mine, but how is that a consolation?

But this bath-time perusal was a mere scratch of the surface. My fundamental flaw is the real reason for Edwin to steer clear. This flaw is my failing as *marriage material*: that mercifully and unexpectedly neutral expression of my mother's; of, I suppose, her generation. More up-to-date and a little less polite: I have *no staying power*. And of course there are other, timeless words, of which *untrustworthy* and *fickle* come to mind. I prefer plain *hopeless*, because that is how I feel. Here I am, married to the perfect man but ruining him, and loving another.

This morning, in the bath, I contemplated how I would feel if Edwin had taken Philip's place, somewhere on the other side of that door. Given time, or perhaps no time at all, I would detach from him, too; and lie to him, and think of leaving him.

I thought, *Well, I would, wouldn't I? because why wouldn't I?*

I thought, *What is wrong with me?*

And then I would be in the same dreadful situation; no, a worse situation, having swapped perfect Philip for hung-up and held-back Edwin. I would be more alone than ever, which is unimaginable. And everything would be worse for everyone else, too. Not only would I have ruined Philip's life, but the lives of two other people; their perfectly adequate marriage. What was unbearable was how much Edwin could hate me for doing that. And, so, there, in the bath, I realised that there is nothing to be done, that everything will become worse, that there is everything to lose.

While I was in the bath, Hal had roamed my bedroom and come across an emery board which he mistook for one of his chewsticks. When I emerged from the bathroom, the damp, bitten emery board lay discarded on the floor. Poor Hal, he must have been thrilled with his find, then sorely disappointed. That was when I decided upon a longer walk, as compensation. I was clipping Hal's lead on to his collar when Philip leaned through the living-room doorway and informed me, 'Message from Fern on the machine.'

'Saying?'

A pause, then a shrug. 'The usual. *Call me.*'

That is what I am going home to, now: calls. Unanswered calls are stacked up around me like incoming, circling planes.

Planes are my overwhelming memory of the Chelsea Physic Garden, yesterday: the screaming, heavy-bellied, Heathrow-bound planes. They passed over us at regular, frequent intervals; probably conforming to one of those quoted statistics, probably one per minute, possibly more. Each passage was protracted, and every time the pitch was higher than I had anticipated. They were braking, held hard against the air, against their own speed. *Turning physics upside down*, my father used to tell me, explaining that planes are made to fly, cannot help but fly, have speed on their side; it is the landing that is problematic. True: if I had never flown, I would never have known that descent is such hard work; I would have thought of landing as a simple stopping. What we were hearing, in the garden, yesterday, was the asserting of control over momentum; a battle. As soon as one plane had passed, another would begin to move down into the airspace, to take over our immediate sky. And then followed the same noise – intensity and duration – but somehow always sooner and more severe than I had expected, like spasmodic pain.

The irony was that we were in search of some peace. We should have known better: London is London, there is no escape. And, worse, the sky of West London is an extended runway. If we had stayed in the Physic Garden for much longer, we would have needed to sample the remedies. We should have gone to a coffee bar in Soho, in the eye of the storm, in a backstreet, a sidestreet: a couple of Italians busy behind the counter, dab hands with the espresso machine, and above, a fan stirring the thick, risen air. There is no escape, but there are lulls: London is full of eyes in the storm. Eddies and eyes.

The garden was his suggestion, when we met at the station: 'I'm a member,' he said; and, peculiarly, he sounded surprised.

Not as surprised as I was. '*Are* you?' I had been there, but I am strictly a member of the public.

As we walked towards the underground, he slid the membership card from his wallet. 'Present from Vivien's sister. The elder.'

'You make her sound like a druid or something.'

'Oh, no, she probably has a mild interest in geraniums or whatever, but her main interest is Chelsea, and I don't think that she knew what else to give us.'

'No: *The elder*.'

'Oh.' And he laughed, that almost-despairing note. 'No, not much of the druid about her. Oh, God, I'm never going to see her again without thinking *druid*. And that's like seeing – I don't know – Patricia Hodge and thinking druid. Like going mad, in fact.'

Joint membership, courtesy of Vivien's sister. To some people, he is a half of Vivien-and-Edwin; unimaginable without her. And to me, he is unimaginable *with* her. Two worlds. Mutually exclusive. In opposition.

'I'm running out,' he said.

We were going down the steps into the ticket hall. I glanced up, across at him. He was peering at the little card. 'Close to expiry.'

'We won't see Vivien there?' What if she decided to drop in on her way home from work?

He slipped a ticket into a turnstile machine. 'No, she never goes.'

I followed.

Was she that predictable, or did he only think so?

'I think we've been once.'

'Oh. That's a shame.'

Looking away, he took a breath, one of his dizzying, steadying breaths; one of those breaths that somehow seem to leave him breathless. Then he said, 'Yes.'

We went into the garden via Swan's Walk, a door in a wall. The houses behind us were Georgian, imposing, roped with wisteria; their views were of the garden. I marvelled, 'Who on earth earns enough to own one of these?'

'That kind of wealth probably isn't earned.'

'These houses must be more expensive than . . . well, than *anything*. . . than *castles*.'

He frowned. '*Castles*?'

'Well, yes, *castles*.'

'You're probably right.'

I laughed. 'I'm always right.'

And he almost echoed me. 'Yes, you probably are.'

Inside, I consulted my plan of the garden. 'This is the Hidcote Lavender Walk. Have you been to Hidcote?'

'No. What's Hidcote?'

'A garden in Gloucestershire.' Gloucestershire: suddenly, nowhere had ever seemed so far away. And unimaginable: a county of people doing . . . doing what? . . . Gloucestershire activities. Thinking Gloucestershire thoughts. Meanwhile, here, the wall turned the noise of the traffic to an aural steam.

'And how do you know about this Hidcote?'

'Philip knew.'

Edwin read from the plan, '*Systematic border beds*.' There was a waspish note in his complaint, 'Do you see anything systematic about these border beds?'

'No, I've never seen border beds less systematic.'

We stood side by side, looking down over an extensive tangle of vegetation.

'A case of the Emperor's new clothes, I think,' he said.

'The Emperor's new systematic border beds. No, Edwin, come on: that's the point; these are *border beds*, not *clothes*, so what do we know? Be fair: what do we know about border beds?'

He was unimpressed. 'We know whether or not they're systematic.'

'You know, these beds are someone's art. To someone, this mess is everything. Including systematic.'

The waspishness was still there, but, this time, relished, when he said, 'You're sentimental.'

I laughed. 'I can think of worse failings. And, anyway, first, you say that I'm cynical; then, I'm sentimental: make up your mind.'

'I'm beginning to learn that the two go hand in hand.'

I was strolling away when I said, 'Ah, that was something that I learned the hard way. We cynics are the ultimate romantics; we become cynics because no one lives up to our standards. If you're looking for my failing, it's forgiveness. I don't do it; don't seem able.'

'That, I don't believe.'

'That's because I overcompensate.'

We reached the tiny fern house. As he followed me through the doorway, I had to warn him – 'Careful' – because he was too close to some lilies, his sleeve was in danger of a gilding with pollen. *Lipstick on your collar*. When we emerged through the opposite doorway, seconds later, I suggested that we go into the house for a cup of tea.

We were served by a man who had the enthusiasm of a volunteer.

Coming away from the counter, Edwin whispered, 'Did I *imagine* that our man's actual words were "Pop up for a top up"?'

'You didn't, but you did imagine the pinny.'

Instinctively, he glanced around; then, as sheepishly, turned back to me with his laugh. 'I didn't. And, yes, that *is* a particularly fine example.'

'A pinnacle.'

He was following me; I was looking for space on one of the many long tables. Behind me, he said, 'My grandmother's aprons were of that calibre.' I found somewhere for us to sit; indicated for him to put down the tray. He said, 'Bought in Grouts: where else?'

'Where?'

'Grouts, in Palmers Green. A shop. Or, *Fancy Drapers*, as I remember they called themselves. God knows what an *un*fancy drapers would be like. My grandmother shopped there for – oh – tea towels, dusters, rubber gloves. There was heavy-duty underwear, too: the girdle kind.'

'Flesh tones.'

'Flesh tones, whale bones: frightening. What I loved were the glass counters; the walls of tiny drawers; the money going along wires over my head to the cashier.'

This was the first childhood memory that he has told me. I have told him quite a few: friends, incidents.

'That shop was still there, a couple of years ago, when my grandmother was alive.' Then suddenly he was saying, 'You're tired.'

'You mean that I *look* tired.'

'I don't. You don't. You have a tired demeanour.'

'I'm not sleeping.'

'Nor am I.' Beginning to pour the tea, he smiled, quoted, ' "Here we are, out of cigarettes . . ." '

I returned the smile.

> *. . . Two sleepy people,*
> *With nothing to say,*
> *Much too much in love to break away.*

'We do have a substantial slice of Victoria sandwich, though.' I took a fork to the thin, flopped end.

'And that's something else I haven't encountered since the halcyon days of my grandmother.' He paused for me to finish my mouthful. 'Any good?'

'More moist than Niagara Falls.'

'Excellent.' Then he inclined his head, and said, gently, 'Sadie, there's something that I should tell you; something that, unfortunately, could further trouble your sleep.' And that was when he told me about the phone bill, about Vivien.

When he had finished, he said, 'To be truthful, that wasn't the first discussion that Vivien and I have had of my friendship with you.'

Discussion; *friendship*: there I was, being put in my place. I was gazing around the room: tall, narrow sash windows; pink walls, the same shade as the custard that we were given sometimes in primary school, custard with cochineal.

'A couple of weeks ago, there was some trouble because she said . . .' – he faltered – 'what *did* she say?' – rubbing his brow with the heel of one hand – '. . . that I'm only ever happy, lively, alive if I've seen you.'

He looked at me; I looked at him. He looked unhappy. Recently, his hair had been trimmed, blunted, and the margin of newly-exposed skin was unmarked but seemed somehow damaged, defective: helplessly stark, like a blind eye. On several occasions, recently, my head has turned to unlikely men: ordinary men, their necks chafed on collars; me, tender towards their painful plainness.

I thought, *So, Vivien knows. She and I know. You can say what you like, but we know.* I wondered what he would say; how he would try to explain away this, this aliveness.

'And she's right.' There were those eyes again, shocking blue, momentarily unflinching. 'You *do* make me happy. Always.'

In my stomach was an odd sensation of anaesthetised pain: a pain without the pain. Carefully, I said, 'Well, that's mutual.'

'Yes,' and suddenly he was cheerful, 'but that's because we haven't known each other for long, so, of course, it's natural that we enjoy each other's company, that we have plenty to say to each other.'

I said nothing.

He dropped a tone for, 'Now look what I've done, I've made us both miserable,' and ventured a weak, conciliatory smile.

I copied.

'Let's try not to be miserable.'

I was thinking, *What you're telling me isn't making sense.*

'And I'm afraid that there's more trouble.'

I looked up; I must have been looking down, because I looked up and there were his eyes, again. For other people, a look into another's eyes is an opening up; but Edwin looks to lay down the law, to put up a barrier, to keep me in my place. The look of his eyes says *Listen to me; because what I say, goes*.

'Vivien's mother is coming to stay with us.'

'Oh.' *So*? This was not of prime interest to me, at that moment.

'For a month.'

'A *month*?' Sheer surprise took over.

'She always comes for a month; shuts the bar, comes for a month.'

'And stays with *you*?'

'And stays with us.'

'But why *you*? What about those sisters?'

'They don't have room: Judith is in a studio; the druid has children. She'll go to them for weekends or whatever, but our place will have to be her base.'

'For *a month*.'

'For a month.' An inward breath before he said, 'So, *I'll* have to call *you*, because she'll be around; and even when she's elsewhere, she bleeps into the machine for messages.'

'*Your* machine.'

'Vivien taught her. The reason is that she has arrangements to make, visits to arrange,' he sighed, 'or, so I was told.'

'Why don't you invite her to open your post?'

He was subdued. 'Well, I do have my suspicions.'

'You do?'

He remained inexpressive. 'Well, I was going to ask you not to send anything; or, to send to work. When she's around, I'll go into work.' Then, 'I do have a sense that she's forever looking for evidence of something amiss in our marriage.'

Her too, huh? This was news: within the clan, there were misgivings; that had never occurred to me.

He surprised me further with a weary, 'But I suppose that people can tell.' And then he was saying, 'She's thinking of retiring back here. The opposite from usual, I suppose: retiring from Spain to England. Odd, to think of her retiring.

Odd, to think of retiring. I have no idea where I'll be, when I retire, or with whom.' The expression in his voice and on his downturned face was one of exhaustion.

All that I could say, a moment later, was a gentle, 'Do you think that you'll manage to talk to me, when she's here?'

His raised gaze differed from the usual blank blue; was hazy; warm. 'What do *you* think? By hook or by crook.'

Since leaving him yesterday, I have been pondering those eyes, humming,

> *Those eyes,*
> *Those sighs,*
> *It's the tender trap.*

I have been reading a book on colours, to try to identify the shade: *ultramarine*, meaning not *ultra-blue* but *from over the sea* because, in medieval times, the dye had to be imported; was so rare, expensive, valued as to be favoured for portraits of the Virgin Mary. Without the book, I would have settled for royal or peacock blue. Cobalt. Delphinium blue. The blue in Dufy's *Baie des Anges*; in Chagall's stained-glass windows. The blue of much that is precious to me, luxuries that I have collected and been given, over the years: bed linen; bottles of bath oil; a tall vase; a handbound photograph album. The blue of my souvenir of my first trip to Paris, when I was a toddler: a pendant, the size of an adult's little fingernail, on which is a representation of Notre Dame. I am disarmed by a delicious, inexplicable thrill and forboding whenever I see that charm: a physical memory, I suspect, of the cathedral – its enormity, its solemnity – or perhaps of being told the tale of Quasimodo. The blue of the fragment of glass which is Sellotaped to a postcard and displayed in the window of our local newsagent with a scrawled plea: *Wanted, a piece of blue glass like this (but bigger).*

I picture my emotions as that colour, a ruinous blue; a blotch of ink dropped on to paper, the paper instantly drenched and dissolved. Edwin, too: I think of our souls as the same shade and consistency. Philip's emotions form his outline in cool, bright, emerald green, but with something more to it, a lustre of barely detectable red threads. Carl is incandescent, a blur of overexposure.

I had coffee with Carl a couple of days ago, here, in the park. When I arrived on the café's terrace, he was at a table beneath the tangled, tasselled canopy of vines, and sunshine was trickling down on to his hair, face, his cotton-covered shoulders, his arms, hands. His smile folded up his eyes. As I fussed with the vacant chair, he reclined in his own. He was cupping a bottle of mineral water, and condensation pooled in the crease between each palm and thumb. He said, 'You look summery.'

'Messy,' rushed, crumpled.

'Bedizened, to use a delicious word I came across, the other day. You know what that means?'

I shook my head.

'Means, *tastelessly dressed*. Not that you *are*, of course, but I've been desperate to say the word.'

'*Bedizened* . . .'

'Old English, I suppose. Like bedazzled.'

My gaze was jolted back into his, which he lowered to indicate my dress.

I deflected with, 'You don't think the colour's too much?' Gingercake colour.

'Ah, colour,' he was doubtful: 'don't ask me, I'm no good with colours; good with shapes, no good with colours.'

I could have said, *But there is nothing to this little dress other than the colour; there is no shape; the only shape in this shift is mine.*

With his fingertip tapping the bottle, splattering the film of slush, he said, 'I guessed from your nickname that you have red hair.'

'But you can *see* . . .' As I said these words, I understood: 'You *can't* see that I've red hair; you're colour-blind.'

'Red/green.' A dismissive hitch of his shoulders.

But I was hooked. 'You're colour-blind.' One of my clear childhood memories is of my mother telling me that there are people – men – who cannot distinguish between red and green. To me, this was more fantastical than any fairy tale, and, ever since, I had wanted to meet one of those mythical men: a man who passes for perfect but has a few flawed stitches in the lining of his eyes, a pinhead cluster of dud cells which makes his whole world alien to me. I will live my life blind to the blurring of red and green which Carl has all around him.

'You don't think I'm horribly defective?'

'Oh, I think you're wonderfully defective.'

His eyelids rose; the corners of his mouth, too. 'Let me tell you: no one, *but* no one, has ever said that to me before.'

'Let me ask you: what colour is my hair? I mean, *to you.*'

'Oh, I don't know . . .' The answer seemed to require concentration; the concentration seemed genuine.

I wondered: what was there to decipher, of elemental colour?

And I recalled the facts: red raises blood pressure, respiratory and pulse rates; red light enables optimum vision, is the light in which air traffic controllers work; red, comprising the longest waves discernible to the human eye, is the closest of all colours to sound.

Eventually he decided upon 'Brownish.'

I laughed, hard. '*Brown*ish? Brown*ish*? No one has ever said *that* to *me* before. Oh, God, I'm in *heaven.*'

He braved a smile. 'You're in a little black dress.'

I have noticed that whenever I look at Carl, he is looking at me. Unlike Edwin, he has no fear of me. He never sneaks a glance. There is never a sidelong glance. He never looks me up and down. There is nothing to that look of his: he looks so as to see; as simple as that. And I like that. He sees me, sees my imperfections but perhaps sees perfections, too. Or, to him, imperfections are *facts*; they *are*; they are *me*. I have a feeling that he sees me as I see these trees. I see no perfect tree. They are trees and that is their glory.

WAYLAID

❧

That most dismal of days – drizzle, bath, unmade holiday plans – was a week ago. The word *dismal* – I remember this from a childhood history lesson – comes from days on the medieval calendar that were marked as unlucky. That day, when I had arrived home from the walk and fed Hal, I listened to Fern's message; the message that Philip had told me was there. By this time, Annie had added another (consisting simply of *Annie to Poppy . . . Annie to Poppy . . .*). Between the two was a faint remnant of a previous message, washed up from the depths of the tape. The voice was Edwin's and his words were, *It's me, and here I am in New York, and I've . . .*

The following words, I remembered, had been, *a little while to spare.*

I played the sequence again but heard only Fern and Annie.

I checked once more, and, yes, there was Edwin, with those same words.

Pressing *play* again, I heard no one but Fern and Annie. Another four presses produced no further sound of Edwin. He seemed to have gone; but had he gone for good? Had Philip heard him? Why else had he been so keen to inform me that he had heard Fern? And if he had heard him, what would he have made of those words? How would that fragment have sounded, to him?

It's me . . . and *. . . in New York.*

Which is the most damning?

Yesterday, I went to a wedding in the West Country. I went alone, because the bride is a childhood friend and barely knows Philip. Her choice of a Friday made excuses easy: across the bottom of my invitation she had scrawled *Don't worry, I don't expect Philip to take a day off work*; and on my RSVP I wrote *Sorry, Nancy, but Philip has taken all his holiday for this year, can't take another day*. There was no excuse for me, though: this one was critical; this would have been one too many invitations turned down. Anyway, I was pleased for a chance to catch up with a few old, rarely-seen friends. So, I arranged to go. Edwin said, 'Shall I come and meet you off your train, on your way across town? for a quick coffee?'

'No –' *you don't understand, you haven't listened*, 'it's a Friday.'

'And?'

I was going to have to say the words: 'Vivien's home.'

'I'll say that I have to go into work.'

'At eight o'clock in the morning?' The wedding was mid-day; I would have to leave Paddington by nine.

'That I have to go into work *early*.'

'*That* early? When have you *ever* been into work *that* early?' Certainly never since I had known him. He had never even been into work on a Friday, since I had known him: Friday was their day – his and Vivien's – together at home.

'Well, no . . .' But then an impatient, 'There has to be a way. For God's sake, there has to be a way for me to leave my own home when I want.'

The day before yesterday, Edwin had confirmed, 'I'll be in that coffee shop near your platform.' But yesterday, as I walked down the platform, I spotted him, ahead, sitting on a thick pipe which runs along the wall a couple of inches above the floor. His arms were folded over his shins. In that position, he looked boyish. I had never before seen him look boyish. I have seen so little of him, though. He had been watching me. Even when he realised that I had seen him, his composure was unchanged, and, expressionless, he continued to watch me. A long look: from a long way, for a long time; longing.

'You said you'd be in the coffee shop,' I mock-protested, sitting beside him, leaning towards him for our formal, ritual exchange of a kiss.

The kiss done, he handed me a takeaway espresso: 'Coffee.' Then he said, 'I wanted to be *here*.'

'And here you are.' I smiled.

'And here I am. You look nice.'

A compliment was unusual from him; unprecedented, even, perhaps. Even he had sounded surprised.

'I *am* nice.'

His laugh was like a cough. He conceded, 'You are.'

The formalities and pleasantries over, I asked, 'Are you in trouble for leaving so early?'

He stared over the concourse, his lips hardened. 'Oh, I'm in trouble whatever I do.'

This was uncharacteristically candid, and I was unprepared. 'I'm sorry.'

'Not your fault.' Then, '*Not* your fault,' as if I had demurred. He dipped his face into his hands and rubbed his eyes.

'You look tired.'

He surfaced from his hands with a rueful smile. 'I *am* tired.' Then, '*And* we've bloody, bloody dinner this evening with Adam and Ginny; why don't they leave us alone? Adam and Ginny, and William and Clare, and Penny and Joe: does anyone else want to invite us to play happy families, this month? Or, rather, to *watch them* play happy families, for which, frankly, neither Vivien nor I have the stomach, at the moment.'

A snatch of song inside my head:

> *Manhattan, I'm awfully nice,*
> *Nice people dine with me*
> *And even twice.*

'And, anyway, that's not where I want to be; they're not who I want to be with. So, all I do is drink. I'm pathetic. The evening before last, I drank far, far too much.'

I was stunned by all this, and warbled a pointless, 'Rory and Lucy?'

He nodded. 'Vivien had to take me home in a taxi. From Richmond. I suppose that I'm still recovering. From the alcohol, I mean. Well, yes, and the fare. For that fare, I could have flown to Paris. Not that I would have enjoyed Paris any more than that taxi ride, in my state. What a shame: I was unconscious for the longest taxi ride of my life. The longest in *Vivien's* life, certainly, as I doubt that she'll ever allow me to forget.'

I had no idea what to think, where to start, or how to come up with a response. He looked helpless: such chaos, for someone usually so controlled. I recalled how he had looked when I had first seen him: untroubled, intact, untouchable. *And now look; look what I have done.* The tender skin beneath his eyes was bruised by tiredness and the barely dispersed hangover. Punch drunk. 'You must feel awful. I shouldn't have made you come here, this morning.'

'You didn't, if you remember.' He turned those dense eyes on me: a look that, I suspect, was intended to be meaningful but because, as usual, he declined to add facial expression, remained blank. *Blank for all occasions*, like a greetings card. Then the gaze flowed away behind me as he said, 'I shouldn't be here, but not because of my hangover.'

I was utterly still in that slipstream; I was sheer anticipation: *he will say something; everything will be resolved; I will know where I stand.*

He sighed, 'I'm *tired* because I'm tired of *this*.'

This . . . this . . . which particular *this*? I cast around. Me? tired of me, of coming to meet me? to keep me happy? Or Vivien? tired of being married to her while wanting to be with me? or of being in love with me while wanting to stay married to her?

This could be good, bad, or in between.

He said, 'This atmosphere at home. The complete lack of civil words between us. Her questions.' He sipped his cappuccino, an action which should have been simple, a stalling action, but which was complicated by the froth: he had to lick his lips, twice, then worry and wipe them. In solidarity, I took a mouthful of my own coffee, but of course came away clean.

'Questions because of the phone bill?' I did not presume to say *because of me*.

'No. Yes.' He winced, 'Not always.' Shook his head. 'Not only. There's so much . . .' A frown. 'There's everything.' Then, 'Hardly helps that her mother's with us,' and an almost-amused, world-weary, 'can you imagine?'

'No,' truthfully.

Then he announced, 'Vivien has decided that she can't trust me, and I can't say that I blame her.'

I concentrated on my coffee.

'And that's hardly a happy state of –' the unsaid word was *affairs*. 'Hardly a happy state. For instance, she doesn't know that I'm here.'

I blotted my response with another mouthful of bitterness. Otherwise, I would have said, *Well, I know that*. I would have said, *Do you think I don't know that?*

'I don't know if I'll ever be able to tell her, ever again, that I'm seeing you.' This was said with some sadness.

I thought, *You don't know what you want, do you?* And realised that, in contrast, I did. I had undergone a thorough, unequivocal change of heart. All that was unclear to me, now, was whether what I wanted would in fact happen, and how. What I wanted was to live with him, to love him, to have him love me. I wanted to discover if that was possible. And to discover if that was possible, I wanted to have a love affair with him.

He was saying, '*She's* trustworthy, you know. Absolutely. But, oddly, I don't respect her for that.'

No, but you will.

And what a cold, hard word: *respect*. He had chosen that moral term rather than *understand*, or *envy*, or any emotive word. He could have chosen *love*.

Oh, but you will, Edwin.

For now, he had to think of Vivien as stay-at-home, stick-in-the-mud, shallow.

In time, you will.

Until then, there would be no telling him. And then, he would think of respect for her as all his own idea. He would never know that I was there before him.

Gently, I checked, 'What do you want me to do? Do you want me to – I don't know – do any different?'

'No. No. I want you the same as ever.' With that, he stood, and I followed. I followed him down into the tube station and on to the train. For the remainder of the journey, he was as full of fake cheer as Christmas, entertaining me with tales of Vivien's mother. Nothing more of his domestic trouble was said.

Until yesterday, I was certain that what was needed was talk; that talk was the answer; that words would lead us step by step from this limbo of unhappiness, sleeplessness, drunkenness. As if words were stones rather than air. Of course I knew that the words had to be a particular type: we needed to talk, but not of the Vivien-scrutinised phone bill. I knew that our words would have to be heavier; fundamental; of feelings. Then came yesterday, and there we were, talking, of feelings; but still, in a sense, everything was unsaid, submerged. His words muddied the situation; they were equivocal, retracted, unexpected: one step forwards; two, back. And perhaps he will never use words of the right kind; perhaps all his words, always, will have that dark blue blur to them so that I have to read between the lines.

Then, yesterday, I discovered that the right kind of talk is not, as I had believed, of feelings, but of wants. We should have had less talk of what *is*, and more of what *could be*: words that can show us a way forward, but commit us to nothing. We need vision, if only, in the end, for us to turn back in the light of it.

Those words, though, yesterday, were *his*: there *he* was, talking, of *his* feelings. Whose fault, though, was that? I chose silence. At home, too, with Philip, I say little. I am sliding into wordlessness. But was that my fault, yesterday? I had to listen hard to follow him; had I tried to join him, to meet him half-way, I ran the risk of tripping up. I am so wary of putting a foot wrong; of stepping out of line, the thin line between reassuring him of my feelings for him and frightening him with them. I have never been so shy of my own words. He needs reassurance, he looks so wounded in my presence. But he is scared of me: I can see that, too. This fearful tentativeness between us is odd because I feel so secure whenever I am with him. That is what I feel, above all: safe; the world, stopped. But the truth is that the world never stops, and our problem is that we cannot stay as we are, nor do we seem able to move. I am reminded of my father explaining to me the principal danger of flying: engine failure on the runway when a plane is travelling too fast to brake but too slow to take to the air.

We do not need words: we need a kiss. In films and books, that is how people wake from this spell. Because a kiss is unequivocal. No, there *are* equivocal kisses; but, still, a kiss is a fact. They exist in time and space; with each one, the world moves on. I am comforted to think of the independent existence of kisses; to think of them out there in the universe, like those medieval angels on a pinhead.

But a kiss with Edwin seems as unlikely as those pirouetting angels. How can all this be so very difficult? *A kiss is just a kiss.* Nothing has ever been so difficult, even when I was a teenager. With Edwin, every word and touch is stymied. He has only rarely touched me, and only ever in passing, to place his lips on my cheek: a hand on my shoulder, or in the small of my back. And today, thinking about all this, I have been followed around by the echo of someone else's long-ago touch: one touch to my arm, from a boy who became a friend on a holiday when I was fourteen or fifteen. He – Ian – was a year or so younger than me. I did not have a crush on him, he was not crushable material, he was nothing special, although, in retrospect, that was what was special about him: my mother's appraisal was that he was *nice-natured, well-mannered, well-behaved*. To me, he was shy, a beguiling mixture of formal and open. One evening, he and I were with a few other friends, walking back from town to the hotel, in darkness, when a car came speeding towards us from a blind bend in the road. As our small crowd moved to one side, his hand came on to my arm: that was all, and just that once, but that touch is one of the fondest memories I have. The protectiveness of the gesture was not what impressed me, but, rather, the unconsciousness, unselfconsciousness: that natural, relaxed, intuitive awareness of me as a companion physical presence.

Yesterday, on the way home from the wedding, I missed a train because, on my way across town, dropping into a department store to buy buttons, I was waylaid. Having taken a wrong turning in stationery, I came up against gloves: hundreds of inanimate, supple, slender, unreal hands. I was captivated by the many sizes, materials, colours. Running a pair through my fingers, slipping my fingers inside, I was struck by their lack of adornment, I realised how hands are more jewelled than anywhere else on the body. On and around hands are the pieces that have most significance: rings; christening bands; even those SOS bracelets. Then, looking down a row of kid gloves, I was thinking of hands on keyboards. Instruments other than keyboards have to be held or steadied as well as played; but on keyboards, both hands make music and do nothing else. As I moved along to eveningwear, my thoughts turned again to Abbe's photographs; in particular, the portrait of Mabel Normand, the only subject in that exhibition whose hand was a blur of movement. The hand on her hip was somehow too much for the slow release of his shutter. She differed in other crucial respects, too: her slouch; her bucktoothed grin; her goggle eyes. My mother's description of her would be *no oil painting*.

Presumably, Mabel could have played this up, could have played the comic; but, no, that smile was bashful, hopeful. The caption beneath the photo had condensed a troubled life: her notoriety; her procrastination of marriage to the man who, for years, everyone expected her to marry; and then her untimely death. That was the word: *untimely*; an eerie word, quite without adequate substitution.

Standing there amid that extravaganza of gloves, remembering that old photograph, I was fairly certain that I could go through the store asking everyone I came across if they had ever heard of her, and find no one who had. For all her notoriety, a mere lifetime later she is gone without trace. On the evidence of that portrait, the notoriety was incidental, accidental; I saw a genuine irreverence, a touching failure to suppress it. Whenever I look at that face, my unvoiced response to the Abbe-coaxed smile is a fond, *I wish you'd been my friend, I bet you could've shown me a thing or two.*

'Go for it,' were Drew's words, the measured and considered words of my friend Drew, down the phone, when I told him about Edwin. An unsettling, disorientating combination: those words, that tone. He followed with a fairly breezy, 'Just don't jeopardise what you have with Philip.'

I said nothing. I could have asked, *How is that possible?* I could have said, *That's impossible.* I should have explained, *That's the problem.*

Having told him the story, though, I had assumed that the problem was taken as read. Perhaps I should have sprinkled clues, key words: *cake*, *can't*, *have*, and *eat*.

He would have laughed, though, and countered, *You live*

on cake. At some point, he would have gone on to use the phrase, *The best of both worlds.*

The problem is that, eventually, two worlds will boil down to one; the one for which I am accountable.

I should have said, *That is not what this is about.* Had he not listened? I could have asked, *How do you know what I have with Philip?*

As soon as he had advised me to lie, to stay, I knew that this was not what I wanted. I said nothing; should have said, *This – the lies, the staying – is what you have, or want to have, with Sarah.*

He was exclaiming, 'Why are you dragging your heels?' No thought went into his words before they were spoken.

I said, 'It's not up to me, alone. And I feel that I can't push him, that there's something that he can't . . .' unfortunately, only one word would do '. . . stomach.' Whenever I am with Edwin, now, that is what I feel I am in the presence of: some failure to stomach.

Drew was dismissive. 'Well, he's mad. Or stupid. Or something.' Then he said, 'Don't leave Philip. Philip is perfect for you.'

There was nothing I could say. I made a small sound of acquiescence. So, suddenly, I was misleading Drew, too. That was all that was required: one wordless sound.

Drew saw me through the winter during which my relationship with Casey came to an end. We were students, we had very little money and one of our main, shared problems was that our house was cold. He introduced me to the Spectators' Gallery of the local pool. *Sod the swimmers*, he would say, *soak up the free sauna.*

We would sit there for as long as we could bear: reading, gossiping, eating cheap, pale, overly-sticky chocolate that we bought from a vending machine. I remember once, when, as we were leaving, a boy stopped at the end of the highest diving board, and his manner of stopping – *only just* – stopped us too. And, so, we were held up there in that gallery, unable to leave before he dived. From his raised and rigid arms, his definite aim, we saw that this was to be a dive, no simple jump. On the ground, similar boys cheered, jeered, turning his failure of nerve into a spectacle. He played to them by standing tall on the lip of the platform and bowing deeply: *Thank you, fans*. Eventually, he had made spectators of everyone. Countless times, he sauntered back to the ladder, to freedom, before the raised pitch of their pleas lured him to return. Then, he would sit on the end of the platform and swing his legs: an elaborate show of making a decision as to whether he could be bothered. Around him, fellow divers came to walk the concrete plank. Some belly-flopped, snapping open the surface; others flew below the water through invisible holes that they made with their fingertips. Up in the steaming gallery, we promised ourselves one more minute, again and again. We worked ourselves up, worked our way through two more bars of chocolate. I remember that he did dive, perhaps ten minutes later; but, oddly, I remember nothing of it.

When I was with George last week, he talked of a woman with whom he had worked more than thirty years ago. 'She was extraordinarily good, had all the makings of an excellent detective, but disaster struck: she fell in love with one of our chaps who was married – had an affair, whatever – and when that didn't work out, turned to drink. Such a shame. Had to leave the Force, of course. A couple of years later, she was done for insurance fraud.'

I could have been listening to a history lesson: in history, people suffered unimaginable, pitiable fates. Modern me would be safe from doom. Unhappiness, no; but doom, yes. Whatever happens, I will escape with my life. That unfortunate woman's loss of self-respect and livelihood was predictable: a downward spiral was what happened to such women; was all that could happen to them. In the fifties, women seemed fashioned for disaster: improbable, hourglass figures;

lethal heels; handbags with clasps that had to be pinched open; clip-on earrings. For me, mention of the fifties never fails to bring to mind that television advert from my childhood – from the sixties – in which the Hitchcockian blonde descends the steps from a plane, lamenting under her breath, *My girdle is killing me*. Incredibly, the suggested solution to her problem was to wear an eighteen-hour version.

When George told me about that woman, I remember thinking. *And, anyway, I never drink to – what is the expression? – drown my sorrows.*

I do remember that: thinking, *what is the expression?*

Drown.

Say it.

Drown.

George had remembered her because he was telling the tale of an arrest to which she had accompanied him: the arrest of a bogus doctor.

'Really?' I had interrupted him, amazed. 'Really bogus?'

He laughed. 'Really bogus.'

'Well, no, I mean, I'm surprised: did you really come across . . . boguses?' I faltered over the plural, wondered whether I should have said bogi.

'Oh, regularly, over the years.' His turn to look surprised, but because of my naivety. 'They're around . . . doctors . . . lawyers . . .' Another laugh. '*Of course* doctors and lawyers; never any bogus dustmen.'

Or housewives.

The story was that the bogus doctor had caused a fuss, had refused to leave his house, so George had told him to report to the police station by eight o'clock that evening. 'And my fellow officer used to say that that was one of the most important lessons that she ever learned: an arrest doesn't necessarily require strong-arm tactics; nine times in every ten, they'll come of their own accord.'

I was unconvinced. 'But how could you know that he'd oblige?'

He gave me that look again. 'Where else would he go? These people have nowhere to go. They're loners. They give themselves up.'

Last week, on the phone, Edwin said, 'I had a conversation with George, the other day.' I went to murmur, *Oh, yes?* but he was already saying. 'He tells me that you have an admirer.' The tone was amused, indulgent, but painstakingly so: a deliberate effort to seem casual. I could hear the echo in the pit of his stomach.

I was dismissive: 'Oh, yes.'

The echo was why I did not laugh and say, *More to the point, Edwin, I have a husband*. That, and the shock that they had talked about me. How had that happened? One of them would have had to raise the subject. Who did that? and how? *Talk about*: that seemed apt; because for some reason, no reason, in my mind's eye they were wandering around me, discussing me as if I were a sculpture. A pleasing vision: I would like to be a sculpture. In that conversation of theirs, I had had another existence. I had had an existence. How did Edwin feel when he heard my name, in conversation? He had had to say my name, listen to the fall of that parcel of his own breath through the air towards George; listen for whatever he could hear. And how did he feel to hear my name in someone else's mouth? For what did he listen, then? Fondness? Awe? Suspicion? Until then, he would have only heard my name from Vivien, if at all, which could have been unpleasant; from which he would have cringed. I had heard his name in my conversation with Drew. I had said his name to Drew, several times, and had had his name said back to me.

Once, Drew said, *This Edwin guy*. I smothered a laugh: is anyone less of a guy than Edwin?

George had been referring to Carl. He had come across Carl having coffee with me on the terrace in the park. I wonder how he knew, though? Probably how I know: and I have no idea how. Carl's adoration is simply obvious, indisputable, primary. Deluded, but with no unpleasantness: the word is *transparent*; the expression, *open book*. Soon, he will discover that whatever he imagines he sees in me is not in fact there, and then he will come to his senses, move on. Get over me. Move on to someone suitable. Younger. Undamaged.

Edwin's call was a bad time to discuss admirers. He was in a phone box, his voice slightly raised over heavy traffic oozing along a road in heavy rain. He had tried earlier to reach me, but I had gone to the corner shop. His message was, 'I'm soaked and miserable and you're not there.' As ever, the tone was even, but I heard his amazement that I was not there: breathtaken, as if my absence in his time of need was genuinely incredible, somehow against the order of things. And he did indeed sound miserable: not petulant or melodramatic, just desolate. When I had heard his message, I dialled his mobile, but the mechanical woman answered with, 'Sorry, the person you are calling is not available.'

A succinct expression of my predicament; I replied aloud to her, 'You can say that again.'

Over our coffee, Carl and I had been discussing admiration: that of others for him. During the past few years, he seems to have had more approaches from men than I have ever had. These bother him less than current troubles with several women, older women. 'Middle-aged women,' he lamented; which, I was disappointed to discover, referred to women in their late thirties or early forties. Women facing the last ditch, the end of the prime, the fall from grace.

I shrugged. 'You're a pretty boy.' *Goes with the territory.*

'So people tell me. But what the fuck does my face matter?' *Not just a pretty face.* 'Because one day, I'll be all jowls and bags, the same as everyone else.'

He will never be the same as everyone else: his lean face will age well; moreover, his is a face to grow into. He is too young to know that beauty is a gift.

'My looks have nothing to do with *me*.'

Precisely the definition of gift.

'I didn't even know until I was sixteen, when my friend Nick called me a good-looking bastard.'

The peculiar, particular blindness of the beautiful. And a man, disinterested, had had to tell him. In no uncertain terms.

Despite his obliviousness, he has lived the life of a beautiful person. There are statistics to prove how such a life is plain sailing: an attractive person is more likely to be given a job; is less likely to be convicted by a jury. A month or so ago, on my London-bound train, there was a man with the most extreme and extensive facial disfigurement I have ever seen. I was *en route* to meet Edwin; but when I arrived, I told him nothing of that man. How could I? How would I have raised the subject? And why? And which words would I have used? The man's face was a physical phenomenon; I would have needed an extraordinary, specialist vocabulary. So, I said nothing of him, and the experience lodged unworded in my throat like a guilty secret.

I had looked away within the same instant I saw that man. Initially, I was pleased with my speed, my skill in glancing away, expressionless; I was sure that I had saved him from something. But from what? From a second or two of staring from one person in one train carriage? How could I have ever considered that, within a lifetime of stares, the aversion of my gaze was some small salvation?

I have lived for almost thirty-two years, and have been in hospitals, and in foreign countries, but I have never seen anything like that man's face. His scarring was like a burn, or an advanced malignancy, perhaps a congenital malformation, some disease of connective tissue; but of another order. In a town nearby to the one where I grew up, there was a woman who had no face: the result, I suspect, of a childhood fall into a fire. Colour and features had been burned off. She had sparse hair above a high forehead. Whenever I spotted her, she was shopping: laden bags; brisk. As a child, I was comforted to see that she shopped, and so briskly; she did me a service by shopping. I had assumed that I would never see a facial disfigurement worse than hers; I was confident that I knew the worst. Nothing could be worse than no face at all. How wrong I was. This man had extra face, he had lumps of scar tissue, in tomato red, luminous purple, livid.

My guess is that small children do not stare at him but turn and run, screaming. Older children will stare, confounded. No adult will ever look into that face twice. How odd, that the most visible person I have ever seen will be made to feel as if he is invisible. How ironic, when invisibility is what he must crave. I keep thinking of places where we are seen; all the places. Post office counters: for some reason, I think of post office counters; perhaps because they are the epitome of nowhere, for me, but will be as impossible for him as anywhere else.

Each of us is our face, first and foremost. I am so thankful that my face was untouched: I carry the memory of that man with me, as a reminder that I must always be thankful. If I stand still, I am easy on the eye. If I do not talk about my life, no one knows that there is anything amiss.

But if we are our face first and foremost, then our shape comes a close second. My unscarred face is nothing special, but what I have in my favour is my figure; or, lack of. Only recently did this dawn on me, and perhaps because this asset of mine has increased in value. The bodies of my peers are childbearing, nowadays: subsided like burned candles. My body seems to have become increasingly childlike: bony rather than curvy. I am having a second childhood. My due, given the first.

In swimming pool changing rooms, I detect other women glancing at me with naked envy and resentment. I should tell them that this is all that I have. No, not even this; this body is not the whole story. But then they see for themselves, as soon as I move; as soon as I step to the lockers, the showers, sinks. They see how I need to concentrate on something which, to them, comes naturally. This perfect body only moves perfectly in water. On land, I am stranded.

Back there on the terrace with Carl, I had protested: 'Listen, prettiness is temporary, but it *is real*. And is your personality more permanent? You could be knocked down by a car, tomorrow, and your brain messed up, wiped clean, whatever.'

Only when he remarked, 'You don't take sugar,' did I realise that there had been a silence, during which I had scooped up a teaspoonful and showered the grains into my cup.

All I could say was, 'Well, today I do.'

'And today you're, um . . .'

I was stirring, hoping that the sugar would dissolve into nonexistence. 'I'm what?'

He pointed to the envelope of the letter that I had been reading before he arrived; pointed to the title, *M Summerfield*

'Oh,' I laughed, realising my mistake: what he had said was, *Today you're M*. 'I'm always M: it's the first letter of my name.'

'You're going to have to tell me, or I'm going to have to make some joke about Sadie having a silent M.'

'Can't you guess?'

His glance was one of appraisal, before he ventured an uncertain, 'Miranda. You look like a Miranda.'

I do? 'Think.'

'Oh, okay, yes, think; this time, think. You know how to make a person feel clever, you know that?'

I gave in. 'Mercedes. Sadie comes from Mercedes.' My real name, which, in fact, feels unreal. Love it though I do, Mercedes seems unconnected to me; like a middle name. Or like something in a drawer; a constant, reassuring presence, but rarely seen; quaint, of sentimental value, handed down.

'Wow.' He stared.

I wondered what he was seeing. 'Do I look like a Mercedes?'

'There's a joke in that, isn't there?'

'Oh, don't stint: there must be several.'

'But seriously, was I stupid, not to have known?'

'People don't know unless I tell them.'

Edwin: the realisation; Edwin does not know.

'Do you have any brothers or sisters?'

'No,' my usual answer, the easy answer, the simple answer. No brother. Not for years.

Carl laughed. 'Because I wonder what they would have been called.'

Last week, George had said, 'You must have had a hard time, alone, as a child, an only child.'

'Yes,' I answered, truthfully.

'My sons had each other to help make up for how little they had of me.' We were strolling through the rose garden. 'I was of the opinion that bringing up the boys was my wife's job.'

'Uh-huh.' Carefully expressionless, I was in fact despairing: *Here we go again*. And, as always, wondering why: why test me, probe me, goad me? Sometimes his drawing attention to our differences – generational, cultural – seems genuine, he seems to want me to update him; but even then, I find this tiresome. Our friendship is tenuous enough, and rather than expose the weakness, I would prefer to enjoy his company: his worldliness, of a kind, a small kind; his stories; his unaccountable, understated, awkward affection for me.

'That was my opinion.'

'Mmm.' *Oh, I believe you.*

'Consequently I've never really known the boys: didn't, then; and now – because there's so much ground to cover – still don't.'

I must have made a sound, because he said, 'No, I don't think you realise,' and stopped still, so that I had to stop, too. 'You don't realise that the little they had of me . . . well, for instance, I never allowed talk at the dinner table. None, not a word: silence. Can you believe that?'

No. I stared, hard, straining to see the shadowy disciplinarian within the familiar avuncular figure.

'So Victorian,' he muttered, suddenly aghast and curious as if discussing someone else; and resumed walking, seemed more relaxed. 'You see, since I've known you, I've realised how bad I was as a father.'

'Oh, George, *no.*' How had that happened? How had I made him feel so bad?

'The last few weeks, I've tried a couple of times to bring all this up with them,' he raised a hand to stop an exclamation from me, 'no, I should know how they feel.' Surprisingly good-humoured, he said, 'And you know what? My wife tells me that they've been discussing whether I'm having a breakdown.' He laughed. 'What she's decided is that I've become sentimental. Imagine the shock, for her, because that's something she's never seen: me, sentimental. It's utterly foreign, to her.'

Foreign. I love the expression *far-flung.* And that, I suppose, was what I was for the year following Jacqueline's death. My final trip was the furthest. I went to San Francisco: I flew across the world, and came down to earth on that most notorious, feared fault line.

Before I went, I said to Annie, 'I need you to cover for me.'

Say what you like about Annie . . . With Fern, such a request would have turned into therapy. With Fern, everything turns into therapy.

Annie's answer was, 'As long as you tell me why,' but she was being mischievous, not serious.

The best I could do was, 'I will, eventually,' checking, 'is that good enough?' and adding, 'It's not what you think.'

'No?' Mock-disappointment.

'If it was, I'd tell you. I need to go away from here, to be alone. I can't explain, but I need to be more alone than I'll be if Philip knows where I am.' What I wanted was to be beyond him.

The problem was that I overshot and ended up beyond myself. San Francisco – my seventh trip in seven months, my final far-fling – was where everything caught up with me. One night, I woke and did not know where I was: a faintly familiar, sickening feeling. I waited the usual second or two, looking around the room. The room looked back. And sometime during that second or two, I realised that I had no memory at all: not only did I not know *where*, but I did not know *who* I was. The loss was sharp, overwhelming and physical, as if I had taken a step, and where there should have been ground, there was thin air. I lay there, nothing but eyes, looking and looking, strenuously draining the details of the room into me, dredging my small world for clues.

Then, suddenly, I was up, out of bed, at the window. Even now, I am reeling from the impact of that jet of adrenaline. Even at the time, I was awed by that instinct to move upwards, outwards, away from trouble, *Go, go, go*. I seemed to believe that if I discovered where I was, then I would know who I was. I was clear-headed, wide awake: wide open to the world, laid wide open.

My view of the room was moon-silvered. Fear, to me, had always been a small, dark place; but in that room in San Francisco, the truth dawned: worse than tightened darkness is blankness, is having no footholds. *Dust to dust*. Worse than sinking into the depths is being washed up, wide-eyed, but seeing nothing that makes sense. What was odd, though, and shocking, was that while I was crossing the room, I was thinking, over and over again, *It's happening*; as if my body had been waiting, had been haunted by this clean, pale oblivion.

I believed that I could survive, that I could become me again, but perhaps only because there seemed no alternative. I aimed for the window because I had to see the world, as much as possible of the world. Somewhere beyond the glass, there would be a toehold. What I did see, in the distance, was Golden Gate Bridge, and I thought, *That's familiar*. Yes, those were the words, I remember thinking those exact words: there was one of the wonders of the Western world, and I was thinking, *That's familiar.*

And then I remembered; as simple as that. Just as everything had been taken away, everything was granted once again. I stood at the window, shaking, relishing my lucky escape. Since then, I have told the tale to several people, all of whom have suggested that I write something down to keep by the bed as a failsafe: perhaps *I am Sadie Summerfield.* But I know that anything I write down is merely words: if I lose my memory, then *Sadie Summerfield* will mean nothing, because who on earth is she? In that room, I learned that there are circumstances in which no one can help, in which there is nothing that anyone can say to help me.

I suspect that, in San Francisco, I recovered my memory of having no memory. Like a playground joke: *I had amnesia, but I don't remember.* And like all good playground jokes, no joke at all. I have no memory of what happened to me when I was twenty-four. Afterwards, I had to believe whatever I was told, which was little or nothing, No one knew much; no one was there. No one except me. A tale has to be told, though, for an ending to be reached.

I think, now, that I took all those trips not because I was running away but because I was moving upwards and outwards, I was searching for clues. I was travelling the world to draw my coordinates, to try to discover where I was when I was at home; who I am. My problem is that whatever I discovered seems to have prevented me from coming back.

WISH

Last year, I watched a television documentary of a plane crash. I watched because even if I know that disaster is pending, I cannot resist the testimony of pilots: their calm, cautious attitude to that most bizarre and potentially hair-raising of activities; their world-weariness, all that talk of *gin-clear skies*. This particular disaster had happened more than a decade previously; the programme was an almost celebratory account of the aftermath, of how the incident was assimilated into the history of aviation, done and dusted. Investigators concluded that the cause was a flaw the size of a grain of sand, and those who spoke to the cameras were keen to convey their appreciation: *Imagine the chance of that*! A chance as small as a grain of sand in thousands of tons of metal. The minuscule flaw remained undetected during routine checks. Then, one day, years later, all of a sudden the damage was done: something ripped, something else came loose, a chain of devastation was unleashed, leaving the plane unnavigable. I failed to follow the technical talk, but the pilot described hauling on levers, using the rudder, banking into the wind: crude mechanics and physical force; superhuman tenacity and skill. A runway was approached, on to which the uncontrollable plane crashed, cartwheeling and exploding into several pieces. We – the viewers – saw this for ourselves, courtesy of an amateur video.

This was the moment of the amateurs: smashing into the ground, the plane entered the realm of bystanders. And this was America, the Midwest, so these eyewitnesses had a wide-eyed respect for the one truth, *The camera never lies*; they shared a beguiling, utterly unBritish assumption that they would be heard and believed. Their accounts contained the same phrase, again and again: *They came walking out of the cornfields*. No one had anticipated survivors, but suddenly there they were, *walking out of the cornfields*. A considerable proportion of passengers had been thrown clear into those fields and their falls broken by that corn.

Later, in hospital, when the pilot regained consciousness, his first question concerned survivors. When told the figure, he turned to face the wall and cried for two days. Eventually, following his recovery, he flew until he retired. He was speaking to the cameras from his retirement: his props were an armchair, a G&T, and, behind him, in the window, Californian sunshine. His demeanour was a charming mixture of pleasure that he was able to help, and regret that he was unable to be of more help. He seemed caught between stressing that the fault was a chance in a million but was nevertheless the precise occurrence for which he was trained: a chance in a million; all in a day's work.

The same phrasing was used by the eyewitness to the accident in which I was involved: 'She came walking out of the water.'

He was asked, 'Who did?'

'A girl.'

'A girl? Which girl?'

'We were in the dark and they were so similar, they were both – look, I don't know – girl-shaped. All I could see was that one had hold of the other, one was dragging on the other.'

That is all I have: someone's replies to someone else's questions. I was one of those two girls; but I do not know which one. One of us was walking. How? I was the only one who ever walked again, but not until much later. A doctor told me that the cause of my problem was bleeding and swelling; the rising pressure of that dammed blood. The damage must have taken time to happen. Perhaps there were moments following impact but before unconsciousness when I could walk.

But if possible for me, then not only for me; I was not necessarily the one who did the saving; I could have been the one who was saved. And even if I did the holding and dragging, how can I be sure that what I was doing was saving? The witness's description was, *had hold*, not *holding up*; and *dragging on*, which strikes me as an odd wording, significantly different from *dragging*. Even if the holding, dragging girl was me, how would I have known which way was up? I could have been dragging her back down, doing more harm than good.

She came walking out of the water: the same phrasing, but there the similarities end. For me, there was only one eyewitness, Eric Allanby Locke, aged sixty-seven, a retired telephone engineer of Cold Christmas, of all places. He and his wife were spending a weekend with his recently-widowed sister, and he had spent the evening in a local pub named The Case Is Altered. Of all places. He lacked the eloquence of those Midwesterners who had gone with their video cameras to watch hundreds of people falling from a blazing sky. Having had three pints, he was heading home along an unlit road; heading for a bridge across an even darker river. There were other differences, for me: no hero, no heroics; no corn to break a fall; no fellow survivors.

And there was the fundamental difference that he did not tell the truth; not the whole truth. I know that there is a missing piece. Whenever I try to remember what happened, I have that sensation of starting to take a breath but having the opening up blinded by water. Mr Locke would have known that no one who was inside that car could contradict him. He was the one who watched as the car skidded on the freezing overflow from the risen river, clipped the parapet, and flew from the bridge into the water. No doubt he reasoned that his omission made no difference; he would have said to himself, *What happened, happened.*

What did happen? The following day, my father went to the scene. He said, later, that marks on the tarmac showed how the car had skidded before reaching the ice. He remarked, too, that there was a dead badger at the side of the road. He mentioned that badger several times: *A big bugger*, he mourned, *in the prime of life, and intact, felled by a simple knock, a clean kill.*

Mr Locke made no mention of a badger. If our chaos had begun with a simple strike to the badger, he would have said so. And certainly he would have known: he was close, would have seen, or heard. And so I wonder: did our problems begin with him as he tried to warn us to avoid that badger? Just as I would have done, probably. Perhaps even my father would have done so. That could have been us: we could have stepped into the road, waved at the oncoming car, assumed that we would be seen in time.

I relied on Mr Locke for the truth and he let me down. He chose self-preservation, even though there was no need. He was not responsible for the unique, fatal combination of factors: the particular location, the lack of skill of the driver, the ice, the water.

This afternoon, I am kicking through a tinderbox of dropped leaves, wading ankle-deep through this dry flood that has followed the hottest summer since records began. From a distance, the grass seems to be covered with scraps of tangerine-coloured tissue paper. The leaves beneath my boots seem too small to have lived and died; they look like baby leaves. Some are ruby red; others, lime green, looking like sea creatures, neither properly plant nor quite animal.

A few minutes ago, I had the habitual exchange with the usual pair of fellow dog-walkers. Our comments, limited to the weather, are nonetheless heartfelt. Today, the man enthused, 'Lovely, again,' and I replied, 'Endless,' although the opposite is true, the end is close: autumn, late autumn, winter. We are on a downward tilt to winter, a list to end a listless summer. As I spoke, some seagulls rose from the grass nearby, and this, on the border of my field of vision, gave an impression of snow vacuumed by wind. Our so-called pleasantries do tend to feature the unpleasant: we complain to each other *Don't like the look of that*, or, *Cold wind, though*. That *though* is despite no one having previously spoken. Similarly, one of us will say *Better than we expected*. How could we know what each other expected? Because all daily dog-walkers check the forecast. I read in a newspaper article this weekend that there is a sixty-seven per cent chance of the forecast being correct. According to the article, there is the same chance of a marriage not ending in divorce.

I read the newspaper all day on Sunday. No music, all day; just a jangle of words. Across the top of the section entitled *Life* was an index: *Sex, gardening, fashion, interiors*. I side-tracked into the adverts; there was one for a Toby jug: *A jug guaranteed to bring a smile at breakfast*. I looked hard into that jug's grotesque face, but no: no smile. There was an advert for *The stairlift company that I trust*. As opposed, presumably, to those that are to be distrusted. The article on risk claimed that for every 500 million climbs of staircases, there is one death from a fall.

There have been no smiles, lately, at our breakfast table. Somehow, plans for a holiday have been abandoned, and we are entrenched now for the coming winter. On Sunday, Philip ventured, 'We need to talk.'

And I thought, *Talk will mean me saying that I'm not in love with you anymore, and that I'm in love with someone else*; I thought, *No, we don't need that*.

'Do we?'

He got the message, said nothing in reply, went from the room talking instead to Hal: that familiar mixture of chivvying and soothing that we use for Hal, *Come on, then, boy, come on, now, let's look for your lead* . . .

While he was in the park with Hal, I went into his study. This trespassing was a compulsion; as if there was something for me to find. But there was nothing for which I was looking. The room is familiar to me, I am often in there; he leaves the door open, sometimes I fetch stationery from the drawers in his desk and occasionally empty the bin. Nothing changes; there are trays of papers that have remained untouched for years. But in another sense, the room is unfamiliar, a home for books, journals, papers and correspondence written in jargon. The room is alien, too, in decor: the dowdiness. He seems comfortable with the functional atmosphere: he never complains; and anything decorative is deposited with disregard, the framed pictures and photographs propped against walls. I know that he loves the room – he seems more relaxed and absorbed, there, than anywhere else in the house – but it is uncared for. It is the heart of the house, for him, but he has little spare time to spend there. It is simply a space that he has reserved.

And that is how he uses space: collected, in boxes; the room is cluttered with caskets and drawers containing nothing. *Saving space* refers, of course, on the contrary, to depleting, compressing, negating space. Philip, however, preserves space. On Sunday, I went to the plywood box – a recent addition – on one of his shelves: the shelf-space taken up, then multiplied as the box consists of four drawers, each perhaps six inches square. Three were empty, but in one was a scrap of newsprint, an obituary. I knew the name: his old boss, first boss, mentor. I remember Philip going to the funeral, five years ago. Around that time, he must have cut the obituary from the newspaper. His boss's name was listed, with names of family members, and the date and place of death; no mention of work.

I was struck again that all Philip's thoughts and feelings are, to me, unfathomable, apart from those of which I am the focus: those, I know; those are expressed; those are simple. The only ones with which he trusts me. He could have come to me with the obituary and said something like, *See this? Remember him? I miss him.*

Could he not have said that? That would have been the very least that he could have said. But what would I have said in return? I have no idea.

It is a relief to be here in the park with Hal; a relief from his naughtiness. Lately, his misbehaviour has been notable. I remember that we were warned by his previous owner; and I remember my alarm: 'Naughty?' Initially, we had been told that he was no trouble. She laughed, and clarified, 'In his attitude; he's stubborn and lazy.' In fact, Hal has a sole vice: he likes to lie wherever he is forbidden. He lies on the prohibited sofas and beds like a pacifist, making his objection, making a spectacle. It is not as if his own bed is uncomfortable: I made sure that he has a designer model; designed to mould to his shape, to retain his own copious warmth. Moreover, he is never forbidden without good reason; the reason being his extravagant shedding of a blondness that is resistant to the Hoover. As Philip says, *Hal's fur abhors a vacuum.* I do try to accommodate his every whim: I did place a folded blanket on the sofa, for his use; but he would stretch ridiculously to reach the uncovered area, or, whenever I was away from the room, move there. Transgression is essential to his pleasure. Whenever he has colonised the forbidden, the world stops, for him: he tosses aside his routine, neglecting to prompt me for meals and walks.

He gauges a scale of naughtiness, with stunning accuracy. And then, whenever he is in the mood for disobedience, he aims for the top: of all forbidden places, he will lie in the naughtiest possible. New additions to the furniture are assimilated into the scheme within a week or so. Whenever we go to stay with friends, he makes observations of some kind as we look around the house or take our luggage to our room, because eventually he will disappear from our company and, moments later, we will find him settled somewhere expensive.

Within a day or two, he will have calculated, from our responses, the most heinous transgression. And from then onwards, unless we close the appropriate doors, that is where we find him.

Lately, I must have been failing to keep watch, or keeping less watch than usual, because every time I turn around, Hal is on a bed or sofa. Usually, he tries to cover up: as I turn the corner or come into the room, he is hurrying to the floor, skulking. Other times, though, he is brazen, rising reluctantly, with theatrical slowness, absurd stretches. Occasionally, he decides to take his chances, and refuses to move. And then, if I try to move him, he lolls, so that I end up calling for assistance: *Philip! Hal's on the bed again and he's making himself heavy*.

On one occasion, a couple of days ago, when we had brow-beaten Hal into leaving the bed, I remarked on this increased naughtiness, and Philip said, 'He senses the atmosphere, I suppose; he's unsettled.' His provocative tone brought me up sharp. I stopped pinching wisps of fur from the canine-crumpled duvet. We stood facing each other across the empty bed; stationed at opposite sides, as if for a vigil. I had never before seen him sullen, but now his expression was heavy on the eyes and lips: eyes, heavily-lidded; lips, slack. He was laying blame. Too restrained to blame me for his own unhappiness, he was blaming me for Hal's escalating delinquency. We were going to discuss the dog because we were unable to discuss ourselves. *What a cliché*, was my immediate, unvoiced response. I smiled, but not from amusement: my smile was because there was nothing to say; my smile was an acknowledgement. Because, yes, the atmosphere, here, *is* unsettling, and that *is* my fault. In retrospect, I am aware of a conspiratorial element to that smile, too: suddenly there was something that we both knew. In that moment, beginning with his comment and ending with my smile, we accepted as a fact that we are unhappy.

What we have, now, I suppose, is an unhappy marriage:

this marriage that, despite my own personal unhappiness, was once perfect. Unhappiness has seeped from me into my marriage. I feel caught off-guard: that is how I feel, even though I am the cause. *Unhappy marriage*: the phrase has the ring of newspapers, biographies, external and rather formal accounts. An expression that I remember from my childhood, from the talk of grown-ups. My own parents would have been said to have had an unhappy marriage. What do we say nowadays? We use words like *mess* and *problems*. And we are specific, diagnostic: the problem is her work, his jealousy, her ex-, his failure to commit. What are our problems, Philip's and mine? Where would we start? The old *unhappy* was a fairly innocuous word, covering a multitude of sins, sparing people, always said with a hush.

A week or so ago, answering the phone to Edwin, I said, 'Oh! I was thinking of you,' and, laughing, added, 'but, then, I'm always thinking of you.' This was no mistake; these words were intended. As I heard them, I recognised their daring, and I did feel a thrill, but a purely delicious thrill, entirely comfortable, utterly relished: no trepidation, nothing tremulous. I was thinking, *I said that*, and, simultaneously, *So what*? because what was there for me to lose?

I was buoyed up by the sunshine, which was gloriously autumnal: angled, aged, on the turn. Soaked in it, the room was blown: walls and windows insubstantial; corners clouded by brilliance. A ray, refracted and magnified by water in a clear glass vase, was bouncing on the wall behind me, which, under the impact, seemed to be wobbling.

Edwin's low, barely-sounded note of laughter had the pleasured feel of a purr. 'That's nice,' he replied, easily, 'and mutual.'

As easily, I said, 'We have to talk,' with unintentional kindness, as if this were a mere reminder of something previously discussed and agreed.

I listened for him to counter with, *About what?* I had no idea how I would respond.

But he said, 'Yes, I know,' and even more surprisingly, there was no echo of reluctance, nor even of relief. He sounded optimistic.

Then he asked, 'When?' and, before I could answer, continued, 'where? Because I'd prefer us to be on neutral ground.' Bizarrely, the tone remained amiable for this talk of conflict.

All that I could manage was, 'I don't know.'

'Well, we can think of somewhere. But in the meantime, do the usual: let me know when you're coming to town.'

And I agreed. I should have commanded *You see me today*; or at least *You see me tomorrow*. I should have objected, *Enough*; or, *Not good enough*. Thankful for small mercies, though, I permitted him his procrastination; his pointless, heartless procrastination.

The following day, which was a Saturday, and a perfect day, a distillation of this stunning summer, Philip asked if he could join me for Hal's walk. His fetching of the collar, lead, and scooper made a joint venture of my usually solitary duty, and his enthusiasm turned the routine exercise into quite an occasion. Hal was delighted because, as far as he was concerned, the pack had assembled. He trotted towards the park with obvious pride. The landscape was slapped with a lacquer of unadulterated sunshine. Freeze-framed in the windows of passing cars, we must have looked a picture: couple with labrador; our backdrop, quintessentially autumnal woodland.

We were strolling, chatting, reviewing plans, engagements and arrangements that had been made for the coming week, when I added that I was going to spend an afternoon in London. Instantly, I was aware of having made a mistake, which was surprising because on so many previous occasions I had said the same or similar with no consequence. And yet this surprise was no surprise at all, like the squeeze of a throat around something swallowed askew. We continued to walk, the leaves continued their jubilant clamour at our feet: ostensibly, nothing had happened, nothing was amiss, but I knew that I had overstepped some mark. From Philip came a sense of concession withdrawn, goodwill depleted.

He said, 'This Edwin . . .' but his tone was, as usual, good-natured, in good faith, interested, disinterested. A beguiling combination, which encouraged me to look at him. I was genuinely, intensely curious as to how he would proceed. For me, having lived for months in anticipation, the mere advent of the conversation was a relief. And already the unsayable had been said. In two words. *This Edwin* . . . That simple. Wonderful Philip. He knew. And now that he knew, surely the problem would begin to be solved. I detected a similar surge of hope from him, too. We had solved everything previously for each other: that was our gift. And now, side by side, making our way across the park, we would solve even this.

He tried again, and tried to be helpful: 'Poppy, is there anything I should know?'

But this was no help: I realised that I wanted a direct question to confront or dodge. Faced instead with this one, I was disoriented: the truth was that I did not know what there was to know. I *would* know, when I had talked with Edwin. I longed to ask Philip if he could wait a couple of days for the answer. The atmosphere between us was so civilised that such an outrageous request was almost credible. I said nothing, helplessly listening to my own lengthening silence, wondering what reply I would hear.

Gently, he prompted, 'Is this a love affair?'

He was trying so hard that he had asked the unaskable.

I said, 'Oh, no,' so glad to be able to give an answer, and one that he wanted to hear. For the moment, the truth was neither here nor there. Then, I thought, *Listen to yourself*: my words came back to me, struck me as a lie. The truth, though, is that Edwin and I have never even kissed: so, this is no love affair. There I was, all of a sudden, in a Wonderland where something that was obviously true – *Oh, no, this is no love affair* – was a lie. Unreasonably, I was furious with both Philip and Edwin for confusing me, for turning me into a liar; I wanted to scream, *See what happens when you leave me to deal with this on my own.* Unreasonable, I knew, because all three of us are on our own: each of us is struggling separately with a problem that is impossible to solve alone.

Ashamed, I quashed the rage, and hurried to make my lie more truthful: 'I do realise that my relationship with Edwin is rather intense.' Focusing on my shoes, my kicks into the leaves, I was nodding: a display of looking grave, of giving due consideration to the problem; I was at a loss as to what else to do.

Philip's response mirrored mine: kicks and nods.

I offered, 'I do realise that.' I did so much want to lessen the lie for him.

We continued nodding: hard to know when to stop, perhaps; or, reluctant to be the first to stop.

'Edwin and I have agreed to have a talk.'

Politely, Philip enquired, 'And when will you do that?'

'This week.'

'That's why you're going into London.'

'Yes.'

We both knew, by then, that the answer to his original question was in fact yes; or closer to a yes than to the no that I had given him.

No more on this was said. At pains to be kind, to avoid offending each other – his dismay, my unreasonable anger – we spoke instead of the weather, Hal, and the shopping that needed to be done. As soon as we were home, I went to do that shopping, and twenty minutes later I was in the high street, in a call box, dialling Edwin's mobile phone.

My message began, 'Listen. Philip asked me, this morning, about my relationship with you.' I balked at using Philip's words, *Love affair.* They could be used against me, if handed over: Edwin could come back to me with an incredulous,

derisive, *You're nice enough and I'm very fond of you ...
but, 'Love affair'*?!

'Oh, don't worry, you're safe: I said that everything's normal.' The resentment curdled into sarcasm. 'I should have said *Quite* normal.'

I was thinking, *Go on, hate me, see if I care*, and the bravado was genuine. As far as I was concerned, if he regarded me as unreasonable, if he failed to meet me half-way on this, then he was worthless.

'I *lied*; I *lied*, Edwin; I lied to Philip, and I hated doing that. I never have to want to do that again.' Despair rattled in these words; despair at Philip's helplessness, and mine. Not that I was the only one who had lied, nor the first: Edwin had had to do the same, to Vivien; he had endured months of tension with Vivien. One moment of awkwardness, for me, and here I was: kicking up a fuss, laying down the law. Edwin had asked nothing of me. Well, more fool him.

'We can't go on like this.'

My gaze went away on a succession of shoppers as flawless as a film-track.

'Like *this*: phone boxes. Mobile phones. Messages. Lies. The pretence that everything's okay.'

I was imploring a void that, sometime later, would be Edwin's appalled apprehension.

'Nothing's okay.' Not least that I had to plead blind in a glass cubicle in the high street.

Calmly, I continued, 'Yes, I know you said you'd talk to me. Next time I'm in town, you said, but that isn't soon enough.' *Isn't good enough* was what I almost said, but did not dare. I had relented, and now into my mind's eye crept an image of him, cornered.

'Look,' my free hand covered my face, 'I know you don't want this talk; I know that; I know. And nor do I; oh, God, nor do I.'

Him, cornered.

'And I hate to make you do this; I never, ever want to make you do anything that you don't want to do.'

Me, cornered, too.

'But we're in trouble.'

Without warning, my time was up; the dialling tone drummed. I redialled; did not listen as the automatic woman gave her perfunctory apologies and instructions. My intention was to finish the call, to say goodbye, but the Pavlovian beep brought a different response: all of a sudden, I was lamenting, 'And something else: how did you ever think that 1471 would solve anything? And why did I let you?'

The usual signings off remained to be done, but in the circumstances seemed absurd, so I simply hung up. Running around me on the glass was that footage of shoppers. I picked up my purse, thinking how likely I was to have forgotten it; which, on this day of all days, would have been unbearable.

The next afternoon, I brought my own mobile with me to the park, and dialled the code that summons messages.

'. . . Sadie . . .' He sounded winded. 'Thank you for your messages.'

Protocol observed, the rhythm faultless, but the tone and volume were weird: faint, inexpressive.

'You're right. About everything.'

No, not winded: devastated.

'I'm . . .' A shake of his head, perhaps; or a bitten lip. '. . . so sorry that you had to lie. I'm so sorry. I've been . . .' His eventual, chosen word had the thud of inevitability: '. . . stupid.' Then he said, 'Yes, we must talk, as soon as possible.'

I wished that he had said something like, *I need to see you.*

'By the way,' he finished, 'I didn't know, but my messages play back in reverse order.' He paused for me to grasp the implication. 'You have to laugh.'

Which I did.

* * *

We spoke yesterday morning to make arrangements: three o'clock, the French Institute. I arrived five minutes early and he was already there, at a table, sitting behind an impressive array of porcelain and stainless steel: cup, saucer, teaspoon, teapot, strainer, jug of milk, jug of water. He had been watching for me; when I stepped into the doorway, he flinched. His stare looked mauve; and, like bruising, both pitiable and unsettling. He was rigid and expressionless except for a slight pursing of his lips. As best I could, I breezed, and my own unwitting smile prompted a reciprocal, tentative twitch. The stare became dazed; his head tipping backwards as I came closer. With his chin raised and eyes widened, he looked more vulnerable than I had ever seen him. My heart took a gulp of blood. I bestowed the habitual chaste kiss to the cheek.

'You okay?' I nodded towards his teacup.

He said that he was, and I went to order a coffee.

At the bar, my back turned to him, I was defenceless against his unheld gaze; I was one big cringe, from my rounded shoulders to the unevenly worn heels of my shoes. For the first time in my life – there has to be a first time – I wondered if I tended to underestimate the size of my bottom.

But he isn't looking, I reassured myself; *You know he isn't the type.*

Did I know? What did I know of Edwin? Edwin: a married man, in love with me, here to see me. This was new: me, turned away, him, behind me. This had never happened before; even this had never happened. So much has never happened: day by day, I come across more. And lately, we do less: he has stopped offering to walk with me to the train. Station platforms are no longer a domain of ours. Lost ground. Lost time, our goodbyes coming sooner.

I wondered whether he had watched me crossing the room. If so, how did it look, the way that I moved? As startling as the first time he saw me stepping down behind him from the train? Or familiar enough, now, to be unremarkable, perhaps even undetectable? How *do* I move? I avoid the word limp, with its connotations of cuteness, like lisp: that sense of a slight missing of a mark. To me, a limp is a mere ambulatory tic: standard movement but with some element overlooked or skimped. My stagger, by comparison, is conscious and strenuous. *Limp* muddles two meanings: one, lame; the other, weak. Lame, yes, I am, well and truly; but weak, no. I have dud muscles, but the others work harder to cover for me. With each step, I have to raise that one hip. Otherwise, the foot would trail along the ground behind me. I would walk around with one foot forever in the past.

I remember the consultant's explanation: 'The line to this muscle has gone dead; the fault's at the exchange.'

I said, 'My foot needs a walkie-talkie.' This was in the days before mobiles.

He said, 'If you like.'

Oh, yes, I'd like.

Years before the damage was done, one of Casey's friends used to refer to me as, *The leggy redhead.* The description could still hold; still summarises me. Edwin must wonder: I am spectacularly lopsided, but unscarred. For anyone in the know, there is very little mystery: this one-sided weakness is the hallmark of a head injury.

I leaned on to the bar, hoping to attract the attention of one of the staff. They outnumbered their clientele: three of them, and no one but Edwin and me in the large room. They were conversing in French: two women, one man, early twenties. The man whipped towards me, but said nothing, gave no smile.

I did the smile for him. 'An espresso, please.'

He was role-playing a Jacobean prince: all glower and athleticism. Lunging to the coffee machine, he said something to me in French: bafflingly brief, this could have been no more than *oui*; but, being foreign, was, by definition, beyond me.

I took a guess. 'Single.'

He glared over his shoulder.

This time, my smile was mere reflex. Helpless, I was thinking, *Please don't do this to me; not today; not here.*

Slapping the coffee machine around, he continued the conversation with his two friends, at high volume. This was a performance. He had given me a minor role: quite simply, *English*. Standing there, I had plenty of time to think back to what I had once read on the topic of how the English are regarded by the French: the words I recalled were *goofy, awkward, gawky*.

His performance was a portrayal of reluctance, of a belief that he deserved better.

I thought, *Don't we all?*

What had brought him here? No desire to practise English. In French, he told me how much I owed him. He took my fiver with disdain: he knew that ruse. Into my palm, he counted the change both rapidly and emphatically.

And I said, '*Merci.*'

Back at the table, I asked Edwin, 'Do you speak French?'

He looked doubtful. 'A level.'

The A that, in the middle-classes, also stands for, *Annual-family-holidays-in-the-Dordogne*.

While I settled (cup, coat, purse), we chatted (my train journey, this new venue). Then he said, 'Anyway . . .' head inclined and gaze benevolent.

Despite the focus, I had a sense of being looked at from a distance. Of being looked down on. His bearing said, *Chin up, old gal*. I wondered how he had looked at his wife when confronted with the phone bill. I wondered if she had ever thrown anything at him. And, incredibly, in spite of all this, I welled with love. Whenever he behaves poorly, badly, I am bowled over by an *only human* response. *Inhuman*, though, comes a close second.

'Anyway, anyway . . .'

I said, 'Yes.'

'Would you like to start?'

Suddenly, we were adversaries, with an agenda.

'No.'

And from both of us came something like laughter, but enfeebled, defeated.

'Well, then, I will.' But first he took a sip of tea, replacing the cup precisely on the saucer.

He started with, 'You're right.'

We shared another flutter of knowing, timid laughter at my unspoken, *I'm always right*.

Cautiously, he continued, 'This *is* out of hand.'

I listened diligently, continued to do so, soaking up the silence, dredging for sense or nuance, because these words of his seemed unlike any that I remembered having said. My listening – measured, thorough – bore no relation to how I was feeling: pulse smacking, breaths fracturing.

Out of hand. My own hands lay below, before me – one on the tabletop, one on my forearm that lay across the tabletop – and I marvelled at their composure.

'None of this is normal.' He sounded rueful. 'I do think that we need to normalise.'

I looked up at him; he looked so kind, careful, trustworthy. I smiled, because there was nothing else that I could do. Conceivably, his life has been a succession of women smiling at him in just such stupefaction. I quelled an urge to reach for his hand because, of course, we have never touched and his use of the word normalise made this moment anything but the one in which to make the move.

Normalise: I considered, *no one, but no one, would believe this*.

That one word would be enough to ruin a scriptwriter's career, *You'll never work in this town again*.

Who would believe it of me? That I had ended up in love with a man who, when discussing our feelings for each other, would refer to a need to normalise. What had I ever done to deserve that?

And, sitting there, I was faced with Edwin's conviction that he knows nothing of life, with two exceptions: loyalty; and his own limitations. The loyalty strikes me as clumsy, unconvincing, contrived; not loyalty at all, but self-righteousness and cowardliness. As for the limitations, this version of himself is exactly that: a version. His life is lived in watertight versions. Limitations let him off the hook.

I wanted to take issue with him, but what could I say? I could not say, *But you love me*, because he had never said anything of the kind. I could not say, *But we're having a love affair*, because we have never even held hands. So I had to sit there and take it. And smile. The smile, like the hands, belied my feelings.

He told me that he would have to leave at five o'clock.

'Going anywhere nice?' He tends to socialise in the early evening: drinks with friends.

He said nothing.

Home.

The shock, for me, was not that he would cut back on time with me in order to be with her, because, lately, I have noticed that he has been going home in time for her return from work. As if that will compensate her. No, the shock was his refusal to say that word *home* to me. The implication was, *Not for you to ask*. Unnecessarily brutal, because I rarely ask; I am keen to respect his privacy. His silence was obvious exclusion; forcible.

We spent our remaining time together discussing new, improved conduct. He wanted rules: no coded calls, and none from phone boxes; all calls to be made openly from home. Then he asked, 'How often do you speak to your other friends?'

With some of those whom I regard as my closest, I have no more contact than a call once every couple of months; with some acquaintances, I speak every few days.

'Depends.' I thought, *Listen, Edwin, you're not my friend, and never have been. My friend is not what you are. And if you could accept that, we could go home, at least for now; there'd be no need for ridiculous meetings like this.*

And all the time, inside my head, I had Ethel Merman and Bert Lahr bawling Cole Porter's *Friendship*:

> *If you're ever down a well*
> *Ring my bell.*
> *If you ever catch on fire,*
> *Send a wire.*
> *If you ever lose your teeth*
> *and you're out to dine,*
> *Borrow mine.*

But somehow, twice weekly was decided upon. That is the rule, now. His rule, not for me to break. I wonder if he will ever call me and say, *I know that I shouldn't, but I just wanted to hear your voice.*

Throughout this dispiriting exchange, he looked increasingly hopeful, and for that look – so rare, from him, of late – I was glad.

At one point, he checked, 'Are you okay?'

Chin up. I went one better: I smiled. *Anything, for you.* I smiled bravely: yes, that was what I did; that was the kind of smile. New, to me. Not that I have never been brave, but stoicism has never been my style. As I made that guarded wince, I had a sensation of time warping: fifty years ago, my head would have been pinned with a small, brimless hat, and my heart with a discreet, stone-sharp brooch. This other me was buttoned, gloved, and accompanied by a thumb-sized handbag. The story was that this other me had made a mistake: serious, but – with guidance, a firm hand – resolvable. One word describes how she was feeling: chastened. The problem was that – as if in a dream – I knew nothing more of the mistake than its incidence: for the life of me, I was unable to recall, or even guess, and, worse, I had a suspicion that I would never know.

As we rose to leave, he asked me, 'Was this what you'd expected?'

The innocence of the question was disarming. As was his openness to my response: across the table, he had stopped, he stood still, relaxed and bright-eyed. Friendly.

No need for me to manage a smile, this time; my face was burned with one, unfailing and unresponsive, like scar tissue.

'More or less, yes.' Never a truer word. My earlier unsaid words – the ones that included *love* and *affair* – rattled, but in a parallel life. They belonged to a language different from the one in which this conversation had been conducted. A language that, for us, was dead. We moved away from the table, and the waiter – officious, suddenly – swooped for our crockery. As we went towards the foyer, I was thinking of asking Edwin if he had ever studied Latin; I wondered if he knows that *to prevaricate* means *to walk crookedly*.

'Names for body parts tend to come from Old English words,' I said to Carl, this morning, over coffee, in the garden.

He was low in his chair, elbows on the wooden arms, chin on loosely-linked hands. Only his eyes moved, to mine.

I laughed. 'Seriously: *hand*, *foot*. . . *ear*, *eye* . . .'

He took a chocolate-covered coffee bean from the saucerful on the table, and his big, bold mouth stretched into a smile. I had had three phone messages from him in as many days – the last was just, *Coffee?* – and, under pressure, had given in, had invited him over.

'No, listen: remember bedizened? Well, I had a browse through the dictionary.' *Bewitched. Betwixt.* 'Can't remember how I got on to the body. But as far as I could see, they all have their roots in Old English: ankle . . . elbow . . . knee . . .'

'Hip?'

He had me there. 'I didn't think of hip.'

'Looks like we need a dictionary.'

From indoors, I fetched a paperback version, which I handed to him.

'Hip . . . hip . . . hip . . .' Pages thudded and chirped, then fell silent. 'Yes: origin, Old English.'

'Aha! Shoulder?'

When he confirmed shoulder, I admitted, 'That, I wouldn't have believed.'

'No?'

'Too sophisticated. Too long.' Coffee darkened and drew hard on the inside of my mouth. 'Face: there I was, going all over the body and I don't think that face ever occurred to me.'

He was laughing at me; but then, a dismayed, 'Latin;' and he quoted, '*Latin, Facies*.'

We exchanged glances, aghast.

'Fits, though, perhaps: being Latin, I mean; face being more of a concept than a thing.'

'Chin,' I said, 'doesn't sound Old English-ish, to me.'

The inevitable pause, before, '*Ah*, but it *is*.'

'*Is* it?'

He was already busy again, 'Mouth . . . mouth . . .' Clumps of dictionary moved from one cover to the other. When the word was found, he started, 'Tongue, tongue, tongue . . .'

Grains slid from the cafetière into my tiny cup. Glancing across, I marvelled at the lip to his lip: his top lip has its own lip, which I hungered to suck into mine.

'Teeth,' I said, quickly.

His fingertips whipped a few pages. '. . . *See tooth*. Okay, I'm off to see tooth . . . and . . . your answer is . . . yes.' Over the book, he was somehow both animated and still. Leaning forwards, he was also, somehow, sitting back, relaxed, in his chair. Made up of outlines and details as delicate as brush-strokes, and as bold. A princely presence, Leonine. There we were: The Lion, The Witch, and The Wardrobe.

'Neck,' I said, 'throat,' and closed my eyes so that I could turn to the heavy sun.

As he found them, he repeated them. '*Neck*. . . and . . . *throat*.'

'See?' I said, 'This is easy.' This hidden language, visceral English beneath the Latin, Greek, French. 'These words are all the same.'

'All short and sweet.'

'Well, all short.' *Nasty, brutish.*

'All wonderful: you know where you are, with them; no confusion, no allusions, they have a job to do, and they do it, and I love that.'

I asked if he would like more coffee.

He raised a hand, performed an exaggerated tremor. 'Just a touch.'

Unthinkingly, I echoed, '*Touch.*'

A tentative smile; nothing withheld, though; none of his face unwarmed.

I was hot, needed shade, went inside to make more coffee.

In the kitchen, I thought of *walk, run, fly, swim,* all from Old English; also, the shortcomings, catastrophes, *deaf, dumb, blind, limp. Crawl* and *stagger,* I had discovered, come from Norse; *stumble* and *struggle,* from Middle English. Another Middle English word, according to my dictionary, is *drown.* Before Middle English, what was the word? There must have been a word. Perhaps that word survived, attached to another meaning, floating through the centuries. Perhaps I use it, unknowingly.

When I returned with the tray – full cafetière, rinsed cups – Carl was triumphant: 'Touch, yes. And finger, thumb, toe, heel. Oh, and hair, and red.'

I ruffled my hair as if I could rub it out.

Into the book, he said, 'Heart.'

I waited for him to find it before I said, 'Head.'

Settling down and unloading the tray, I failed to notice for a moment that the dictionary remained in his lap; he was looking at me.

'What?'

He glanced at my crossed legs and said a considered, 'Calf.'

Automatically, I hooked the elevated foot behind the grounded ankle: hiding.

He began to leaf through the dictionary, but checked, 'How do you spell that? Just – you know – *calf*?'

'Yes, just *calf*.'

Within seconds, he looked up, gravely. 'Old Norse.'

'Much the same: pillage people.'

'We didn't have calves, then, in Old England. We had . . .' he shrugged, '. . . bits of leg, I suppose.'

I said, 'Spell.'

'Hmm?'

'*Spell*.'

The eventual answer was that the verb is French, with English origins for the two nouns: spell of weather; magical spell. His attention stayed with the book, he was searching for something else; seconds later, he looked up to tell me, '*Wish* is an Old English word, you know.'

'I didn't, no.'

His small, flawless eyes seemed all iris, all barely-blue, no impression of whites. They gave an even reflection.

I looked away over the garden, the focus of which was the back wall of the house, the Boston ivy. I had assumed that the brilliant leaves were red, orange, but, in fact, they were pink, very.

'What about the seasons?' I asked him. 'Autumn?'

Latin, apparently.

I suggested that we try fall, and was right. We went on to spring, summer, winter.

And earlier this afternoon, for something to do, I went through dark and light, day and night, dawn and dusk, twilight, sun and moon, shadow, water, rain and snow, Heaven and Hell. But back then, this morning, in the garden, when we had whisked through the seasons, I said,

'Life is:' I already knew, from my previous search.

'Is it?'

Love and lust were the two words to which my earlier

investigation had then taken me: logical, and nearby. Of them, though, I made no mention to Carl.

He laughed his apology, 'I have to ask: is death?'

'It is.'

Sleep: even if I could do nothing else, I was adept at being dead to the world. But lately, sleep is no longer my solace, no longer visits me. I am abandoned to darkness; impoverished urban darkness. Supine, I keep my hands on my concave stomach, because, somehow, that curve is a comfort to me. Often, I go downstairs and listen to music, putting the *Goldberg Variations* to the use for which they had been commissioned all those centuries ago by the insomniac Baron von Kayserling. Although I can hum every note of that recording, I am still always surprised by Glenn Gould's own few notes of humming; I still look up, around, for whoever is there in the room with me. Two nights ago, returning to bed, I glimpsed my reflection in the mantelpiece mirror, and was shocked; not by what I saw, but by seeing anything at all, as if I had assumed that the mirror would be deserted, like everywhere else in the house. My reflection was quite alien, but, surprisingly, not unappealing: away from harsh lighting, I was drowsy and rumpled. When I went back to the bedroom, Philip, unwoken, was holding on hard to an armful of duvet.

Home. And wife, the origin of which my dictionary notes as *Old English*, *wif*. And widow, spinster, mother. Sister is a derivation of the Old English *sweostor*, so similar to the *schwester* that my little German friend taught me, all those years ago. All so similar, these women words. *Woman*: *wifman*.

Carl was looking at me, again: that appraising, appreciative look.

'What?'

'Wool.' He nodded towards my skirt.

'Wool/silk mix.'

When he had investigated both words, he said, 'Gold. You wear gold.' He could have said *always* or *a lot*.

When that was confirmed, I asked him to look up jewellery. He shook his head. 'Too complex for Old English.'

I was less sure: 'Jewel?'

His scepticism, though, was well-founded: 'Latin, from *to joke*.'

On cue, I laughed.

'What?'

So I told him: 'I used to be a goldsmith; that was what I used to be.'

'Oh:' cautiously interested.

'And I was well aware that my line of work was – shall we say – of no consequence. You know: *Let me through, I'm a goldsmith*! I used to worry, to wonder why I didn't want to be a doctor or teacher or something. And all I can think is that, knowing I couldn't change the world, I'd gone to the other extreme.'

'Sort of, If-you-can't-beat-'em, make-'em-easier-on-the-eye.'

'Sort of. Well, no. Make life a bit less . . .' *like life*?

'Nasty, brutish and short?'

'Nasty and brutish. No evidence for the increased longevity of the bejewelled. Unfortunately, because business would have been booming. I was good at it, I was good at – well, I don't know – the design, the intricacy, I don't know; at putting enough shine and mystery into those little pieces. I was good at it, so I did it, and enjoyed it.' And perhaps life is that simple.

Was.

Was?

'And now?'

Ah, now. Well, now is a different story. 'My hand.' I had no idea what to say; I lowered the hand, palm upwards, on to the table, between us.

'Your hand.' He had no idea what I meant; there was nothing to see; we were both looking, for some seconds.

'It looks . . .' He could have said, *normal*, or *fine*. '. . . perfect.'

I said, 'It's weak.' A moment later, 'Very. No good for goldsmithing.' What I should have said was, *Good for nothing*. 'I was in an accident.'

As I watched – as we both watched – his fingertips came to mine; the tips of his fingertips. With the slightest of pressures, almost none, he drew my fingers outwards; opened my hand.

Still looking down into my palm, he murmured, 'You'd never know.'

'Unless I told you.' I spoke slowly, almost in a whisper, although there was no one to overhear. 'That's not where the damage is. Connections were messed up. I had a knock to my head. I was in a car.' Only when I had finished did I realise that my brief telling of the tale was backwards.

Just as gently as he had touched me, I took my hand away; returned us to how we had been, having coffee.

An hour or so ago, Drew took hold of that hand with something between a squeeze and a shake. He had dropped by, unannounced, on his way home early from work. I was in the kitchen when the doorbell shrieked. Instantly, Hal was in the hallway, doing his Dangerous Dog Act. This never fails to amuse me: that he has taken it upon himself to guard us, and embraced the self-imposed duty with fervour. As far as he is concerned, our postman's intention, daily, is to add forced entry to the service provided; and every morning, his canine commotion saves the day.

I went to the hallway, where he had fallen silent: the caller was known to him, had spoken to him. For Hal, as for all dogs, a person is either friend or foe; and once a friend, always a friend, of whom the very best is thought, and for whom every allowance is made. His quivering nose was in the letterbox. When I had managed to ease open the door, Drew stepped across the threshold, acknowledging Hal with a deflatory, 'Mate.' For me, of course, a kiss. His smell was a confusion of body-warm linen and the static-stiff materials of his car. He said that he was on his way home; I said that two-thirty seemed early. He shrugged, his briefcase scuffing the wall. His hand-raked hair was a shambles. I noticed, for the first time, the folded skin around his mouth and nose. I was struck that he looks quite distinguished.

'I'm knocking off,' he said.

'Wish I could.'

'Why? What're you doing?'

'Nothing. Hence, I can't knock off.'

'You should knock *on*. Have a change. I should take you somewhere.' He was taking off his jacket. His eyes were rimmed with the same shade of pink as his nostrils, and there was little difference in size. 'Alas, I'm going home to prepare a presentation. To slave over a hot presentation.'

'I'm unloading the dishwasher.'

He was genuinely and excessively sympathetic: 'Pointless. Loading, yes: labour-saving. But unloading! – it's all over, and there's still . . .' he winced, thinking hard for the word, decided upon, '. . . *involvement*,' quickly adding, 'don't.'

'Don't what?' I knew, though.

'Don't tell me that's the story of my life.'

I turned, for him to follow me. 'That would be facetious.'

'It would.'

The sun had gone from the garden; we took our coffee into the front room, to the sofa. We chatted for a while about nothing very much before he asked, 'How's your love life?'

My immediate intention was to treat the question with scorn, to refuse to answer, but the temptation of a listener was too much: with scarcely a missed beat, I was saying, miserably, 'I can't think of two less appropriate words.'

'Why? What's happened?'

'That's the problem. Nothing's happened.'

'Still?' He was confounded. 'What's wrong with this bloke?'

'Maybe it's me.'

'It's not you.' He took my hand, gave that squeeze, shake, and I assumed that he would then let go; but he kissed me.

And so there we were, kissing. One moment, no kissing; the next, nothing but; and of the instant between the two, no trace, glossed over and swallowed. The easiness astonished me. He had shown me how easy, and, in gratitude, I kissed him more. His mouth, moving on and into mine, made a swirl of impressions: dry lips, lavish saliva; a peppermint steam above a burr of tobacco. As I opened up and closed in on that mouth, the tobacco kicked in, kicking up long-buried responses, legacies of my earliest, illicit kisses, of smoke-sour boys. Meanwhile, beneath my fingertips was a smooth forearm, a faint grain of hair; next, the linen of his sleeve, granular; then his hair, which was the surprise: the silkiness of his hair, his baby-hair.

Something of me was being tested: a sensation similar to that of running, years ago, for a bus, or, in childhood, swapping hands to write. I marvelled at the workings of my body, uncomplicated and obliging, mysteriously neither quite voluntary nor involuntary. A sensation similar to that of swimming submerged: a transformation called for and duly coming, just as absolute as the water.

What was happening to me was lust. Pure and simple. Chemical. A gilding of lust; and inside, coarser, ticking down into the depths of me. Drew's own physical response was unmistakable, but in another sense there was an utter absence of expectation. He was surprised to have been taken up on this, as far as this. Where we went from here was my decision. Even as I turned his tongue around mine and sloshed my hands through his hair, I knew that in some minutes' time, I would look at him and think, *Why am I doing this with this person?* And at thirty-two, I am too old to be doing that; I have been doing that for long enough.

I demurred. I lessened my ardour, increased my affection, and eventually slipped from him, took the tray back to the kitchen. He followed, and tried his luck, took liberties, but these few remaining kisses of his were scrupulously playful, conducted with the combined frivolity and formality of a dance. His parting kiss, though, on the doorstep, minutes later, was exuberant. I knew that he knew that this was the last.

When he had gone, I sat on the sofa, to cool down, to settle, to take stock. *So, this is me, now*: in love with one man, lusting for another, kissing yet another, and married. Months ago, it was true only that I was married. I had fractured, since the summer, but something fundamental had now fallen into place: *desire*.

Desire: Latin, *of a star*.

Sex had never been a problem; I had had my fair share of pleasure. But that was all that sex had been: no problem; an act, with a response. A pastime, more pleasurable than most. I had taken – *how* had I taken? – thirty-two years, twice sweet-sixteen, for lust to make sense to me.

And that was when I remembered: my mother *did* offer me advice on marriage, once. No, not advice: a comment, made in passing and concerning someone else, perhaps a relative, perhaps a public figure, a politician or a film star; I do not remember, I did not want to hear, I did not listen. I was a teenager. She said that nothing is more important in a marriage than sex. No: she said, *I suspect*; she did not know. But for me, a teenager, love was everything, falling in love would be everything, would include sex. And for a teenager, any sex is good sex. No: there was some mention from my mother of *fascination*; I think what she said was that sex was the source of a fascination that could keep a marriage alive. I had dismissed this as the embarrassing ravings of an old woman. She must have been in her mid-forties.

* * *

This afternoon, shadows of trees streak the park like spilled, dried ink. Beneath the trees, the sunshine is filtered and strained by leaves, is opaque and fluid on trunks. Anyone strolling there is cloaked in airy black lace. My own shadow, glowering over the path in front of me, looks more substantial than I feel. In this unclouded, angled sunshine, everything is doubled; even this, a discarded tin can, nestling with a dark twin. Most impressive is the stretch of railings, the perfect replica on the tarmac. This tumbled sun is blinding, confounding; the world crisscrossed, treacherous.

Coming in my direction is the man whom I watched, one day, guiding a group of attentive, middle-aged, warmly-dressed people around the park; the man on whom I was eavesdropping when he said that he had joined the Parks Department thirty years ago.

Today, as on the day of that tour, he is bony and stately in a suit, and walks with a stick. On that day, he stopped his audience beside a bush to tell them, 'These are my particular interest, we've been building a collection of them here for the last nineteen years.' And I thought, *You're adorable*: the boyishly thin blond hair; the fragile skull, and specs, golden-framed pebbles of glass; his slow pace, his painstaking patience. I longed to follow him around the park: this gentle-manly, ascetic botanist with a niche in public life. And now here he is, dusted-down and promenading. With him is another man: stocky, ruddy, Barbour-clad. They are relishing the sunshine, their faces turned into this vast, upturned blue basin of sky. The other man has a slim, glossy folder tucked underneath one arm. As I pass, I hear him musing, and discern the words *project* and *exciting*. The folder-bound project could have something to do with the lottery grant: notices appeared, a month or so ago, tied to railings and pinned to tree trunks, informing us of a *Public Meeting to discuss the Lottery Grant*. Posters appear fairly regularly, here, to advertise demonstrations on techniques such as pruning. Beside the dahlias there is a notice entitled *Companion Planting*, inviting us to telephone for more information. I worry that no one does; I wonder whether I should, to be polite. This morning, the dahlia bushes are being hacked down by the hobbling gardener: time for something new, according to a schedule of planting that is a mystery to me. Passers-by are picking over the debris, coming away with impressive bouquets of lurid pompoms. I would love to do the same, but am afraid – ridiculously – that this is somehow unacceptable, that this is pilfering, barely tolerated by the gardener; that I will be the unlucky one who faces his wrath.

I am thinking, still, of what I saw earlier: two people – a man and a woman – playing a game of catch from which they excluded their dog. They never glanced at the animal, which pranced desperately between them; their noisy enthusiasm was for each other and the tennis ball. Each throw was extravagantly high, but precisely-aimed. The dog fluttered, lamb-like, its gaze riveted to the ball throughout the protracted trajectory. This was no lamb, though; this was a Doberman: tremendous strength and speed suppressed hard, in good faith. The scenario held me, helpless, for several minutes, watching for an occasional concession, some cursory inclusion, my hopes dashed with every thud of that ball into a hand. An eventual turning away proved no escape from their whoops and swoops, the tottering of that animal. Hurrying in the opposite direction, I was quite unable to stop willing the dog to turn on them, even though I knew – as did the dog – that, if vindicated, they would show even less mercy.

MAKE NO BONES

❧

Today's forecast ended with the words, *This afternoon, staying cool*. It is the end of November, there are no afternoons, the days drop from lunchtime into darkness. And *cool*? Today, as on every previous day for weeks, there is no sky. Cloud cover is entangled in the tree tops. Bare branches hairy with twigs.

The tree across the road is what I remember of the first time Philip and I were alone together in our house. The house was unoccupied, in limbo between exchange of contracts and completion. The estate agent reluctantly lent us the key – to be dropped back through his letterbox by morning – because we had bought a bed which had to be delivered on that day. The bed arrived in the afternoon, but we went back into the house later, late. The thin-spun mid-summer twilight enabled us to make our way up the stairs. By the time we stepped onto the landing, our thrilled whispers had settled into silence. We sat side by side on the bed. The view from the window was the horse chestnut tree. For the half-hour or so that we were sitting there, we watched the eddies of leaves in a breeze that, down in the lane, was nothing.

That tree – us, sitting, watching that tree – is one of Philip's memories, too. Whatever happens between us from now onwards, I suspect that neither of us will ever again say, easily, fondly, as we have done from time to time over the years, *Do you remember: us, sitting, watching that tree*?

This dire weather has ample compensation for Hal: smell. At this time of year, everything lies down to die in the abundant, clinging moisture: so many lives flashing before Hal's nose. He drinks down the decay, arrives home exhausted but exhilarated. And then, slumped, he is a whisker from consciousness; sated with sleep, ready for action. In contrast to me. Nowadays, I am rarely anywhere but bed: going to bed early and getting up late, the unaired bedroom either dark or dim. Bed is purgatory: no sleep, no waking. Getting up, I lug weariness with me. Philip has always gone. I never hear him go.

I am not enjoying this walk, I am still perturbed by what happened on the way here. I was driving, having been to the garden centre for potting compost, and turned from the main road into a side street. Sprinting along the pavement in the direction from which I had come, was a little girl, three or four years old. Her anorak was flapping over an eye-catching, rather old-fashioned, elaborate party dress: zips and toggles over frills and bows. One arm was raised; and beyond the fingertips, a piece of string tied to a balloon. Her expression was anguished, the mouth wide open. Running behind her was a man with an identical expression, focused not on that balloon but on her. She was a couple of steps from the main road. She flashed in my rear-view mirror, and was gone; a car loomed. I was driving; I could not look around. I had to drive on.

Before yesterday, I had not seen Edwin for weeks. During those weeks, he had been abroad twice, for work (a conference in Salt Lake City, an archive in Stockholm). We had decided – he had decided – that we should resist meeting every time I am in London. He seems to have no idea how rarely I would be in London if not to meet him. During those weeks, I went once, testing the water. Edwin-less London was alien. Visiting my old favourites – streets, shops, cafés, galleries – I was flustered, exhausted, disoriented. And worse: bored. I spent the day biding time until I could – respectably – go home. In the end, my departure fell short of respectable: the four-twenty train.

Yesterday, I had an arrangement to visit Fern. Just as when Edwin first came across me on that train. I made sure that this trip was on a day when I knew that he would be around. Lately, he has been busy: *keeping busy*, in his words. Planning my visit, I contacted several friends, but none was available: various appointments, engagements, occasions. Fern was my last resort, and was a captive audience: she is staying at her parents' house, in a distant suburb, looking after their dog while they are on holiday. Why did I go at all? I could have – should have – lied; simply *said* that I was going.

Fern was amazed by my proposition; she wailed, pitiably, 'But I'm *here*.'

'You're *stuck* there. Let me come and see you. I'll pop up.'

Pop up? A train from central London, then a bus.

Edwin was reluctant to make an arrangement; he suggested that I call him when I arrived in town. I did, but we had problems with our connection. When he warned, 'You're breaking up,' I made a snap decision. I had been mulling over venues in Notting Hill, but the names slipped my mind and I was hazy on directions. So, I said, 'Holland Park. Café.'

The café is an old haunt of mine, I was a frequent visitor when I was a student. Somehow untouched by the eighties, it has none of the excesses of cappuccino culture. There are pastries on paper plates covered with polythene. Having arrived before Edwin, I wiped a porthole in the condensation and gazed outside at the wooden tables, recalled sitting there once with Annie, recalling her informing me that she had become a vegan. It was on a Sunday afternoon; had Saturday night's conquest been a vegan? I was unable to overlook the Danish on the plate in front of her, and broke the news: 'I can't imagine that's vegan.'

A cheerful, 'Are you *sure*?'

While I considered how to answer, she took her first bite, and said through the mouthful, 'You had me worried.'

That was so many years ago. Edwin arrived with a head-ache, wanted fresh air. Outside, we sat on a bench. There, with the usual, pained sigh, he suddenly asked, 'Were you in the same accident as Jacqueline?'

My stomach was squeezed by surprise: *what's this? where's this going?*

'Yes, I was.' I tend to think in terms of having no fellow survivors because Jacque did not survive as she was; I feel very much that I survived that accident alone, that I alone lived to tell the tale.

His enunciation of her name had been respectful; clear and careful, a password to the conversation that he hoped to have.

I said no more; he was asking the questions.

'Were you driving the car?'

'No.'

Seconds later, 'Did you play the piano –' stop, start again, – 'Is the accident why you don't play?' He was focused resolutely on the horizon.

Another acid wavelet of surprise against the walls of my stomach. He *had* noticed my hand, my dead, curled hand. No one had ever before asked *why* I do not play; why I do not do what I love. I answered with the truth: 'No, I don't play because of my brother.'

He turned to me, expressionless but wider-eyed than usual.

'My brother was the piano-player; piano-playing was *his*. He was amazing. Well, seemed to me that he was amazing, but I should say that I was seven when I last heard him. That's what I remember of him. All that piano-playing. That's all I remember.'

When I said no more, he asked, 'Did he die?' He stared at me, his lips pressed together.

'I don't know.' That was the honest answer. 'He disappeared. No, I mean, I *mean*, he did *leave*,' voluntarily, with his belongings, or some of them. 'He was seventeen. So, that's . . .' I did the calculation, 'twenty-five years ago.' When had I last done that calculation? I recalled thinking, *Twenty-one years, now*. So that was four years ago. What was I doing four years ago? I was writing wedding invitations. I said,

'Anything could have happened.' Including my forty-two-year-old brother ending up married with children. Perhaps his unorthodox departure was a hiccup, perhaps he settled down, his life unravelling in the opposite direction to which mine seems to be moving.

Gently, Edwin suggested, 'Chances are, he's alive.'

'Chances.' I shrugged, dismissive; I am always unimpressed by the main chance.

'No contact, ever?'

'Never.' I revised, 'None that I know of.'

'And you've never searched for him?'

'He went, and then never contacted. I think it's clear that he didn't want to be found.'

'Is it that simple?' The question sounded genuine, not rhetorical.

'Is it that complicated? Is there anything less complicated than cutting loose?' But is there anything less true than what I had just said? Cutting loose leaves holes in lives; lives thereafter never better than cobbled-together. Cutting loose leaves every possible question unasked and unanswered.

I began to backtrack. 'Perhaps if I hadn't been seven . . .'

He gave me a look. 'I meant *later*.'

I returned it. 'I *know* what you meant. *I* meant that I never knew him. To me, he was some big bloke who played the piano, and smelled of cigarettes and –' I puzzled, '– *damp*, you know how teenage boys seem to smell *damp*? *Is* it damp, that they smell of? That's what I remember: the smell of him, the sound of him – the piano – and that he was big. And he probably wasn't big at all. No one else in my family is big.'

Edwin was nodding, as if he agreed, although he had seen no one of the family but me.

And now I was agreeing with him, 'But if I hadn't been seven . . .' He continued nodding.

'Well, that would have been . . .' No need for me to finish, surely. 'To him, I suppose, I was just a little girl.' I remembered, 'He had girlfriends; there were girls around.

Daisy.' What I had remembered was that there was a Daisy; I had no memories of her.

Edwin remarked, 'Daisy! The invasion of the flower fairies.'

I had a sudden thought: did my nickname start with my brother?

'And his name?'

'Lind.'

'Lyn?'

'Lind. Lindbergh. Don't ask.' I challenged, 'And, anyway, how often do you see your sister? And you *know* her.'

An inward breath, from him.

I filled the vacuum with, 'Yes, okay, I know: that's *why* you don't see her.' A flutter of his eyebrows: rueful confirmation. 'My brother went and never came back or contacted to see if I was okay and I'll be damned if I'm going to go and look for him.' That was the other version. Or the extended version. I am never sure which is true, or more true.

Quietly, he asked, 'So, what happened? Why did he go? Do you know?'

'We'd been on holiday – me and Mum and Dad, in Spain – and when we came home, he'd gone. I *know* that, but I don't *remember*. A policeman came to our house, he had a cup of tea in the living room. Cup, saucer, biscuit: the works. That, I *do* remember. But whether the policeman was there on the day that we came home, or sometime later, I don't know.'

'Do you think he's alive?'

'I don't. Think.' Then, exasperated, I said, 'This is why I don't tell people: because I disappoint them.'

Why assume that we are haunted by those who were significant – or deemed significant – for us? I am dogged by recollections of people who were incidental. Lately, I have been thinking of Caroline, a hairdresser in the local salon, to whom my mother took me for trims when I was – what? – seven? nine? She wore a charm bracelet, which narrowly failed to compensate for her compliance with my mother's instruction that I should be given a feather cut. And yesterday, sitting there on that bench with Edwin, I was thinking of the Jose Vidal Quartet, which had played every evening in the dining room of the hotel where we had that holiday when I was seven. The four men lavished attention and kindness upon me. The singer looked like Captain Kirk. Dad bought me their record, a forty-five. I wonder how old these people are, now; I want to extract them from my amber memories, to update them. Caroline? Not much older than I am; forties; and probably looks the same, give or take the odd facial line. And the men in the band, twenty-five years on? In their fifties? Do they still play in bands in hotels? Does anyone, nowadays?

'You want to know the truth? Shall I tell you what I feel – really feel – about the loss of my brother?' Because suddenly, at that very moment, I had realised. 'It's this: that it would have been nice, to have had a brother. That's all: could have been nice. That's all I know.'

After a moment, he asked, 'Was there no warning?'

'They hadn't been getting on, if that'll do as a warning.' Raised voices, complaints, slammed doors, absences. In my family, no one ever got on. And my mother seemed less able or willing to get on with me after Lind had gone. I took his place in her line of fire. *Get out of my sight*!

But this yell of hers had a catch: I was denied the choice of where to go. The cellar was where I spent those afternoons. The light switch was on her side of the slammed, bolted door, and she never obliged. Usually, the darkness was total; only rarely were there golden splinters in the doorframe. In that cellar, I kept moving, hoping to repel the indiscriminate creep of spiders. The pacing, tapping and jiggling was exhausting. Sometimes I was taken there during an afternoon and fetched back into an evening.

One day, when I was down there, sitting on the top stone step, my father came home, unexpectedly: in the hallway was his voice, a casual enquiry, 'Poppy around?'

My mother's reply was, 'Sophie's,' and she sounded as if she believed it. How I would have loved to have been at Sophie's house. I wondered if my confinement was somehow my own mistake, and mine alone; known only to me. And yet I knew that I must not shout out; I just knew. I had to wait for him to go again, for her to be released from her spell and to release me from mine.

'My parents married because of my brother. I mean, because my mum was pregnant.'

'And then there were ten years between the two of you.'

'I was last-ditch, I suspect.'

'And were you a success?'

'They're still together, if that's what you mean. Less to do with me, though, probably, than to do with . . .' I paused, considered, and then admitted defeat, '. . . whatever keeps people together.'

'History.'

I was doubtful, 'Oh, I don't know. I don't know that their history was much of a draw.'

'Habit.'

'Ditto.'

'Nowhere else to go.'

True. 'Life without the other one was unimaginable, I suppose, after a while.' After a while? Perhaps from the beginning. Perhaps they had never had anywhere else to go.

'Empathy,' he said. 'Loyalty,' he said, to the horizon. 'A pact.'

'Well, that's what marriage is, isn't it.'

He turned, blank, unblinking.

'Isn't it? Partly? Basically?'

He did not seem to have heard me. 'I've been looking at flats.'

Flats? My brain skidded on the word, kicked up images of shoes, of tyres, of marshes.

'Just in estate agents' windows. To see if I could afford to move, to leave Vivien in our place and move into a studio.

And I can. Afford to.' He seemed surprised and pleased, or perhaps relieved. 'We've been talking, Vivien and I, a little, about how we'd manage if we separated. She'd stay, for now, and I'd go.'

I thought: *they talk*. About feelings; about the future. With her, he does something that he fails to do with me. And of course he does: she is his wife; he owes her. He owes her everything. The future is supposed to be hers; his feelings, too. Me, he owes nothing. To my disbelief, I found myself pondering the position in which they do this talking: does he hold her hand? does he hold her? I was unsurprised by what he had said, although I was listening hard, with every sense, including the sixth. Why no surprise? Because I had been waiting a long time for this, but would wait quite a while longer before I believed that this was indeed what I had been waiting for.

He looked down into his lap, contemplated his limp hands. 'What do you think would happen between us if we were –' he frowned, '– unattached?'

The question was a test. There should be no question; my answer should have been, *We're in love, so what do you think would happen*? What I was thinking would happen was that I would visit him in his studio flat, where we would have supper and sometimes I would stay over. The usual. The unremarkable and wonderful usual. In my imagination, I saw a room, a smallish bed, and I was moving towards him, having arrived a moment ago and buzzed the intercom; I was damp with rain, I was London-smudged, but I was inside those four walls and then his arms, for a kiss. Kiss, supper, bed. I did not care how often I would call on him, what we would have for supper, what we would do or not do in bed.

What would happen? This: I would be with him, he would be with me; we could be together, alone, in private. Unlike now. The prospect of four walls to ourselves, and he had to ask what would happen? The question required caution. So I said, 'I don't know.' And this did the trick.

'I think that's right.' His own caution was enthusiastic. 'To make assumptions would be wrong, I think.'

Fine: I would do everything required of me, including nothing. More worrying to me than assumptions was my lack of imaginings: a moment ago, in my mind's eye, I had crossed that room towards him, but gone no further. How could we ever move, now, from facing each other over tables and sitting side by side on benches, to even simply taking hold of each other?

Suddenly, he said, 'I wanted to call you last night.'

He would have remembered Philip's fortnightly evening meeting.

'And why didn't you?' I knew that the question should have been, *What did you want to say?*

'I would have broken the phone box rule. So, instead, I . . .' he shrugged, '. . . walked.'

'Walked?'

'For hours.' But then, quickly, he was asking, 'How's *your* home life?' In his concern was a twang of curosity.

My poor attempt to convey the atmosphere was, 'Philip watches me.' Philip says little; his conversation, with me, now, is minimal, functional. Not grudging, but fearful: the fear of saying something wrong, of betraying his feelings or provoking an expression of mine. His gaze, though, is unchecked, and unabashed, slides everywhere with me, even for the most mundane activities, perhaps particularly for those activities – changing pillowcases, drawing curtains – because then, he supposes, I am unguarded. Perhaps he supposes that, in those moments, I am his, again; or, as I was. Or even, perhaps, as I will be. The eye of the storm. I never expected stealth from Philip: stealth, I expected least of all. And he seems to feel similarly: he skulks as if he is the wrong-doer in the household. I wonder what he expected least of all from me. There is no animosity in his eyes; none that I have seen. There is nothing much. When I said those words, *Philip watches me*, I realised that his gaze is in fact everywhere before me, laid down before me, a declaration and a reproach.

Edwin murmured, 'He watches you?' Then, 'He watches you.' Then, 'I'm sorry, I'm so little use to you in all this.' Something like a smile, but apologetic, ironic, before he continued, 'No assumptions, but do you think that you'll leave him?'

'I don't know.'

I don't know how. I would have to be sensible, rational, I should juggle figures, I would have to find a job.

I don't know why. I saw my house; Philip, sitting on the edge of our bed, having just asked me to marry him. Dishevelled, he was radiant, the shade of blood beneath warm skin. I blinked back the vision and there was Edwin, cold and cautious, all his colour drained into the tip of his nose.

I thought, *I am topsy-turvy.* And, *I cannot right myself.*

I should have said, *Let me answer your earlier question. No, I wasn't driving the car, but I should have been. Jacqueline didn't drive; I did, but the roads were icy and I lost my nerve, or lacked the nerve, ordered a taxi. We were sent Paul Brown, twenty-nine years old; by day, a cook at the hospital, and, on that evening, working his second-ever shift as a cab driver. He had a wife, Lisa, a three-year-old daughter, Clare, and a ten-month-old son, Daniel. I was – am – a good driver, a very good driver; I was taught by my father. I should have known how good a driver I was. I don't know for certain that I was a better driver than Paul Brown. But probably I was less tired than he was, and less rushed. Certainly, I was better acquainted with that road. I played safe, though, and look what happened.*

Edwin was saying, 'Vivien would never, ever leave me.'

I wondered if anyone can ever know anything with certainty.

He said, 'Seems to me that the world is made of two kinds of people: those who settle, and those who are perpetually dissatisfied.' Then, 'We're both married to the wrong kind of person.'

I had to say it: 'No, we're married to the right kind.'

We sat there a little longer, in silence; we two pact-breakers. Our spouses had no faith in us, and now we had no faith in ourselves or each other.

We moved on when Edwin suggested returning to the café for coffee.

I was surprised: 'You're going to have coffee?' Magic mushrooms would have been as likely.

'No, *you're* going to have coffee. *I'm* going to have a nice cup of tea.' Suddenly, there was the old Edwin: his navy-blue eyes shone, and there was the tightening of one corner of his mouth.

An expression which I reflected as I said, 'Just like old times.'

But he reacted as if struck: a nod and an intake of breath so sharp as to seem perilous. The opening and closing of his mouth were both definite, the latter a revision of the former. And then, only then, did he look at me: eyes shining, but no smile. We had old times: they were good, but they are gone. He looked for two, perhaps three seconds. He said nothing. There was nothing to say. Or, nothing and everything.

We spoke only once on our way to the café, and only one word each, when the sole of my shoe rushed on a slime of leaves. Catching hold of me, he checked, 'Okay?' and I said, 'Yes.' My skid, stopped, never happened. His arm – beneath, inside mine – was a grip, unequivocal, absolute; his relinquishing of me, measured.

In the café we recovered ourselves to some extent, warmed by our drinks, and freed from our earlier discussion. Buoyed by my narrow escape from a fall, I was chatty again. I remembered what I had omitted from the account of my brother. 'I'll tell you what my brother used to play for me. "You're The Top." That was what he used to play – sing – for me. Years later, I heard it again, and realised that was what it was; what I'd thought was just a load of nonsense.'

Faintly, he repeated, '*You're the top.*'

'You know: Cole Porter, "You're The Top".' I spoke, did not dare sing:

'"You're Mahatma Gandhi . . .
You're Napoleon Brandy,
You're the purple light of a summer night in Spain."'

He said,

'"You're the National Gallery,
You're Garbo's salary,
You're Cellophane."'

'Yes, that's the one.

"You're an old Dutch master,
You're Mrs Astor,
You're Pepsodent."

And is this when we leap on to the table?'

He laughed, one nervous note. 'It *is* a load of nonsense.'

I quoted, in my best, brittlest, haughtiest Gertrude Lawrence, '"Strange, how potent sheet music is . . ."' Then, 'It says it all. Because what – sensible – can you say about love?'

'That's what you were, to him.'

I failed to follow. 'What?'

'The top.'

'Oh.'

'Oh, I imagine that you were.' The words were resonant but distant. He sipped his tea. As I watched him, his head bowed, his eyes closed, the song continued inside my head:

I'm a toy balloon that's fated soon to pop,
But, if baby, I'm the bottom,
You're the top.

* * *

The homeless man crosses my path, plods away behind me, and I turn to watch him go, drawn around by his odour, which is solid enough to obscure him: he is nothing but that foul smell. The trainers, hair and beard are the same as ever, but his face has altered, the features pulled downwards, twisted, unanchored: an expression of wretchedness. Enveloped in that stink, he is now beyond the everyday world, the world into which everyone else steps even if only on occasion, even those of us who spend some of each day here: the old lady who throws the naked doll for her dog; the unbalanced, motorbike-damaged man; the much-pierced, khaki-clad teenagers. Even a toddler – even a baby – will know how a person is supposed to smell. No one, confronted with that raw stench, will grace him with the most basic look of recognition, human to human. Nor even with the benign regard in which we hold the dogs, here; even the aged dogs, stout and swaddled in coats; or those with bandy legs, or three legs, or docked tails. And there is no going back, for him: he has no bath or shower, no change of clothes. As he disappears between the trees, I am sickened by my complicity. Even if there was never much that I could have done, I should have asked if there was any specific trouble that I could try to relieve. Who knows what small favour would have broken his fall.

Later, yesterday, after leaving Edwin, I travelled as planned to Fern. Opening the door to me, she announced, 'We're going to take Pavlov for a quick walk, before it's dark.'

I fussed the spaniel's ears, and broke the news, 'It *is* dark.'

She revised, '*Properly* dark,' and slipped into a cashmere tent of a coat. 'Ingrid's here, with the girls.' Her sister and two nieces.

Ingrid appeared fleetingly in a doorway further down the hall, calling a greeting. Genially bespectacled and big-bottomed, for years she has looked a generation older than

Fern, who is in fact a mere eighteen months her junior. Behind Ingrid was the prattle of children's television.

Fern added, 'Making scones.'

I cooed my appreciation.

Gloves slid on to Fern's hands with an ease that would have been impossible for me; I resent and struggle with every layer of clothing. Tiptoeing around Pavlov, who was weeping with joy, she reached to a rack for a hat: wide-brimmed; a graceful curve within which she was transformed, dignified and resplendent.

'James is asleep – for now – so all's well with the world.' She ushered me back over the threshold.

On the driveway, I said, 'So, Ingrid's here.'

'They live – I don't know – half an hour away.'

'Couldn't Pavlov have stayed with them?'

'Both work.'

'Oh, Ingrid's back at work?'

'Four days.'

Across the lane was a gate, which she unlatched. Pavlov dived ahead into darkness, the undergrowth crazed and uproarious. How Hal would have loved this copse. He would have loved the whole day: the travelling and the parks.

Fern said, 'It *is* dark.'

'I warned you.'

'*God* is it dark!'

Rutted, too, and squelching.

'Are you okay?' She was eclipsed by the hat, by the swoops of that brim as she resecured the gate and took her bearings.

'Yes.'

She stumbled.

'Are *you*?'

'Come on, let's get this over with.'

We were breathing hard, working our way across uneven, unstable ground. Pavlov's exuberance drew us onwards at quite a pace. My focus was on footholds and the bleeding of shadow that indicated a clearing, the footpath.

Fern asked, 'How are you?' and her breaths infused the question with urgency.

Perhaps that was why I switched from a casual, conventional, *Okay*, to, 'Not okay.'

'Oh,' high, half-formed, quizzical.

'I'm in love.'

'Oh,' dampened down a tone, and quavery.

My words were stark in the gloom; and with them, for once, all at once, came every one of the feelings that I had ever had about the situation. The scorch of elation was sluiced with despair.

Beside me, Fern was puffing; her striving, a sea in the shell of my ear.

'And I'm married to Philip. Who is perfect. And perfect for me. But this man – Edwin – is . . .' *make no bones*, '. . . imperfect. Married, too.'

Instead of *Oh*, came a murmured, 'Edwin.'

And where was he, as his name joined us in the knotted blackness? Far away, unimaginably far from the bumps and crevices which, with the bones of my ankles, were sparking pain.

She said, 'Tell me. The story.'

And so I did. My story of nothing – a love story of love unspoken, lovers untouched – rattled around us, amassing from questions and answers, punctuated by Fern's calls for Pavlov as he splashed away into littered leaves, and by occasional, ear-shocking cracks of the tree-lidded dark.

At the first crack, Fern had said, 'What's that?'

'Nothing.' Nothing important.

But there were several more noisy punctures of the sky. 'What *is* that?'

'It's . . .' What did it matter? This was a place of weirdness underfoot and overhead. I was trying to answer her question, *What's the wife like?* I wanted to do justice to the question, to Vivien; to remember everything that I had ever known about her, although I knew that a list would make little sense, or not the kind of sense required by Fern. I would be trying hard, but she would think that I was making light. What is Vivien like? I know something of her job, her family, her upbringing. I know what she looks like; or, to be more accurate, what she looked like when I saw her. What else? She toasts marshmallows and makes a mean baked banana, but otherwise hates cooking. Drinks gin and tonic. Was vegetarian, once, years ago, for ten days; stirs a half-teaspoon of sugar into her tea, unable to give that up; smoked during her early twenties. She has no wisdom teeth, has hayfever and migraines, had glandular fever when she was sixteen, depression when she was twenty. She wants to be buried rather than cremated. She bought an expensive pair of boots last Saturday, on Edwin's credit card because once again she has reached the limits of both of her own. She listens to the Bach cello suites when distressed. Watches breakfast television every morning. She would like their bedroom fireplace opened up. Whenever possible, she naps during the afternoons, a habit acquired from her mother. If not Vivien, she would have been a Barbara; her middle name is Stephanie. Her birthday is in late December. I cannot remember the exact date. I wonder what she knows of me.

'Are they gunshots?'

'Of course not.' That, I knew: why would there be gunshots?

'Fireworks?'

'Fireworks, yes.'

Suddenly she said, 'Max is imperfect; if that's the word we're going to use, then, yes, he's imperfect. And it doesn't matter. My opinion is that he's lazy, forgetful, infuriatingly uncommunicative; he'd say that I'm the opposite, making heavy weather, storms in teacups.'

'Mountains from molehills.'

On cue, a stumble, so she laughed, 'As if molehills aren't bad enough.' Then, 'We do have a hard time with each other.

There's nothing particularly tempestuous in our relationship, but there is . . .' she considered, '. . . a lot.'

In the wake of another explosion, she wondered, '*Is* it fireworks?'

'Think, Fern: it's November.'

'Oh, yes.' But she turned around, and tugged me to follow. As we retraced our steps, she said, 'Poppy, you don't have to stay married to Philip. I adore him, so I'd be very sad to see you separate. But you don't have to stay married to him *for me*.' I heard the smile. Then seriousness: 'Listen, the world is full of divorced people. Why do we expect to succeed first time and early on in our lives? When Ingrid met Paul, he was married.'

I had some vague recollection, 'Oh, yes.'

'She said that he'd been getting by for years, in that marriage; ticking over. Most men will settle for so little, expect so little. And give so little. Remember: selfless people give the least.'

I slowed up, confused.

Her arm linked into mine, drew me onwards; her brim bobbed on my ear. 'All that Paul gave of himself was his shoulder to cry on. Ingrid said that all the emotion in that relationship came from his wife.'

'I wonder what would have happened if he hadn't met Ingrid.'

'Nothing.'

'What happened to the wife?'

'Remarried.' She reminded me, 'Almost everyone does.'

'Not always happily, I imagine.'

'That isn't your responsibility.'

'No?' Glancing sideways, I noticed the extravagant vapour of our breath; marvelled at how, so far, I had missed that.

'You can't live your life to please someone else.'

'Not even the sickness-and-health person?'

'That's no marriage. You can do your absolute best by that person, you can have that person's interests foremost at heart:

yes, fine, and good luck. But live your life to please them? No.'

We trudged, wordless, for several seconds, until the gate was within sight. Fern yelled for Pavlov; then, quietly, so that by comparison it was almost an aside: 'You've been so unhappy for so long.'

The truth, yes, but I hated to hear the words, to feel them in the air, real, frightening. 'That's because of everything else, though, isn't it?'

She shrugged, as if that were irrelevant. And that was my second surprise: the first was that she did not assume that I should stay with Philip; the second was that the causes of my unhappiness could be irrelevant to the decision to leave, to move on.

Fumbling with the gate, she gasped, awed, 'Those gunshots! What if we'd died, here? What an odd end that would've been!' In the same tone, as she stepped before me into the lane, she said, 'I've never doubted that I want to be with Max, you know; never. And thank God; thank God for that.' Her eyes were illuminated by the streetlamp, I saw that they were glossed with fear. And unfocused: she was not afraid of me, as I had expected, but of the possible, accidental loss of her good fortune. That fear had a hollow look; faced with it, I recognised, *That is where I am, so very far from safety.*

GOOD AS GOLD

❧

This is what happened. Edwin rang me and, in a voice thickened and fractured, said, '. . . Sadie . . . you know what I'm going to say, don't you?'

I had no idea. Less than twenty-four hours on from Holland Park, I was utterly unprepared.

He said, 'I can't leave Vivien; I'm not going to leave her; I can't do that to her.'

I think that I said, *I never asked you to.*

I know that I said, 'I never expected you to.'

At that point, I would have settled for anything. I was still waiting for the kiss that I had never had; I still had never been told that he loved me.

He said, 'We can't be friends, Sadie. We can't stay in contact.'

I knew, then, why he was crying; I knew that he was crying, and why. My reaction was amazement rather than alarm.

I was thinking, *Endings are for books, films, for fictions; not for real life.*

I was sure that he would see sense.

He said, 'She hasn't asked me to do this.'

She, Vivien, unlike me, had been granted that for which she had not asked.

'I've behaved despicably, with an utter lack of regard for her.'

Ah, self-loathing: this, he could do.

And so the tables were turned: I – not Vivien – was the mistake. With this one phone call, Edwin was undertaking the messy business of correcting his mistake. From this call onwards, his life would be straightforward; his future, rosy; or, if not rosy, clear. Hard work, undeniably, but edifying, and with just reward. His intention was to regain her faith, and restore his commitment. Good words. Good deeds. Edwin, atoning; Edwin, creeping up on to the moral high ground: this was what I had to listen to, and the sound sickened me.

I said, 'Don't do this,' with the kind of calm that comes from a gun held to a head: his head, my gun.

Because where did his grand gesture leave me? Atonement was not an option for me: I could never retrace my steps to Philip, I had no way to make good the pain I had caused him.

He said, 'I'll never forget you.'

'Oh, well, that's okay, then.'

His response was a hurt silence, which struck me as bad form. But no doubt he had considered my sarcasm to be inappropriate; I sensed the unspoken admonishment, *Behave like an adult*.

He, though, was behaving like a contrite husband.

'My worry isn't that you'll forget me, Edwin; my worry is that you'll hate me. If what I did, and made you do, was so terrible, then – in time, if not now – you'll hate me.'

He whined, 'I won't hate you, I will never hate you. I don't hate you, I'm a million miles from that.' He stressed, 'Sadie, I don't hate you.'

I think that he said so twice more.

And that was all that I took away with me from the person with whom I was in love and who, I am certain, was in love with me: an assurance that he did not hate me.

He said, 'No one did anything wrong. We followed our hearts.'

And of course we did: because what else is there to follow, in matters of the heart?

I had a more pressing problem: George; I was due to go to George for lunch and was already late when I had answered the phone. I told Edwin, and he asked that I call when I returned.

* * *

George seemed delighted to see me, remarking many times on the interval since our last date. He said that I looked much better than I had, then. The irony nearly winded me.

Making sure to smile, to agree, to thank him with good grace, I was thinking, *You so nearly saw me happy; you don't know how nearly*.

I was steeled, focused inwardly on survival, feeling invincible when in fact I was so vulnerable; taken in by my own illusion of composure. For George, I enthused and chattered, determined to give him his due, to avoid merely going through the motions; determined that he should not suffer because of Edwin's failings. In turn, George obliged with stories: the sixties rock star, his death in a swimming pool, the journalists' suspicions of murder, 'But as I was forever telling them, I went to the post-mortem, saw the liver: size of –' he glanced around the room '– a coffee table.'

I was unimpressed. 'Depends on your coffee table.'

He looked pointedly at me over his bifocals.

'No,' I said, 'I suppose not.'

When I came home, I rang Edwin. He picked up the phone immediately.

'It's me,' I said. 'Are you okay?'

'I've had some lunch.'

'Good.'

'And thrown it up.'

'Oh. Oh dear.'

'You?'

'George had rustled up a ploughman's, and so far, so good.' Then I checked, 'Are you sure? about us having no contact? Isn't that a bit drastic? Can't we salvage a friendship?'

There was a silence, before he began, 'I feel . . .'

'Congratulations,' I said, in the pause.

'I feel,' he continued, very slowly, 'that we can't be friends while you're still in love with me.'

'Oh.' So, that was how the talk of love happened, in the end: as talk of mine, and of a lack of his. I wondered when he had stopped loving me: because that was the implication, loud and clear. I took him at his word, the truth of it did not matter; what mattered was that he had said it and would have me believe it.

I said, 'Well, I'm not in love with you, really, wholly; not now.' And there was some truth in this. He had made himself unlovable.

Could I have misjudged his feelings, to such an extent? I was unable to trust his feelings or my own judgement; and all this was so sudden.

He said, 'Nevertheless, I think that we should forego contact for some considerable time.'

I had told him what he wanted to hear – that I was no longer in love with him – and he had refused to believe me. And so I was indignant, now, on behalf of the grain of truth.

He said, 'And I'm talking years.' Said firmly.

I was cowed, wondering in vain what I could say to give substance to that truth. I would have said whatever was required to secure him. Words were nothing to me, by now: a devalued currency.

But in fact I said, 'Well, if that's how you feel.'

'Thank you for being so good about this.'

Oh, but I am always good; as good as gold.

I took a last chance: 'Edwin, I won't disappear just because you don't see me.'

'I know. I know that.' Misery reverberated in his voice. 'But I'm going to try hard to put this behind me. We're going to have a long holiday, next month.'

A second honeymoon. A second, sad honeymoon. I remembered those lines from *Private Lives*,

> '*I'm on my honeymoon.*'
> '*Very interesting. So am I.*'
> '*I hope you're enjoying it.*'

'It . . . it hasn't started yet.'
'Neither has mine.'

'And, next year, we'll probably move home.'

I thought, *Welcome to the new dawn, Sadie; the one from which you are excluded.*

Plans had been made. They had had discussions. Had those discussions been lengthy, recriminatory, had bargains been driven? Or had there been very little to say, with forgiveness in full flow? Who was I, in their discussions? a vamp? Or was I vulnerable, to be pitied? Which particular shortcomings did I have, in their eyes, in their understanding of the situation, their collaborative story? Was I naïve? impetuous? intense? calculating?

Edwin said, 'I do know that this is going to take me years.'

I thought, *Your whole life, I hope.* I asked, 'So, why do it?'

'I'm married.' This was said in an odd mix of tones: definite and surprised. Then, quieter, 'I gave her my word.'

And there was no answer to that.

Ultimately, there is only so much that can be done with the word *goodbye*. Nothing much was made of that relatively small, relatively quick word with which all contact between us came to an end.

I had been sealed into a story, an ending. Replacing the receiver, that afternoon, I was at a complete loss. I walked around the room, several times, but the walls were overbearing; my breathing, a struggle. I reached for the phone again: my lifeline. Forbidden to call him, I had to call someone who knew about him. Fern was more likely than Drew to be home, and more likely to sympathise.

When I told her, she exclaimed, 'Oh, he's a stupid, stupid man,' and sounded so disappointed that I felt obliged to lighten the load for her by defending his decision. She remained utterly unconvinced. 'He'll regret this for the rest of his life.' And for that, I loved her.

But our conversation was brief; there was little to say.

I lamented the frustration of my urge to throw objects at him.

She said, 'Post them to him; everything that you want to throw, post.'

And I smiled to imagine the tinkling, sopping parcel.

When Philip came home, that evening, I told him that Edwin had asked for no further contact. He looked sceptical. I was unprepared for that. And so there I was again, acting as Edwin's mouthpiece; explaining for him, and, ultimately, defending him.

Then Philip looked faintly disgusted, and said nothing. He did not ask the question, *What does this mean for us?*

I sensed that he was determined to salvage our marriage, despite the damage, whatever the cost; he was biding his time, hoping that I would recover and return to my old self.

I did not say, *I was never who you thought I was; you must know that, by now.* And for the first time ever, I saw him as misguided, foolish, selfish.

But how hard for him: all this, over a man who seemed to him loveless, spineless. It must have seemed perverse. It was perverse. Over the next few days, I resisted an urge to say, *This is me: perverse. Not pitiable, not adorable.* Instead, I did my best to hide my mourning. Around him, my manner was brisk and I did not cry.

Hal bore the brunt. Not even his happiness mattered to me: a carelessness which, for both of us, was alien, alarming, and depressing. During walks, I yelled at him for minor or perhaps even imagined misdemeanours, yanked on his lead, and turned back earlier than usual. Back home, he was keen to appease me, but perplexed as to how. So, he fell back on that old favourite, the first action that he had learned to perform to command and for which he had been praised: sitting. He took every opportunity to present himself and perform with formality. In his nervousness, though, he would forget to stop wagging his tail, which twitched on the floor. He seemed to understand that sobbing was distinct from giggling: the two presumably look and sound similar, but the giveaway, I suspect, was my face in my hands. My face was in my hands for privacy, because whenever I was sitting crying on the floor, Hal was sitting in front of me, looking anxious and embarrassed. The expression was nothing new – that habitual mixture of puzzlement and disdain – but, for once, was appropriate. And pointed. He was only inches away, all haunches and haughtiness, staring into my face.

I began to write a diary, the first entry was *Day two*. The second day of all those that remained to be lived. No mention of *Day one*. No memories, either. Gone. Lost. *Day two*: I remember thinking those actual words as I walked into the park, that morning, with Hal. And so I must have gone to meet the day, I must have risen to the occasion, albeit with reluctance. A day, I suspect, I could manage; I could see my way through a winter's day: that meagre, feeble display of light from daybreak to darkness. A small occasion; not much more troubling than a sleep. What terrified me were the years: the years that would come lumbering along, joyless and demanding. All that exists in the diary of that day are the words, *Day two*.

Day three: Walking wounded.

Day four: Have you landed? He was, I remembered, due to fly to Glasgow; due to land, I remembered, mid-morning. *Are you stepping down the steps from the plane, as I write this?* How odd, that no connection – him, at touchdown; me, scribbling – was, nevertheless, to me, significant. The only other word that I wrote was, *Dentist*.

I remember how, when the dentist fetched me from the reception area, she exclaimed in her ever-striking Welsh accent, 'You're pale today, Sadie.'

She is the palest person I have ever known. Incredibly, she remains jolly – incredibly, she remains *alive* – while working seven-hour days on people's pulpy mouths and then going home to her two toddler boys and student husband.

As I replaced a *Marie Claire* on top of a *New Statesman*, she was asking, 'Are you okay? Are you well enough for this? Sure?'

Shake, nod, nod: I wanted to avoid being sent away. Because what was there for me to do at home? And would I ever again have enough energy to make another appointment? Whereas if I stayed, I would be kept company, cared for, and cured of the trouble that was one more than I could bear. A problem shared? This one, I could give up in its entirety to Nadine's ready, shrink-wrapped hands.

Having examined me, she declared that a previously-filled tooth was the cause, shrugging off my surprise with, 'Repairs don't last forever.'

'Then there's no hope for me,' I realised, as she went to pick over tools and materials with her husky, burly, school-leaver assistant, Lauren, whose T-shirt was printed with the words, *Rage Against The Machine*.

In passing, she sympathised, 'No, you're not blessed.'

When my mouth had been numbed, I was reclined so that my head was slightly lower than my feet. My topsy-turvy view was the paint-swollen plasterwork, the ceiling's chalky fruits and garlands. With a little effort, I could glimpse the window behind us: the radiant blue of a sky that – contrary to this tropical appearance – was the coldest of the year so far. We were shielded from the sun's menace by a deep fold of wooden, white-painted shutters; and warmed, in our shade, by an electric heater on the hearth of the boarded-up fireplace. A Motown compilation was playing on the tape deck. Nadine and Lauren sang along, murmuring melodiously down into my open, stopped mouth:

> '*Destination, anywhere*
> *East or West, I don't care.*
> *See, my baby don't want me no more*
> *And this ol' world ain't got no back door.*'

I was flinching. Nadine asked a few questions, then decided, 'Comes down to a toss-up.' I could either endure sensation beyond the numbness, a tapping on the tomb of my nerve; or choose the certain savagery of steel and its deadening hiss into the roof of my mouth. I chose to shut up and put up.

She was puzzled, troubled by my vulnerability: 'This isn't like you.'

I was failing her, and this failure was beyond my control, was physical: a confusion of anticipation of pain with pain itself.

To distract me, or perhaps to pass the time, or perhaps as an antidote to the chill, she began talking of her summer holiday: a week at a camping site in France. She lamented her younger son's fascination with the washrooms, her eventual discovery that he drank from the toilet bowls. She told us that when the week was over and they had packed, all the other campers gathered to wave: 'to cheer'.

She explained, embarrassed, 'My boys do seem to be uncommonly noisy.'

The campers watched tiny, contemplative Nadine and her tall African husband squeeze with their two rowdy toddlers into the teenaged car, which backfired for several minutes and went nowhere until the arrival, four hours later, of a tow truck.

While she talked, she pinned my tooth. My mouth was crammed with cotton wool wads, metal clamps, and my own spittle, but never her hands; never did I detect her touch on my lips. Patched, pinned, and grateful, I was pitched from the couch into the day, or what remained of the day, what persisted, what roared around me as I walked along the high street: a day demanding to be lived, and, to that end, to be serviced. Shopping had to be done. I went into a supermarket. And there, on the fourth day of discovering circumstances unconducive for crying, I made an addition to my mental list: *With half of my face anaesthetised*. Not only crying in public, again, but unable to cry properly: my face an insensate sponge, I cried chaotically and unchecked; I leaked, I was a mess of mucus. Not only leaking mucus, but, I discovered at the salad counter, displaying a rogue sticker on my sleeve: *reduced item*. I remember thinking, approaching the cereal aisle, *I am sick of this, I am sick of this*. And this was only Day four.

And only early on Day four, with worse to come. Leaving the supermarket, I bumped into Carl. He was all smiles, from that bloom of a mouth to the tips of his ears, which rose. The usual unstinted smile. His usual frank look, frank adoration.

I recoiled: did he not see that I was a mess?

He was enthusing, 'How are you? Are you okay?'

I was feeble, wrenched and bruised; and hungry, having had no food for hours. 'I've been to the dentist.' Disoriented by my own slurring, I had an impression that I swayed.

He began sympathising.

I thought, *I'm going to faint*.

Fainting comes rarely, to me, but always like this: with a clear, articulated warning. *Oh, fuck, I'm going to faint*.

My sight was draining with the blood supply from my brain; the visible world dissolving, darkening.

I said, 'I'm going to faint,' but this was devoid of panic: a mere dutiful passing on of the fact. A faint is a fact.

I had only one concern: *Get down, don't fall*.

He had hold of me, somehow: the dynamics of my descent were altered; presumably he had hold of me. He would be trying to hold me up, but I had to be down, on the ground. He would have to see me through, now; he could not, now, drop me.

I was saying, 'Don't let me go, don't let me go,' and I can hear, now, in my memory, how the stress was on the first word – *Don't* – rather than, as I would have expected, on the last.

Don't . . . Don't . . . Don't . . .

I was willing him, not pleading.

He had hold of me but I reached for him; grabbed, hard,

his hand, a handful of bones. My nails on his skin caused him to exclaim. But he held tighter. And so I was suspended, going slowly to the ground, to my knees; my forehead on my knees. And then on my head was a stroking: the warm, soothing flat of a hand where the faint had constricted and frozen. My ears roared with returning blood-flow.

Day five was the last of the days designated by number. There is only one word recorded for that last day: *fog*. Hal and I walked as usual, but stayed close to the road, to streetlamps, in air that was wringing with sound, with birdsong, footfalls, wheels and engines. From this distance, the park's trees looked like tiny nuclear clouds. Headlamps threaded the road with single golden beams, which, on my damp eyelashes, beaded and broke into halos. Traffic in one direction was stationary. From one car came Radiohead's 'High and Dry'.

> *Don't leave me high,*
> *Don't leave me dry.*

The driver – a woman, twenty-something – was singing along. Her words – behind glass, and pitched against the amplified, plaintive vocals – were inaudible, but piled into the air as steam.

Further on, I saw the cause of the hold-up. Three people were on the opposite side of the road: two young men – silhouettes of layered clothing and long, braided hair – standing aghast, braced, vigilant; below them, a bobble-hatted woman was kneeling over a prone, motionless puppy. She was touching the little black dog, probably massaging its chest, and sometimes bowing to its mouth. With no haste nor hopelessness, she was thorough and measured in her ministrations: the stroking, breathing; the tending. Closer, I noticed that she was wearing a sling in which was a baby, newborn, a bundle that swooped unprotesting to the puppy.

I had to walk by; I knew that I had to walk by. They needed no help. They needed privacy, as much as was possible on that busy roadside. A stationary bus was the cause of the congestion. Its windows displayed perhaps twenty watching faces. I could see from the driver's expression that he had not been the cause of any accident. The passengers' faces were reflections of his: not distressed; just – what? – *stopped*.

I walked by; I had to walk by. But from a distance, I watched. The woman looked up at one of the men, and he joined her. Lifting the puppy from the ground, he held it to his chest, bowed his head, then buttoned the body inside his coat. His friend accompanied him slowly down the road. *What now?* How far away was home? The woman had stepped on to the bus; the bus was gone. In its place, the usual succession of cars.

The next day, I left the country. My destination was the studio in which I had spent a sunny week of the previous midwinter. This, I could do: disappear at a day's notice; find a flight, a room. So, in a sense, all those clandestine trips were practice for this one. This one, though, was not clandestine: the evening before I went, I told Philip; said that I needed to go away, to be alone for a while. Keen to oblige, to indulge me, he was the one who took Hal to Dodie, so that I could pack. Ever-hopeful, utterly unable to contemplate the alternative, he understood only this: the sooner I went away, the sooner I would return. From the bedroom window, I watched them cross the road to the car: Philip, relieved to be busy; Hal, thrilled by the prospect of the journey, giving no thought to the journey's end until his exile was upon him.

For travelling, timing was in my favour: few people go on holiday so close to Christmas. I was going against the flow, away from London. A couple of evenings beforehand, the television news had reported a record number of shoppers in London, the screen showing a foot-level view of a pavement, an undulation of shoes. Cradling my coffee cup, I had wondered: *Is Edwin there? Am I looking, now, at his shoes?* There was a chance. Because he had to be somewhere.

Where I had wanted him to be was in the park, waiting for me. That, he could have done: he knew my routine, I was easily interceptible. He could have tried even harder, contrived to pass through the station in London on the off chance, second-guessing when I would arrive, if I would arrive. Was he ever – even once – in one of our haunts, even if only faintly hopeful of seeing me? What was the chance of my seeing him somewhere, anywhere? Philip had spotted Annie at London Bridge Station, two days before I went away. Annie, Philip: what was the use of that?

He could have called from the phone box on the corner. That would have been good, a good ending.

Edwin! Where are you?

Actually, I'm in the phone box on the corner of your road.

Easy. And not an unreasonable expectation. Because that is what people do. In books? In life. Books, life. People: they admit mistakes, and make leaps of faith.

Travelling to the airport, on a train, I marvelled at how everyone around me looked intact. By comparison, I was an open, weeping wound. I turned from their untroubled, drowsy faces to the window. A towerblock balcony shone with garden furniture, glorious concrete-coloured sky above railway tracks and industrial estates. Earlier, we had passed a sign on a fence, *Is this a dream?* and I took several seconds to understand the connection with the enfenced cul-de-sac and the other, vaguely threatening sign, *You could live here.*

At one stop, the tranquility of the carriage was rattled by a pair of buskers, exuberant and tinsel-decked.

And here's to you, Mrs Robinson.

I smiled, and smiled, surrendering my coppers.

Having made a hit with us, they clattered off at the next station.

When I stepped from the train into the airport, I thought, *Yes, here's to you.*

I was leaving Vivien and Edwin to it, to the rest of their life together. She would know, now, that he would never leave her. Because if not now, then never. And how did that feel? To come so close to loss, before reprieve. Did she feel more secure, now, than when she had married? or less?

Their life had changed, and stayed the same; stayed the same, and changed. Mine was wiped: no going back; nothing in the future. That was how my life seemed to me as I waited in Departures, sipping coffee. There were no departures: the fog had deepened. The airport held its breath: no incoming or outgoing flights. Check-in staff were expressionless, directionless, stumped; runways, leeched, no longer pulsing with planes. I knew that the planes could descend blind, using instruments, with air-traffic control calling the tune; but then, landed, tiny-wheeled, would be unable to trundle in nil-visibility to the terminals. And even if they could arrive, the terminals were missing potential planeloads of crews and passengers who were stranded on the M25. In this unearthly quiet, I was drinking coffee, killing time, writing the diary that had begun to lose track of the days.

You have cut me dead: I will have written those words amid numerous carousels of payphones. If I had picked up one of those phones, I could have found Edwin and Vivien at the end of the invisible line; I could have found them in their home, twenty miles away, having their life. Having coffee, probably, on that cold Saturday mid-morning. Life going on. For them. Him, thankful for small mercies, for the small mercy of her handing him a cup without reproach. He did not know where I was. He did not know that I was in no man's land, a drowned airspace. He did not know if I were alive. He would never know that I had died. He had given me up to fate.

You have left me for dead.

But I will be at your deathbed. You know that, don't you.

Dead or alive, I'll be there. Looking my best. You can be sure of that. And what will you see? Is it true that our thumbs make us human? I am looking, as I write, at the skin between my thumb and forefinger; a fold that has always, to me, seemed most inhuman. Your hand has never been in mine. As I write, I am biting my nails. Nothing of you has ever been inside my mouth. How will that feel, never to have had those touches? They persist, you know, unlived; laid over them, your happened life is a mere, fast-melting snowfall. I am not quite as other people. But you knew that, didn't you. You think that I am all heart, and I am, but not as you think: think again, of a heart, a real heart, it is a fist-sized muscle. I am not as I seem, but you never suspected the extent. Only now, from your new distance, are you getting the measure of me. Frightening, isn't it: the thought that I might walk on water, or fly. Physical laws do have twists, catches, clauses, hitches, backwashes. Think of planes: what goes up does not necessarily come down. This is a truth: abandon me, and never be free. I am stating a fact when I say that no one has left me for dead and lived to tell the tale.

My delay was one of the briefest, the flight not dependent on an incoming craft or crew. When we had boarded, the plane was de-iced. A tanker drew alongside, and men in oilskins wielded hoses. Our wings roared, steamed, and for several minutes our porthole views vanished.

Hours later, I was in twenty centigrade of sunshine, on my balcony. Each of the following seven days, I saw in from that balcony. By midday, it was in shade; so I spent the afternoons in company, in the crowd on loungers by the pool. Evenings, I was in bed by nine, having coped only so far.

Edwin, I am in a dark place.

The entire contents of my head had been addressed to Edwin, for a long time, but now he was gone. Nights were silences into which I was drained and by which I was buffeted. Mornings found me unmoved, braced.

Have you thought, Edwin, how I will come across your name so much more frequently than you will hear mine?

That is in the diary, written sometime during those days; days which rattled with his name or similar: a luggage label, *Mr Edward Adams*; name-badged *Eduardo* in Reception; and in the harbour, a boat, *Eddy*.

You condemn me to have some other man's child; have you thought of that?

Every morning, I woke to a life upon which I could make no start; a life for which I had no heart. Any sleep had been sucked into a recurrent dream: my heart being hauled from me and thrown into water. The pain was no more than a sticking plaster ripped from skin; the terror was the sound of my heart like a stone.

One morning, waking, I scribbled in my diary, *I don't want to die of this, not like this*. I suppose that I meant, *After everything I have survived*.

Mostly I had no sleep because of a fear of spiders, the constant dread of a dark scudding across the floor or bed-clothes. Even the innocence of my folded clothing was suspect, everywhere a potential lair for an incubus, a launchpad for its unfathomable trajectories. My own skin betrayed me, crawled in anticipation of arachnoid scampers and clings. Lying motionless in the dark, I was particularly, intolerably vulnerable.

Then, one morning, I was, as usual, at the rock pool: a basin, no deeper than a metre, mostly natural, partially constructed; a pool washed up on the rocks by a calm sea, but otherwise submerged, sometimes submerged for days. I was sitting on a rock, watching the few, elderly bathers, the water flushed from time to time by spray from waves on rocks below. Their swimming was as stately and strained as that of horses. The surrounding rocks were occupied by German gold-medallists in tanning. The atmosphere, as ever, was reverent; no sound other than that of the turning sea. Then, I saw, on a far rock, a tarantula. Bewitched by the shiny wink, the sinister morse, I was struck cold, stuck fast, unable to scream. No one else seemed to have seen; everyone was unsuspecting of the poison in our midst: the angular outrage, the muscular grip, the crouched creature of prey that would outrun us all.

And then I realised: *It's a crab*.

I am by the sea; this is a crab.

For God's sake – what on earth is wrong with me? – it's a crab.

What was there to fear from a crab? Perhaps the horror, for me, was the laborious, averted motion: an echo of my own. And, anyway, what was there to fear from spiders? There were no spiders, I had never seen a spider on the island; an island blown clean of them.

> *But O, selfe traytor, I do bring*
> *The spider love, which transubstantiates all,*
> *And can convert Manna to gall.*

Let loose on me was fear, taking the form of my oldest dread. As I picked my way back over the rocks, I saw, in a dip, a tiny dead crab: the colour of bleached bone, the shape of a slice of cabbage; white cabbage sliced across the stem. A creature that had lived in the ocean, survived an ocean, but died trapped in a mere handful of water.

I had been burying myself alive: that was how I had been surviving. I knew that, in theory, I would live and love again; but my feeling was that all this – the life, the love – would happen to someone else. And perhaps that was true.

A year on, I swim in the rock pool. I totter over stone, moss, sand; dip, and rise ablaze with chill. I go early, to be alone, and then even the view is mine: the skyward sea; the cliffs, precarious trees. An irregular hollow is no place for my exacting lengths; when a few minutes of lolling and paddling can be spun no further, I return to the rocks and sit with my feet in the water, the rest of me drying and tightening in sunshine and salt. Above the far wall, volcanic eruptions of spray, vapour; below, at their faint touch, the surface strung with ripples, struck with an inaudible chord.

Philip's first ever touch was to my foot. I was in hospital, in re-hab, relearning to walk. He was a social-work student, on a placement. When I first saw him, he was hurrying towards me, he seemed to have been looking for me and I seemed to have been missing; he was saying, 'I can never catch up with you.'

I was in a chair; a physiotherapist was manipulating my slack foot. I said, 'You surprise me.'

I swear that I glimpsed a smile.

He said, 'I'm supposed to discuss your case.'

The physiotherapist immediately began explaining my injury to him; and, offering up my foot, said, 'See?'

Philip asked me: 'May I?'

I noticed the opalescence of those eyes. I made a small sound of assent.

Kneeling, he took my heel into the palm of his hand.

And that was that.

I know, now, that I will never again love as I loved Philip in those early days, those first years. Such a love – unreserved, unquestioning – was of its time, its place in my life. And having accepted that, I have begun to move on.

He has moved on, too; moved away, moved in with the new love of his life. The love of his new life. In London. Everyone says that he is very happy. And of course he is, because loving is easiest of all, for him; is what he needs and loves to do. Philip's flaw is the oldest in the book: he needs to be needed. And by all accounts, the new woman is up to the job. (Annie's considered opinion was, 'So drippy that I nearly drowned.') So far, I have declined invitations. Philip would like us all to be friends, but, for now, I seem unable to oblige. An odd, unexpected ending for us: friendly to a fault when we were married, now unmarried and unfriendly.

This, for me, has been the biggest surprise and deepest sadness of the past six months: my apparently effortless replacement as Philip's wife. Earlier this morning, sitting with my feet in the wave-nudged, molten water, I recalled the myth of Narcissus: falling in love with his own reflection, while, behind him, Echo faded to just that. As Philip's wife, I was an echo; and I remain that echo, whatever happens from now on, and whatever else I become.

Today, my last day: several cups of coffee in the bakery; the best coffee in town. On my way from the rock pool into town, on this winter solstice, I passed morning glory on tree trunks like sugar violets, and bougainvillea as gaudily and uniformly pink as party decorations. At the bakery, I chose a table in the rear, by the open window; the view, a courtyard, three white walls of dark-shuttered windows. Serving, were the usual two women whom I presume to be sisters. Both wield a proprietary air; although the younger, barely more than teenaged one, less so. They both have lank, brown hair, brittle with highlights, snatched back into elastic bands; long, narrow noses; half-closed eyes.

This year, the elder sister is pregnant. She billows in dresses, shuffles in sandals, and stretches occasionally to correct her posture. As last year, the little sister is anorexic: jeans and T-shirt depleted of curves, the face a graze of acne. Both sisters pout, seem sorely put upon. With their customers, they are brisk but watchful, resentful. All this, I endure for the coffee. I am never enticed by the absurd pastries, those piles of berries in glutinous glazes.

This morning, the third member of staff was there. Broad-faced and blonde-maned, she is closer in age to the bony girl but in size to the pregnant woman. She is there less often than they are, and never for long. Whenever I see her, she is going to or coming from somewhere, cradling canvas bags or folders. In her presence, the lugubrious sisters relax. In passing, she undertakes a task, such as clearing the tables, with neither reference nor deference to the sisters. Today, she took a mop from a bucket and sponged the floor around the counter. This was done effortlessly, expressionlessly, in no time, and then she was outside, smoking a cigarette.

As ever, her appearance took my breath away because she reminds me so much of Vivien, of the little that I saw of Vivien. But how? how can that breezy, blasé, gum-chewing girl remind me of Edwin's wife? This morning, I tried hard, watched her smoking, and decided that what strikes a chord is her lack of self-consciousness, her somehow rather unrelenting physical presence. This is the second year that she has evoked Vivien for me: and so we have a history, now, and I have a grudging fondness for her.

She finished her cigarette, returned for her folders. Only then did I notice that the occupant of the table closest to the door was a woman of my own age, alone, reading a book. Incongruous. Odder still, the book she was reading was one that I had been reading this time last year: Alice Munro's *Lives of Girls and Women*. But there, I think, the likeness ended. Rather than girlish, she was womanly. Beneath the long, full skirt were well-turned ankles, well-shod feet. She turned a page; on that hand, a wedding ring. Instantly, a breeze rang chill into the room. Within the same instant, my gaze was at the window, into the courtyard: but nothing; nothing but white walls, dark shutters, blue sky. Beyond my view, though, were the cliffs. Sometimes a smooth, clear sky puckers at their touch, and bruises, leaks. Back inside, two faces – reader, waif – were similarly upturned, expression suspended; all three of us caught unawares. We surrendered our separate vigilance to a shared smile, the unspoken conclusion: *rain*.

Rain: a relief; an interlude.

Starting the journey home, today, was easier than a year ago. That day, I joined the queue for check-in behind two women; women of around my age, but much bigger: the tops of the arms; backs of necks, tops of shoulders. I glimpsed *Peter-*

borough on one of their luggage labels. One of the women was parting from a lover. He was a local: I could tell from the sky-blue, short-sleeved shirt. She was frantic, noisy with grief, her face inflamed and sodden with make-up. The friend, in the supporting role, vacillated wordlessly between self-importance and mortification. The crying woman knew no words of her lover's language; and he, none of hers, ours. His dismayed incomprehension verged on a smile. He seemed glad of her, proud of her, sometimes drawing her head to his shoulder and administering a pat.

She was trying to tell him something, the shouted words illustrated with gestures – *You, phone, me, twenty-eighth, six o'clock* – and punctuated with wails of terror – *Oh, no! Oh, my God, no!* Whenever she faltered over a sign, or failed once again to make him understand, she grabbed for her friend, snatched at the friend's arms, hands, shoulders; and then the two women faced each other and conferred, needlessly continuing the staccato, exaggerated gestures. The man's mouth remained open, eyes wide, head nodding and shaking randomly. She wanted him to ring her on a certain date, at a precise time, because then her husband would be at work.

Whenever she said *husband*, she jabbed her wedding ring, the moans becoming shudders. *He'd kill me, he'd kill me*, she would announce to her friend, me, the man.

This was too much. I asked if I could translate for her; I knew enough words. I began, and, for my sins, I missed the opening of another queue.

With me, the man was diligent in his efforts to understand; he focused, politely, and even asked questions: what time was the flight leaving? could he accompany her into Departures? When told no, he turned to her and shrugged.

'What's he say? What's he say?'

As I told her, she spoke over me, offering me apologies, explanations: 'I'm in a bad marriage, I married young, I've never been with another man until now.'

When the three of them stepped aside and I took final place at the check-in desk, she was calling, 'Thank you, oh, thank you, so much.'

I said, 'Good luck,' because I felt that I should, but I doubt that she heard.

But this year, this afternoon, behind me in the queue were an elderly couple, the man wearing a Panama hat and a cravat. They passed the time discussing whether the massive construction high on the far wall was a duct for the air-conditioning system, or a sculpture.

'Definitely just something modern,' the woman decided.

The man was unconvinced. 'I suspect it *is* something, you know.'

I was allocated a window seat. From there, I watched baggage-handlers cradling long, narrow, white boxes labelled *Flowers*, stowing them into the hold. Over the intercom came the obligatory chitchat, the effete flutter, pilot-polite and proper: 'Good news and bad, today, ladies and gentlemen.' Airily, 'The good news is that we have the advantage of a tailwind and should be approaching London slightly ahead of schedule. The bad news is that during our approach, we'll run into quite a bit of turbulence.'

And sure enough: half an hour ago, ten minutes into – half-way through – our descent, the trouble began. We had been drifting down, engines droning, sounding paradoxically aimless and powerless. Suddenly there was a thump, the hard impact of thin air, the first of the unpredictable blows. Then, between jolts, came lulls which were anything but, they were swells, a rising or falling of the plane, some quick, others slow, I never knew which, and so my body lagged behind; my stomach, a bobbing balloon. The cabin seemed airless and I thought only of the ground, the touch of the wheels to the ground, the release from nausea.

But then, worse: we had begun circling. I am always badly thrown by circling. And that was when the woman started; the woman sitting next to me, from whom I had heard no word, whose every word so far had been for the husband or companion who was suddenly rigid, unresponsive.

Bizarrely, she said to me, 'I love your sailor suit,' and within those few words, her fear was audible, even above the engines' deafening whine, the rattles of hatches and trolleys, the whoops and exclamations of other passengers.

Unable even to turn, I smiled, a feeble smile, kneejerk gratitude for the compliment.

All that I knew of her was the mauve cardigan in her lap, and the keeper ring bracketing the engagement and wedding rings on an arthritic finger, a sun-spotted hand. If I could have spoken, perhaps I would have told her that both my mother and grandmother wore keeper rings, passed down from their own grandmothers. That was what I was thinking, was all that I was thinking.

She said, 'Whenever this happens, I think we're going to die, I think we're going to run out of fuel. Do you?'

'No.' I wished that I could have done more for her. I could have told her that every plane carries enough fuel to reach an alternative airfield. Instead, I thought of Amelia Earhart's final signal: *circling . . . cannot see island . . . gas is running low*.

'You travelling alone?'

'Mm.'

I tried and failed to emulate the husband.

'Holidaying alone?'

Did my reticence make me enigmatic?

'Uh-huh.'

'That's unusual.'

'Keeps me sane.' *Will that do?*

'Children?'

'No.'

'Not married?'

'No.'

'On your own?'

'No.' *Will you stop?*

But she was unable to stop, and, in turn, I was unable to stop answering.

She asked, 'You're living?'

Or I thought that she did. When I looked at her, she asked, 'What d'you do for a living?'

'Oh. I'm a goldsmith.'

'With that hand of yours?'

'No, with the other one.'

That shut her up.

I could have told her the history, the truth of my trips. For a laugh, I could have quoted those lines from *Private Lives*:

> '*I went round the world, you know, after –*'
> '*Yes, yes, of course I know. How was it?*'
> '*The world?*'
> '*Yes.*'
> '*Very enjoyable.*'

But she would have asked me if I miss Edwin. People do ask.

They ask, *A year on, do you miss him*?

Always, I give the question some consideration; I am genuinely curious: *Is that what this is – a missing? Is a missing what I am feeling*?

Because whatever I feel, nowadays, regarding Edwin, is second nature. High days and holidays are, by definition, exceptional: then, there is almost an obligation to wonder where he is, what he is doing, how he feels. There has been a change of government, since we last spoke. How late did he stay up to watch the election results?

Those high days and holidays are when people ask.

They ask, *Do you wonder what he's doing, this Christmas*?

More people know about him, now that it is over; but the longer that it has been over, the less often the questions.

Has he gone the way of every previous crush, into insignificance and beyond comprehension? For a long time, I missed his reticence in the hurly-burly of the world. What I had seen in him was the darkness in me; my own lost heart. His most tangible absence is on my phone bill, in the list of numbers designated as my five most frequently dialled. Every three months, that list arrives, detailing the hours of calls made to each number. Beside his, a blank.

Does *he* miss *me*? I suspect that my absence comes to him, sometimes, in the small hours and in quiet moments, when he is most alone and also when he is least alone: in wells of sleeplessness; in pockets of solitude on social occasions. Perhaps sometimes when he loses the thread for a moment, he winds up with me. Nor is it beyond my imagining that, on certain special days, he wonders, *Where is she today? What is she doing? Is she thinking of me?* Perhaps on wedding anniversaries, he thinks, *What if . . .?* Because I am forever in that marriage, in its history; I am part of what makes that marriage what it is, for better, for worse.

And then I imagine that he does not miss me at all: that he regards the end of last year as a narrow escape and the preceding months as a silly escapade, or, at best, an inevitable, misguided interlude before he wisened up and settled down to the real business of his life.

And so I imagine that he misses me and does not miss me. Both seem equally likely. And I am equally content with either. I have no interest in him missing me: what would I gain, by having him miss me? I cannot pretend, though, a lack of interest in the question: *Does he miss me?* I ponder unabashed and fearless, wanting a scientific measurement of a physical phenomenon. I would like to ring him, and ask.

Do you miss me?

But, of course, he would misunderstand, he would take the question as an appeal.

If I could ask, though, and if he could understand, perhaps he, too, like me, would be perplexed.

What do you mean, 'miss'? Do I cry? No. Do I wish that I were with you? No. Is 'missing' the word for this mishmash of what I'm left with, to live with?

I suppose that is what I would love to know: *What is it, Edwin, that you're left with? What do you live with?*

My father told me that the early pilots were told, *No heroics. If in trouble, get down, just get down. No heroics.*

As we began our final approach, I remembered Amy Johnson, her wreckage, her disappearance in the Thames Estuary. So close to home. This time last year I was in a tailspin. In the end, in my diary, over and over again, was the appeal, *Talk me down.*

I am coming through Customs, now, pushing my luggage trolley, which pulls me along. My headphone soundtrack is *Original Jelly Roll Blues*, the happiest sound that I know. Around the corner, ahead, and across the hall, on the far wall, is a board on which, I imagine, my message to Edwin remains. Because who would know, who would presume to remove that little fold of paper? Unread, unanswered. Infallible. Indelible.

Around this corner, we returning travellers are going to parade, done up in our tans, in front of a crowd.

Hal! I can see Hal. He is imploring passers-by with his practised, perfected look, *Not-just-for-Christmas.*

And Carl. I can see Carl.

Yes, I landed on my feet. But he keeps me on my toes. If that woman, up there in the plane, had asked me for the story of my falling in love with Carl, I would have said that there was no fall: I rose to the challenge. I would have said, 'Carl's another story.'

If she had pressed me, I might have started, 'Some months ago, I looked at him –'

She would have interrupted, 'And you thought, *Where have you been, all my life?*'

No: what I thought was, *Where have I been?*

And if she had asked me why I love him, what would I have said?

'He is the only person who hears me out and answers me back.'

And, of course, 'It's physical.'

So, there he is: the most alive person I know.

I would have to say that I am the luckiest person I know.

He is signing to me, speaking to me with his own special digital technology. A split-second delay while I decipher, because I am a beginner. And now I laugh, loud, forgetting myself, deafened by Jelly Roll Morton. A couple of people look up, around, but see nothing.

What I saw was this: Carl, making good use of a bad old English word.

As bold as brass.

Suzannah Dunn

Venus Flaring

'Suzannah Dunn is a gifted writer'   *The Times*

Ornella and Veronica are the very best of friends, inseparable throughout the trials and minute details of their lives, sharing everything, hiding nothing. They grow up and find their way into the world together – Ornella, flamboyant and domineering, becomes a doctor, Veronica, observant and self-possessed, a journalist. But then something goes horribly wrong between them, and what was once the truest of friendships disintegrates into an obsessive nightmare of smouldering resentment that can barely be controlled. As Ornella's loyalty fades, Veronica's desperate need for reconciliation becomes a matter of life and death – and if you can't trust your best friend with your life, then who can you trust?

In prose that soars and fizzes with startling truths, Suzannah Dunn has created a deliciously disturbing and stylishly compelling tale of loyalty, love, memory, obsession and ultimate betrayal.

'Dunn writes with a warm attentive style which makes her characters compellingly real.'   *Time Out*

'Suzannah Dunn writes in loaded and knowing prose, like a hip Edna O'Brien or Muriel Spark in a gymslip.'

Glasgow Herald

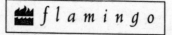 *flamingo*

Suzannah Dunn

Tenterhooks

'I really love *Tenterhooks* . . . Divinely sarcastic and packed full of perky observations, it is very hard to resist.'

PHILIP HENSHER, *Mail on Sunday*

In *Slipping the Clutch*, Miranda walks out of Boots one day into beautiful, beloved, fast-living Uncle Robbie who, years beforehand, taught her to drive in his Alpha Romeo and then died in his Lagonda. Well, what's past is past. Or is it?

In *Stood Up and Thinking of England*, Gillian's family are refugees from the 70s recession, bankrupted in Britain, surviving in Spain. But then from back home come the King family, very definitely on holiday. And it is at the local disco with Tracey King that Gillian catches sight of Pedro . . .

Possibility of Electricity, was the dubious claim made for the Spanish farmhouse that becomes the Paulin family's holiday home. Arriving the following summer as company for Renee's frazzled mother is Auntie Fay. Bond-girl blonde, injecting insulin, tanning to the hue of a blood-blister, and telling Irish jokes. Summertime, but the living isn't easy; and, soon, electricity is the least of their problems.

'Dunn has a sharp eye for the quiet moments of conversation that contain emotional truths.'

SYLVIA BROWNRIGG, *The Times*

 *flamingo*

Suzannah Dunn

Quite Contrary

Elizabeth, a young, overworked hospital doctor, gets a phone call from her father late one Friday night telling her that her mother is dangerously ill. Over the weekend that follows, Elizabeth, on duty as ever and confronting the barely controlled chaos of a busy casualty ward, finds moments to reminisce about her childhood, its joys and its miseries. Past and present are interwoven into a series of vivid tableaux, drawing the reader into an intimate understanding of Elizabeth's life as a whole.

'In this vivid picture of "normal" life, Dunn's Elizabeth, the oldest of three sisters, is a witty, down-to-earth female whom you really care for. *Quite Contrary* isn't a weepy slice of bedtime reading, it's a well-observed chapter on growing up – and it proves a touching and remarkably unpredictable read.'
Time Out

'The writing is loaded with vibrant, visual images of so strongly evocative, so poetic a quality that they seem about to burst and to yield up a weight of hidden meaning.'
Literary Review

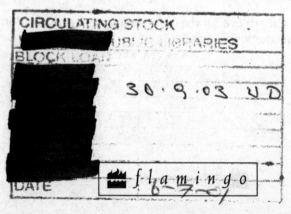